There's No Home

ALEXANDER BARON

Sort Of
BOOKS

Alexander Baron in Eighth Army uniform, 1943

There's No Home

A NOVEL

ALEXANDER BARON

AFTERWORD BY
John L. Williams

THERE'S NO HOME by ALEXANDER BARON

Published in 2011 by
Sort Of Books
PO Box 18678, London NW3 2FL
www.sortof.co.uk

Distributed by
Profile Books
3a Exmouth House, Pine Street,
London EC1R OJH
in all territories excluding the United States and Canada

10 9 8 7 6 5 4 3 2

Typeset in Sabon (9.7/14.2) to a design by Henry Iles

Printed in the UK by Clays Ltd, St Ives plc
on Forest Stewardship Council (mixed sources) certified paper.
288pp

A catalogue record for this book is available from the British Library.
ISBN 978-0-95630-860-3

Contents

There's No Home

There's No Home

Then fare weel ye banks o' Sicily,
Fare ye weel ye valley an' shaw.
There's nae Jock will mourn the kyles o' ye.
Puir bliddy bastards are weary.

And fare weel ye banks o' Sicily,
Fare ye weel ye valley an' shaw.
There's nae hame can smo'er the wiles o' ye.
Puir bliddy bastards are weary.

from The Highland Division's Farewell to Sicily
by **Hamish Henderson**

Chapter One

THIS is not a story of war but of one of those brief interludes in war when the almost-forgotten rhythms of normal living are permitted to emerge again; and when it seeps back into the consciousness of human beings – painfully, sometimes heartbreakingly – that they are, after all, human.

Which war? It might have been any war; the war we knew, the war our fathers knew; or it might be a glimpse, foreseen, of tomorrow's war. It makes little difference.

But since most people like to know when a thing happened, and where, let it be recorded that this story takes place on the island of Sicily, in the town of Catania, and that it begins on the fifth day of August in the year 1943.

All the morning the British soldiers had been streaming into the town. They came clattering in through the Garibaldi Gate, down the steep and narrow Via Garibaldi, always in straggling single file. Their boots and gaiters were white with dust. Their dark denim trousers were filthy, shapeless and torn. Their khaki drill jackets showed black patches of sweat and their faces, scarlet or glistening brown with the heat, were ugly with stubble and sores. They were bowed and weary beneath their packs and weapons. The rays of the sun fell upon them like hammer blows from above and bounced back at them from walls and pavements in dry gusts of furnace-like heat. The saving shadow had been banished; every corner of creation was flooded with a blinding white glare that hurt their eyes and made their heads ache; so that it was only occasionally, and with little interest, that men glanced about them, at the town which they had fought so long and suffered so bitterly to capture. The obsession of battle – that strange sense of trance in which all the superfluous faculties and emotions are anaesthetized – was still upon them. At the moment, only their soldier's senses functioned, keeping their tortured bodies in motion, guiding them over the hillocks of rubble which spilled across the streets, searching the ground before their feet for mines, watching roofs and windows for ambush, recording through their ears the sharp, distant sounds of battle from the foothills north of the town which told them that the German rearguards were still in action, falling reluctantly back along the coast towards Messina.

At the foot of the Via Garibaldi they struck left along what appeared to be the town's main thoroughfare, a broad street in which fine buildings, shops and tree-lined squares alternated with enormous mounds of ruin. High above the street hung the sun, a splash of unbearable incandescence that filled half the sky. At the street's end, appearing deceptively near, rose the blue immensity of Etna, mocking them with its cool tranquillity, as it had done throughout the days of slaughter they had endured on the parched plains which now lay behind them peopled only by the dead. All the morning they came; armoured cars, moving without haste along the street as if their crews were sightseeing, gathering speed noisily as they approached the far side of the town; tanks, lorries, water-trucks, motor cycles; and the bobbing files of infantry, with their indefatigable, spring-heeled walk. The sun rose ever higher above their heads. The last breaths of wind died, murdered. The air became so charged with heat that it seemed that it must ignite and shrivel them all in a great flash. The daylight disintegrated before the men's eyes, its radiance shimmering with curtains of darkness and coloured fire, so that the white walls and the bleached pavements seemed to waver.

A company of infantry came trudging round the corner into the main street. Their commander moved in front of them, as dirty and anonymously attired as any of his men, yet unmistakably distinguishable even from a distance by his height, his splendid bearing and the vigilance with which he looked about him. Even from a distance this seemed to be a man who was recording everything, measuring everything; even the set of his shoulders hinted that the first whine of a bullet would find him prepared; the length and firmness of his stride spoke of determination. It is always inspiring to see a man who is born to lead; there was a fascination about him that brought life back even into the dead eyes of the civilians who had crawled from their shelters to stand abjectly on the far pavement, and which led on the men behind him as surely as if he had them all on a rope.

A motorcycle roared past his men and skidded to a spectacular stop across his path. He raised his hand and the column came to an untidy halt. He conferred for a few moments with the motorcyclist, pushing his steel helmet back as he spoke to free a mass of hair which was of the same red-gold colour as his thick moustache. He spoke a few words to the subordinates who had hurried to his side.

The men began to move again, like sleepwalkers, as if it were difficult for them to get into motion once they had stopped. They shambled on for fifty yards until they came to a large and pleasant square. Here they turned off from the main street and moved along the three walls of the buildings that lined one side of the square. Commands were spoken, without any particular vigour or emphasis, and the men broke ranks. They threw their packs down and stood their weapons noisily against the wall. There was the clank of falling equipment and the pop of water-bottle corks. Voices were raised; the rhythm of the march was broken. They were free men, men at once aware of their exhaustion; they sat on the pavement, backs against the wall, legs outstretched, faces averted from the sun and covered by caps or handkerchiefs. They showed no curiosity about their surroundings or the reasons for the halt. They were inert. Only their commander, standing on the kerb and watching the rest of the army stream by, preserved in his stance a soldier's tension and vitality. With his legs apart he threw his head beck and stretched his arms upwards, wearily yet tirelessly, as if to display by this gesture his defiance of the sun; a human being strong and undefeated.

§§§§

There were only about sixty of them. Less than four weeks before, when they had waded ashore from their landing-craft, there had been twice as many.

4

The first to stir was a stocky youngster who, even at this time, looked a little neater than his comrades. Already he had tucked his jacket inside the waistband of his trousers like a shirt and he had wiped some of the dust from his boots with a piece of paper; quite irrational, this last act, for his face was still plastered with sweat and white dust. The eyes that gazed out of this pallid mask were grey and steady, with that combination of keenness and innocence that characterizes a whole breed of peerers into the innards of cars and radio sets. His name was Geoffrey Jobling. He climbed stiffly to his feet and set off to explore his surroundings.

The man next to him, who watched him fondly as he went, bore a close resemblance to him. They were both hewn in the same shape, they both had the same brush of upright black hair that contrasted oddly with the same grey eyes and gave to both their countenances an air of comic wryness. The man who remained seated, however, looked older; his build was heavier. He appeared, as he sat up to look after the other, more deliberate in his movements; and his eyes were lit with a maturer intelligence. Harry Jobling was thirty years old, his brother's senior by seven years.

Geoffrey came back. 'That big building's the University,' he explained, 'Catania University. Grand-looking place, isn't it? They call this street the Via Etnea. It's the main street.'

'I don't want to know,' grunted Harry. 'Tell me where I can find a glass of nice, cold beer an' I'll sit up and take notice.' But there was a note of affection beneath his raillery, for he was proud of his young brother. Wherever they went Geoff was off like a terrier – he had always been like that – to look for information. He would tell his comrades proudly that a church they were passing (they had probably not even turned their heads to look at it) was built in the fourteenth century, or that a heap of ruins in their path (just like the leavings of a yesterday's battle) had once been a Greek temple, or that Mount Etna was 10,712 feet high, or that sixty per cent of Italy's exports came from Sicily. He would talk in a devout voice of the armies that had passed this way, Greeks, Romans, Normans, Saracens, the liberating legions of Garibaldi; and the other soldiers would listen respectfully, for although they were not in the least interested in the facts, they revered knowledge for its own sake and they would say (how proud it made his brother Harry to hear them!), 'Aye, there's no mistake, he's an educated boy is young Geoff.'

'Don't be running about so much,' said Harry. 'Sit down and rest. We've been through a bit these last few weeks. Better take it easy while you can.'

'What? With old Jerry on the run?' Five minutes rest had recharged Geoff with all the restlessness of youth. 'We'll be up on our feet in a minute and after him.' Then there would be more towns, more enchantments, more villages perched on crags, more white roads winding magically up into the hills; more grandeurs and bright colours than a boy brought up in the Kent coalfield had ever seen. He sighed happily. 'Oh, this is something to write home about, all right!' The phrase had a literal significance for him. His letters home were long and detailed accounts of a wonderful tour of strange lands. Harry's letters to 'the old lady' were briefer and more painfully composed, and consisted mainly of assurances about his younger brother's well-being. It had always been his main preoccupation in life to help and protect 'the kid', not only because of the fierce if undemonstrative love that he bore for Geoff, but because as he expressed it in his thoughts – 'it would kill the old lady' if any harm came to her last-born. Ever since their father and their elder brother

had been killed in a pit accident Harry had watched over
Geoff, at first in the pit and later in the Army. Throughout
the battle from which they had just emerged he had lived
under a double strain. They had slogged up across the plain,
fought their way across the bloody Simeto River, driven a
fanatical enemy from farmhouse to farmhouse, from ditch
to ditch; and at every step, every time a man fell, every
time a shell exploded, Harry had felt a fresh anguish at his
brother's danger. Yet there was nothing of all this, nothing
of the heat, the stinking polluted water, the sweat and dust,
the flies and scorpions, the sores and dysentery and malaria,
in their letters home. 'Dear Mam,' wrote Geoff, 'today we
saw in the distance a castle on a rock. It looked just like
the Gibbs' Dentifrice advertisements. It is called Bronte, and
Lord Nelson lived there once.' 'Dear Mam,' wrote Harry,
'the kid is all right. I made him take the Liver Salts you sent.'
Just now Harry was feeling tired; more tired, more drained
of energy than any of the other men; the lifting of his private
burden had left him limp with relief and exhaustion.

'It's all right for you,' moaned a little man who sprawled
near them. 'You got nothink to worry about. I got responsibilities. Five kids I got. I shouldn't oughta been 'ere at all.'

'You still singing the same old song?' Geoff laughed. 'It's
time you started to make the best of it. How long you been
in?'

'Ten months. Ten months too bloody long, I'll tell yer. It's
all a mistake, that's what it is.' The little man looked as if
he were about to cry. 'They should never of took me. When
I went up for me medical the old doctor bust out laughing.
"Don't you worry," he says, "they'll never make a soldier
out of you."'

'Nor they won't,' interrupted Harry, 'not in a lifetime.'

The little man – his name was Ling – repeated his plaint. He uttered it as frequently as the chirp of a bird, and with the same shrillness; perhaps that was why his comrades called him Sparrow. 'It's all right for you. They should never of took me.'

'I know,' said Geoff, 'you got five kids. Well, you're here now. Fifteen hundred miles from home. Why don't you pipe down? You only make it bad for yourself moaning.'

Harry looked up. 'Don't be silly. It's what keeps him going. Eh, Sparrer?'

Sparrow's bald head was corrugated with wrinkles of resentment. He shrugged his puny shoulders. His grievance was, in fact, what kept him going; his grumbling was the audible manifestation of the incomprehension, the bewilderment which protected him from reality. The other men found it hard to understand how he had survived what they had just been through. He had not fought his way through the battle but had wandered through it in a wide-eyed daze like a frightened child. Yet, of them all, he was the only one now who was unmarked by experience. Most of the company still sat slumped in an utter weariness that was of the soul, with deep grooves of horror in their countenances. Sparrow's face was puffy and tired. His fatigue was the restless, fretful weariness of a frightened urchin. There was nothing in his expression but the resentment and the surprised innocence that had been there since he joined the battalion.

'What about our grub?' he grumbled. 'Three meals a day, that's what we're entitled to. I know the ration scale. I know my rights. We 'aven't sat down to a proper meal for weeks.'

'You don't say!'

They looked up. Sergeant Craddock was standing over them. 'Sparrer,' he said, 'you're a lucky man. You got no imagination. No imagination at all. I wish I was you. We're all dying of fright in a ditch with a machine gun traversing over our heads, an' you're worrying about when the next pay parade's going to be. We're walking through a minefield, poor buggers blowing up all round us, and you start grumbling because you got blisters on your feet. We're surrounded at night, and there you are telling the world that a man's entitled to his eight hours' sleep. Tell you what I'll do. Next time we're up the bloody line and Jerry's putting down a mortar stonk on us, I'll set you up a table and chair, with a nice dean cloth and some flowers, and I'll get old Monty to come and serve your dinner up to you in person.'

'Garn,' muttered Sparrow, 'yer barmy.' He settled sulkily back against the wall.

'Well,' – Sergeant Craddock addressed the platoon at large – 'do you like the look of this place?'

The riflemen stirred. Some of them growled comments. 'Because you'd better get used to it,' Sergeant Craddock added, 'Captain Rumbold just told me. We're staying here.'

§§§§

The traffic no longer streamed by in a grim, continuous pageant. The broad street was quiet, sodden with the white, narcotic sunshine. There were more civilians abroad, prowling warily about like famished cats, gathering sometimes in shrilly disputative groups. In the distance could be heard a clamour of women's voices and people came hurrying past laden with armfuls of clothing or brightly coloured bolts of silk that contrasted with their ragged clothes; they were looters, hastening away from the deserted shops into which a mob of lean and famished slum-dwellers had broken. Occasionally a column of foot soldiers would come plodding into the town, the men bowed, white with dust; or a convoy of lorries would appear and vanish with a rush and rattle; but now they were not all going in the same direction. They were emerging from, or turning into side streets. Military policemen were whitewashing arrows and symbols on walls. Hour by hour the captured town was being turned into a base, and its garrison was arriving in the wake of the pursuit.

The company formed up in the square. The men did not feel refreshed after their rest; they were stiff and tired. Even to move was a victory of the will. They were aware now that they were filthy, and their dirt, their sores, their sweat-sodden clothing became an agony to them. The battalion, Captain Rumbold told them, was going to have a rest. It had been left behind to perform garrison duties. The various rifle companies were going to billets in different parts of the town. Soon they would be taken to theirs.

Captain Rumbold surveyed his exhausted men. 'Get those backs up, lads, and put some snap into it. These Dagoes are getting their first look at British soldiers. They're a scruffy lot. Show 'em something that'll shake 'em. It won't be long now. You'll soon have your boots off.'

The men straightened their backs as he looked up and down the ranks. Some cursed him under their breaths. Some grinned at each other and muttered, 'He's a mad sod!' – the highest term of praise they would accord to any man – or, equally approving, 'Silly old bastard!' When they moved off, however, their apathy returned. They trudged wearily after the guide, out of step, so that their steel-shod boots made a tremendous din on the cobbles, setting up echoes that rebounded from wall to wall of the narrow streets through which they were now passing. The column – they had formed up in threes – twisted through a maze of filthy turnings. The men lost all sense of time and direction and began once more to march automatically, as if they had given up hope of ever reaching a destination.

They were penetrating into the huddle of slums that bordered on the docks. Occasionally they glimpsed the sea and the masts of naval craft at a street's end. It was cooler now, for the streets were so narrow that the sunlight was excluded; but there was little relief in the air, which was heavy with a graveyard dankness. Great heaps of refuse stank against the walls and the air was full of the reek of urine. The houses leaned crazily against each other, their rough plaster walls cracked and dirtied and stained with red and green patches of lichen. Wooden doors hung open to reveal dark and cave-like interiors. The windows were mere holes, unglazed and barred. Water dripped from ancient pumps on the street corners. In the doorways and on the steps crowded children, filthy and half-naked, their faces pale and bloated with hunger; children in such multitudes as the men had never seen crammed into so small an area; all staring and subdued. The women were gathered on the balconies that projected from the upper storeys; gaunt, dark-skinned women with black and unkempt hair, screeching to each other across the narrow streets to add to the clamour of the soldiers marching below. Even worse than these streets were the alleys which the passing soldiers sometimes glimpsed, so narrow that a man might touch both walls at once, unpaved, and lined with one storey dwellings that were little more than caves of crudely hewn lava blocks. The people who lurked in these alleys stared out at the sunlit world with hate.

At last the head of the column reached the corner of a street leading down to the waterfront. It was a short street, but broader than most – broad enough to admit the glare and the warmth of the sun. It was lined with single-storey dwellings, which all leaned away towards the far end of the street as if struggling to support the two taller buildings which formed the seaward corners of the street. One of these buildings had been wrecked by a bomb but the other, on the left-hand side, was intact, although its walls were chipped and battered. It was a four-storey tenement, built around a central courtyard into which a big wooden gate gave entry. In the middle of the cobbled roadway there rose a tunnel-shaped air-raid shelter, around the door of which were clustered some civilians. There were the usual piles of decaying rubbish against the walls, but the light afternoon breeze that came from the sea challenged the stench.

'Here it is,' said Captain Rumbold.

Sergeant Craddock looked up at the name-plate at the street corner. 'Via dei Martiri,' he read.

'That means the street of the martyrs,' Geoff Jobling informed his neighbours.

Private Ling's comment was a characteristic one. 'It don't 'alf pong,' he observed, and leaned unhappily on his rifle.

Chapter Two

THE people of the Via dei Martiri had been standing in the sunshine, listless, trying to absorb the fact that there would be no more bombardment. When the sound of tramping boots had come to them, only thirteen-year-old Ciccio Martinelli had possessed the energy to cry, 'Soldiers!' and to hurry towards the street corner. He had come running back. 'Englishmen!'

Paloma, a young woman dressed in widow's black, with a big bosom and brawny arms, was the first to respond to his cry. She exclaimed, 'Men!' With both hands she swept a tangle of black hair back from her full, handsome face. She smoothed the dress down over her body and stepped out of her house on to the pavement.

There were a score of men and women waiting in the street. Another dozen or so emerged from the shelter. They had been living there for the last three weeks, never daring to come up out of the darkness, stifling in the foul air and the accumulation of human filth. They were so weak and dazed that even now, several hours after the need had ended, they had not yet bestirred themselves to plod back to their own houses. Thirty or so women and old men (the young men had been scattered by war) and a clutter of children; these were the only inhabitants of the street. The rest had fled from the city, during the three weeks of shelling and air bombardment, into the surrounding hills.

The soldiers marched into the street and halted in three ranks on one pavement. The people fell back and gathered in silence on the opposite side. The two groups looked at each other.

They studied each other with a hostile curiosity. Each group looked the same to the other: filthy, exhausted, more animal than human, the soldiers swaying over their rifles, the civilians at bay before their houses. Each was looking at 'the enemy'. There across the road (on whichever side one stood) were the people responsible for these last three weeks of suffering. The roadway was wide – miles wide, it seemed at this moment – sunlit and empty. A baby squalled, and the children began to creep out from amongst their elders. The people looked at their children with a dullness that was worse than a visible agony. The distress that came into the soldiers' eyes was the first human feeling they had betrayed since their arrival. The children all had the same appearance; heads that seemed monstrous on their shrunken bodies; big, appealing eyes; twisted, scabby little legs; and flesh whose colour, beneath the dirt, was a deathly toadstool whiteness. A couple of the children tottered out into the roadway, tugging at the restraining hands of their parents. Others pressed their faces into their mothers' thighs and whimpered. One broke loose and went tumbling across towards the soldiers. The officer who was moving up and down amongst his men, a tawny, terrifying giant, raised his hand and roared an incomprehensible threat that sent the little boy scuttling back in terror. More children ventured forward, approached to within a few yards of the soldiers and halted timidly. One of the men leaned forward over his rifle and made conciliatory noises. The officer snarled another command, and the man straightened up; but the children, encouraged, advanced. The officer seemed to be angry. He spoke again, and NCOs pushed the children back, moving self-consciously and without roughness. The children, excited, suddenly came to life; they squealed and dodged and screamed joyously at the soldiers. The officer turned abruptly and struck at a small boy with the back of his hand, and the children came streaming back to their parents in a pack. A woman snatched up the little boy who had been struck, soothed him and dried his tears. The other people muttered. But the children were not annoyed, for several of them were already sucking bars of chocolate; and the rest were hopeful.

§§§§

Captain Rumbold was pleased with the billet. The big tenement building was scarcely damaged. The courtyard was big enough to accommodate a company parade; at least, until reinforcements arrived. The wooden gates were strong and could be closed every evening at Lights Out to prevent nocturnal wanderings. The tall porchway had rooms on each side, with barred windows, which would serve as guardroom and cells. The captain indicated to his clerk, who trotted at his heels, in which corners of the yard latrines and ablution benches were to be erected, and which rooms on the ground floor were to serve as company office, stores and cookhouse. Piggott, the clerk, followed the captain through the gloomy corridors marking the doors with chalk to show which rooms the three platoons were to occupy.

The captain climbed up through a skylight on to the roof. 'Nice sea view,' he said. 'Make a note for Orders, Porky. I want a couple of tarpaulins up here tomorrow morning to cover those damaged patches. I don't suppose they get much rain here, but we won't take chances.'

On his way down to the street he looked into the rooms, telling Piggott to open the French windows which gave on to the balconies. 'Let's have some air in the place. Get the smell of these blasted garlic-eaters out of the building.' He stood for a while on the fourth-floor balcony, testing the rail with his hands and kicking with his heel at the joints of the stone slabs on which he stood. 'Doesn't feel too safe,' he remarked. 'Probably loosened by the bombing. Take a note for Orders. Men to keep off the balconies for the time being.'

He dictated instructions for fatigue parties. After his men had had a meal, a wash and a night's sleep there would be little leisure for them for two or three days. Everyone would be kept busy turning this gloomy, malodorous cavern of echoes into a soldiers' hive, well-organized, spotless and bustling with life. Captain Rumbold would have done this if his men were twice as exhausted and if only half as many had survived.

He grimaced at the sunlight as he emerged into the court-yard. 'Here. Who are they?'

A group of civilians had crept in through the gateway; a withered old man, three old women, two younger women, all laden with children and big black bundles.

'Clear out, you!'

The civilians huddled together, a tableau of consternation. They all began to jabber.

'Scram! Go on, beat it!'

The clamour increased. It expressed incomprehension, inquiry, entreaty. None of the people moved.

'Here,' said the captain over his shoulder to Piggott, 'get Craddock. He's picked up a bit of their lingo. No, wait a minute, I know.' He pulled his revolver from his holster and brandished it. The civilians fled, screaming. There remained a little puddle where one of the babies had crouched. The captain laughed. 'What a shower! Come in here.'

Piggott followed him into the room they had chosen as company office. The captain indicated a dusty, rickety table. 'One more note for Orders.' He paused, put a cigarette between his lips and tossed another across to Piggott. 'Head it, "Civilians". I want it displayed prominently, at the bottom, double-spaced and in capital letters. All right, light your fag up. Okay? Ready?

He dictated: 'This street is inhabited by civilians full stop Unfortunately full stop They are dirty, diseased and treacherous full stop They are cadgers and cowards full stop They are your enemies full stop Their countrymen killed your comrades full stop Have nothing to do with them full stop' He put his unlit cigarette down on the table. 'Right. You find the portable and start typing that lot out. I'll get the men into the billet.'

He strode out through the gateway, ignoring the men and women who squatted despairingly among their bundles.

He gave an order. A platoon officer spoke, and the soldiers began to file into their new home.

§§§§

The people of the Via dei Martiri had little to do. The town was still stunned; there were no shops open yet, no bars or cafés to visit.

They were too apathetic to spend much time cleaning themselves or the hovels to which they had returned. For the moment they were content to sit on their doorsteps, giving themselves up to the sunshine, watching the comings and goings of the soldiers, and chattering.

The day's glare mellowed into the gilded softness of evening. Above the stillness of the sea, the empty blue of the sky was invaded by streaks of purple shadow and a subtle stain of pale green light. The murmur of military traffic passing through the town was continuous and soporific; the thudding of field guns was too distant to be disturbing. All the afternoon soldiers had been hurrying up and down the street, too intent on their business to linger with the natives. Messengers came on motor cycles. A truckload of rations was unloaded. A senior officer arrived in a car (Rosario Dell'Isola who, as a deserter from the Italian army, knew about these things, said that he was a colonel), was greeted with a salute by the sentry who now stood in the porchway, and emerged ten minutes later escorted by the tall, red-headed captain. From within the building came sounds of activity; voices raised in discordant song, the scrape and bump of furniture being moved, the clatter of cooking-equipment, and an occasional command slashing through the cheerful noise.

'These are strange men,' observed Paloma, as she watched a British soldier crossing the street. 'They seem without heat.'

Her neighbour, Graziella Drucci, who sat at her street door suckling a baby, said, 'If that were true it would be a disaster for you, eh, Paloma?'

'And for you? Aren't you a woman?'

'I am a wife.'

A wife without a husband.

'Without news. That is all. He will come back. In Africa many are missing. They are not all dead. Many are prisoners. They will come back.'

Paloma laughed. 'But when, Graziella, but when?'

Graziella turned her head away and watched the soldier until he had vanished round the corner. 'They walk without pride.'

'The Germans had too much pride. They would not even look at us. We were dogs to them. At least these come to live among us.'

'*Ba!*' The twanging, explosive exclamation came from Rosario, a tall, gaunt young man with wild, black hair who lounged among the ropes of garlic in the doorway of his mother's tiny shop. 'Look who speaks! Paloma, widow to one man, wife to the whole world!'

'Not yours, you ape,' Paloma replied without rancour.

Rosario laughed derisively. 'You've been running after me long enough!'

Paloma grinned – a sly, man's grin. 'And who have you been running after?' She looked meaningly at Graziella.

'At least,' Rosario mocked, 'these come to live among us! That pleases you? These thieves? These murderers? They have bombarded us. They have starved us. Now they have come and taken our neighbours' homes. No, they are not proud. They are simple men. They will take our homes, our bread, our wine, our women. They will be among us to punish whoever speaks against them. But all that, it does not matter, for they have flattered us, they have honoured us, they have shown themselves willing to live in our midst. Madonna!' He made a clawing gesture of despair with both hands. 'Give me the proud ones who leave us alone.'

Graziella had been buttoning up the neck of her blouse. She made the baby comfortable in the crook of her arm and spoke again. 'My father was in the war of nineteen-fifteen. He says the English are good.'

'The Americans are better,' said Paloma. 'They are all rich. They give food, they give cigarettes.'

'You prefer the Germans?' Graziella was addressing Rosario.

Rosario shrugged his shoulders. 'One Pope dies, there is always another. They are all the same. All governments are evil. All soldiers do their bidding. Soldiers are evil.'

'You were a soldier,' said Paloma.

'My husband is a soldier,' said Graziella.

'Your husband is dead. He was a fool. I saved my life and my dignity. I deserted.'

'All the same,' said Paloma, 'these do not seem bad men.'

'For you,' said Rosario bitterly, 'there are no bad men. There are only men.'

'Porco Dio! We have need of a few men in this street. How many have we now? Only you – the saints have mercy on us!'

'There's always Francesca's man,' jeered Rosario. 'He's been here a whole week – haven't you been able to lay your hands on him yet?'

'That one! She won't let him out of the house. What jealousy! Or perhaps she keeps him too busy.'

'Who is he?' asked Graziella.

'Who knows? She never talks about him. I've seen him a few times, through the door. He looks a sullen brute.'

'Never mind,' said Rosario, 'there will soon be plenty for everybody.' His voice was harsh. 'A dog for every bitch!'

'Mother of Jesus,' muttered Graziella wearily. 'Is that all you think about? When will they bring milk for the babies?'

§§§§

The men on guard were drawing their rations. Private Fooks, just off duty, looked at the four hard biscuits and the crumbling lump of pink and yellow corned beef that the guard commander had dropped into his mess tin. 'Here! What d'you expect me to do with this?'

The guard commander said, 'Stick it.'

'Funny, ain't yer? Tickle me feet an' I'll die of laughing.' He thrust the mess tin under the guard commander's nose. 'Look at it. It won't fill the 'oles in me teeth, an' me so empty I can feel me backbone touching me bellybutton.'

'Drink some of that tea,' the corporal advised. 'That'll take away your appetite.'

Private Fooks sipped noisily. 'Gawd! I'll say! What they done? Run a pipeline orf the nearest stable?' The guard-room was crowded and the scrubbed floor was still wet. He walked to the door and seated himself on the step. 'You don't need to eat this. You get fed up just lookin' at it!'

'There's a hot meal coming up in a couple of hours.'

'Yerss. 'Ot meal! I can imagine! They'll give us the same again, an' a dollop o' mustard on top of it. That's all the 'ot meal we'll get tonight.' He broke a biscuit and began to gnaw at it. 'Must be gettin' 'ard up for grub in Blighty. They're puttin' cement in the biscuits instead of flour.'

'Hand 'em over,' said the corporal. 'I'll eat 'em if you can't manage 'em.'

'You go an'—' said Private Fooks, and busied himself with his meal.

It was pleasant to sit here eating and drinking; like sitting on the doorstep at home, on a summer evening, after a hard day's work on the wharf. The sun's warmth was a benign touch against the skin, and the cool breeze from the sea reminded Private Fooks of idle hours on the Wapping waterfront. This street, now, it was kind of nice to look at; not grey and neat like his own little street among the Thames-side docks; it was dirty, and untidy, and – well – foreign – but there was something about the way the houses were all jumbled up, all different sizes, like crazy boxes, the way they lounged against each other, just like the Italians, and the way their mouldering plaster walls glowed pink and green and yellow in the dying sunlight. All day long he had been shut up, mentally as well as bodily, within the four walls of the billet; for the first time the noises of the street entered into his consciousness. It was good to listen to the shrill chatter of voices and the slap of wooden-soled women's sandals on the pavement. These were the sounds of humanity going about its lawful business; they were the sounds of sanity. Without knowing why, Private Fooks found himself able to relax fully for the first time for weeks, and he puzzled at the tickle that he felt in his arms and stomach, the first inarticulate stirrings of bodily pleasure. He leaned back against the warm wall, his head lolling on one side, and stared at two women who were talking in a doorway across the road. He looked at them with delight but without hunger. He had always imagined that Italian women were plump and beautiful. Not these; they were lean and strong-looking, in their long, black dresses, and their faces were pale and without expression. Except, he thought, as the women returned his stare, for their eyes. There was something about their eyes that challenged a man and made him angry; even at this distance he felt it. New emotions were moving in him, but they were familiar emotions and he grinned, promising himself a stroll across the street later this evening.

'Signore.'

The voice had been croaking at him for some time, and he had been vaguely aware of the bulk of a human shape at his side.

'Signore.'

He turned his head. An old woman, so stooped that she seemed to be bowing deeply to him, was grinning at him with pale gums. Her eyes were hideously filmed and tracks of wetness were creeping down from them among the multitudinous wrinkles of her face. Her hands were clasped in front of her. An old man with a hideous purple growth on his forehead hid behind her, trembling violently as if terrified at her temerity.

Private Fooks swallowed a mouthful of biscuit and scooped at the corned beef with his spoon. The first taste of food had sharpened his appetite and he was impatient to satisfy his hunger. 'Hallo, ma.' He bent to his meal again.

She whispered something. Her nearness was unpleasant.

'Signore.' Her open jaw was quivering horribly. She whispered, 'Biscotti.'

Fooks understood the word. 'Eh?' he repeated sharply. 'My bloody biscuits? Gah way!' He hesitated, and sighed. 'Here, sod you!' He gave her a biscuit. She clutched it with both hands, sobbing, mumbling and dribbling from the mouth. The old man extended a shaky hand.

'You too?' Fooks gave him a biscuit. 'My name's Joe Muggins all right. Ought to 'ave my 'ead examined, I ought. Now sod off, the pair of you.'

The old couple did not move, but stood weeping and sucking with their gums at the biscuits. The woman laid her hand on her belly and moaned, 'Fame. Fame.'

Private Fooks turned his head stubbornly away and broke his last biscuit.

'Fame. Fame.'

'F— off!'

The mumbling went on; it sounded like prayers in front of an altar.

'I said f— off!' Private Fooks rose to his feet. 'I can't stand this!' He turned to go back into the guardroom. He halted in the doorway. 'Here, sod it!' He scowled at the old woman and thrust his mess tins into her hands. 'Take the bloody lot!'

§§§§

Night came; a warm, velvet darkness studded with stars. The guard commander strolled along to the street corner and stood on the sea front, looking northwards across a wide, shadowy bay. To the north the white gunflashes were flickering, and he could hear the artillery, faint waves of sound borne on the night breeze. It was comforting to stand in peace and watch the battle recede.

The street slept, the civilians luxuriating in the verminous warmth of their beds after weeks in the foul shelter, the soldiers enjoying the novelty of sleeping under a roof.

Of all the women only one was awake, Paloma, restless in her wide bed. Of all the men only one was awake, the sentry, leaning on his rifle in the porch.

A sound was born in the dark remotenesses of the night, a thin, vibrating murmur. The sound grew louder, an angry drone that crept into the street, invaded the houses, disturbed the dreams of the sleepers, awoke them. The civilians felt themselves go cold with terror in the warmth of their beds. This was the sound they dreaded. It was the sound that brought bombs. They had thought that, with the Germans gone, the war had gone. Would there be German bombs every night now? They trembled and prayed. The soldiers heard, too; in them the sound aroused only a weary resentment, a sense of unfairness because perhaps they were not to be left alone, after all. The noise of aircraft swelled until it filled the night. The ramshackle houses shook and crumbs of mortar pattered down into the courtyard from the balconies of the tenement. The Sicilians and the soldiers lay and waited for the bombs. The noise moved slowly over their heads like a thundercloud. The vibration lessened. The noise dwindled. The soldiers muttered, 'Ours!' and pulled their blankets over their heads. The civilians sighed shakily, muttered grateful prayers, eased their aching bowels and surrendered again to the enveloping warmth of their beds.

Paloma stood at her window. She was wearing nothing but a shift, but she was weak with the heat within her. She opened her front door and enjoyed the coolness of the night. The doorstep was cool to her bare feet. She saw the sentry in the porch, a black, bowed shape. She shook her hair back and thrust her breasts forward against her nightdress, showing herself to him. She saw him raise his head, and she imagined that the white smudge of his face mirrored her own longing. Perhaps, perhaps... But he did not move. She sighed. Stupid soldiers, stupid men, stupid war... She went back to bed.

Chapter Three

FOR the next three days the soldiers were confined to their billet. They saw something of the town when they marched to Battalion Headquarters to change worn-out clothing at the stores, when they went down to the sea to bathe, and when Captain Rumbold took them for a trot along the sea front; otherwise they were imprisoned, occupied with parades and domestic duties.

In their spare time they crowded at the windows which overlooked the street, throwing toffees down to the children and whistling after the women who, contemptuous or indifferent at first, soon thawed sufficiently to answer with shrill and incomprehensible sallies. Already, on the window-sill of a house across the way, a soldier's khaki drill tunic and shorts were hanging out to dry. Private Fooks had taken advantage of an off-duty spell during his period of guard to slip across the road with a bundle of dirty washing. He had accosted a plump and handsome young woman on the pavement and followed her into her house. Their negotiations must have been protracted, for he did not emerge until a half-hour later. His comrades' subsequent inquiries elicited no reply from him except for a complacent, 'Now, now, Nosey!' or a pitying, 'Why don't you grow up?' Once, in a confidential mood, he mentioned that she called herself Paloma, and went on to refer to her as 'ol' Poll.' Now when she stood in her doorway she smiled up at the soldiers with the replete sleekness of a cat full of cream. Her hair was combed and gleaming, and she wore a scarlet flower over her left ear. Many of the soldiers had since prepared bundles of dirty washing. Some had already managed to dash out and find themselves laundresses. The rest were impatient.

From time to time the captain sent runners to Battalion Headquarters, and NCOs went out on different errands. All of these took advantage of their brief spells of freedom to explore the town, and they returned with tales that increased their comrades' restlessness. The town was coming back to life. Thousands of civilians were coming back from the hill villages to which they had fled some of them were appearing in the Via dei Martiri with their bundles and pushcarts – and crowds were beginning to flow again through the once-deserted streets. The shutters were coming down from shop windows. There were queues in the markets for fish and fruit and, for the first time, exorbitantly-priced supplies of bitter black bread and flyblown meat. Some of the rubble had been cleared from the main streets. A corporal had discovered a palatial barber's saloon and had treated himself to a haircut, shave, manicure and shampoo. He spoke of the place as if it were a palace out of the Arabian Nights. One of the medical orderlies described ecstatically an enormous and many-coloured dish of ice cream that he had bought. Others spoke of bars, cafés and pastry-cooks. A few miles away the armies were still engaged, but throughout this sprawling city thousands of people were bustling about, wiping away from their streets, their habitations and their own minds the traces of war as they might clean up the mess after a drunken party.

Somebody came back to the billet with the news that the jocks were in town and raising hell. It seemed that the stocky and ferocious Highlanders, closer than most to a martial past, found it harder to cast off the savage spell of battle. The billet resounded with legends about their exploits. One man swore that he had seen some of them driving past with a lorry load of screaming women. Another said that they were plundering whole streets to furnish their billets. Another said that they were hunting down Italian policemen – scruffy little men, these, in shabby uniforms, who lounged about with hands in pockets, cigarettes drooping between their lips and ridiculous miniature carbines slung from their shoulders and throwing them through shop windows or into the nearest fountain.

Private Fooks returned from one mission with a magnificent silver wristwatch. 'You never seen anythink like it!' he announced. 'There was some little geezer in the street – one o' these black market blokes –'e was selling watches on the sly. You should o' seen 'im, 'ad 'em 'ung all over 'im, 'e did, dozens of 'em. Up comes a bunch of jocks, gets round 'im, says they'd like to 'ave a look. 'E passes the watches round, pleased as a dog with two choppers, 'e was, silly little bleeder. I got one. Then we all strolls off. You should o' seen 'im, dancin' an' prancin' up an' down, wavin' 'is 'ands about, screamin' blue murder. Cryin', 'e was! I ain't a-kiddin' you!

On my life, 'e was cryin' like a baby. None of us takes a blind bit o' notice. Then this little bloke sees an Italian copper, an' 'e starts complainin' to 'im. Know what? This copper takes one look at the jocks an' 'e runs for 'is life. Couldn't see 'is arse for dust. Laugh? I pissed myself!'

On the afternoon of the fifth day the company was allowed out.

§§§§

A few men went off to get drunk. Some departed in search of women. But most of the sixteen surviving members of Sergeant Craddock's platoon kept together throughout the afternoon, straggling through the streets like a party of peace-time tourists. They indulged in little outbursts of horseplay among themselves and occasionally a chatter of animated conversation would spring up among them, but for the most part they were timid and subdued. Everywhere in the town were little groups of men like this, men from the front, hesitating on street corners or clattering along in bunches that overflowed from the pavements into the cobbled roadways, their uniforms bleached and faded, their boots scrupulously polished, displaying the painful good behaviour of schoolboys.

The war flowed past them. Landing-craft bearing reinforcements were gliding into the harbour and mooring in closely-packed lines. The docks, seen through ruined gateways, were a brown ferment of uniforms. Lorry convoys formed up and started off for the forward areas and for the dumps that were being established in the outskirts of the town. Columns of marching men toiled through the narrow streets. Hundreds of soldiers squatted among the debris of a customs shed brewing tea. A military policeman daubed an arrow on a triangle of broken wall and added the inscription: 'To the Forward Area, Ten Miles.' When he had gone a soldier chalked underneath it an arrow pointing in the opposite direction and wrote: 'To Blighty, Fifteen Hundred Miles.' A passing sapper shouted to Sergeant Craddock, 'They've captured Acireale!' and Sergeant Craddock answered, 'You don't say!' – for all this activity made little impression on him and on his men; they did not feel part of it any longer; they felt withdrawn and only mildly curious. Standing on the sea front they could see for miles across the bay in the marvellous clarity of the Mediterranean air. It was possible to see the coast road on which the battle was still being waged. Warships were bombarding the enemy rearguards. The sound of the guns hardly entered into the consciousness of the men, and when the sergeant pointed out to them the flashing splinters of light in the distance that were made by the sun reflecting on the windscreens of the enemy transport, it was only in an instinctive, absent-minded way. They saw white puffs of shell-smoke blossom among the German columns and Geoff Jobling cried, 'Good shooting!' His brother grunted, 'It's the Navy,' as if that explained everything. They did not look up when two Messerschmitts appeared briefly overhead to the accompaniment of an outburst of anti-aircraft fire.

They stopped alongside some troops who had just landed. One of the newcomers shouted, 'You blokes take this place?'

The sergeant answered, 'Yes.'

'Bad?'

'Pretty rough.'

'What's it like here now?'

'Cushy.'

'How long you been out from Blighty?'

The sergeant had to stop to think. It seemed a long time. 'Four months.'

'We been out two years. Africa. What's it like in Blighty?'

'No bloody beer.'

The newcomers began to call out, 'Any Rochdale lads among you?' 'Anyone there from Cardiff? 'Any o' you blokes from Hackney?' Ling found a couple of pennies in his pocket and offered them to a Bethnal Green man whom he had discovered. The other man said, 'Thanks, mate,' solemnly, and put the coins into his wallet.

Sergeant Craddock led the platoon back into the town. He behaved with his men as with equals, without self-consciousness, yet he had the air of being abstracted, apart from them, as he walked at the head of the group. He was five feet nine inches in height, taller than most of them but, because he was broad of haunch as well as of shoulder, appearing almost squat. He walked with such a deliberate uprightness that he seemed to be leaning slightly backwards, and he swung his arms with the palms of his big, ugly hands turned outwards as if he had them on display. His hair was chestnut in colour, wavy but dull and rough, and set closely against his skull, with a few locks straggling down over his forehead. The skin of his face was a light, rough red, and his cheeks were pinched out above a lumpy jaw as if a sculptor had scooped some of the face out to slap it on below, giving a cast of countenance at once gaunt and aggressive. The brutal lines of his face were redeemed by his eyes, which were mild and always hit by the beginnings of a smile, as if they saw a joke in everything. 'Well, what d'you want to do, lads?' he asked.

'Any pictures open?' someone asked hopefully.

'Not much chance of that,' he laughed. 'Let's try for a drink.'

Most of the shop windows in the Via Etnea were still shuttered or empty of goods, but a few hundred yards along they came to a bar, a big place, very smart, swarming with plump and prosperous civilians who even in the summer's heat were all wearing long, beautifully-cut overcoats and rakish trilby hats. The soldiers stood outside for a while, timid and abashed as they stared through the big, plate-glass windows at the deep, green leather armchairs, the chromium fittings and the white-jacketed barmen. The civilians within returned their stare, insolently. 'Hell,' said the sergeant, 'what we waiting for?' and they went in. Some of them lounged at the bar, and some found armchairs, almost aching with the ecstasy of reclining at ease. They drank vermouth and cold, pale beer. It was wonderful.

A thickset civilian with a portfolio under his arm sidled up to Sergeant Craddock. 'Good day,' he said in English, 'welcome.'

Craddock said, 'Thank you.'

'A drink? You will take a little vermouth with me?'

'No thank you.'

'I am anti-fascist. Salvatore di Pietro, avvocato.'

'Oh, yes?'

'You want silk stockings, bread, a signorina?'

'No, thank you.'

'You give me a cigarette, yes?'

'You speak English?' asked the sergeant.

'Yes.'

'Then f— off,' said Sergeant Craddock, 'before I crown you.' Ling said, ''Ere, sarge, this lot's a bit different from the people down our street.'

'Lice,' the sergeant answered, 'they just come crawling out of the woodwork. This lot's the reason why the people down our street got nothing to eat. Drink up, lads, and let's go.'

They strolled through the streets, taking their time in the dry, fierce heat, squinting their eyes (except for a few who owned captured Afrika Korps goggles) against the sun's glare, asking for nothing more to enjoy than the sight of crowds of people going about their daily lives. They stopped for minutes at a time outside every shop window that had any stock in it, whether it was an ironmonger's, a haberdasher's or a bookshop in which every volume was incomprehensible to them. To each they devoted the same solemn attention, discussing the goods on sale as if they were doing their own household shopping in their own High Streets. They went into one or two of the shops. At a stationer's, they bought all kinds of things which none of them wanted, nibs, postcards, sealing wax, paper-clips, just for an excuse to lean across the counter and handle things, for the joy of spending money and having change handed to them by a smiling girl. At this and other shops which they entered, Sergeant Craddock was their interpreter.

A man of little education, he had an intensely active mind which was always seeking something on which to exercise itself. At home it had been the garden, and a hundred household gadgets. Here he had concentrated on learning Italian. Most of the men, in the month they had spent on the island, had acquired a considerable vocabulary and were already masters of a strange patter of English and dog-Italian, which enabled them to carry on fluent and animated conversations with the peasants and townsfolk among whom they moved. Craddock had gone about it the hard way, poring for hours at a time over an Italian grammar which the padre had given him, studying rules each of which took him prolonged thought to understand, and painfully memorizing conjugations, genders, lists of pronouns and other mysteries.

Throughout the campaign, even in the forward areas, he had taken every opportunity that offered itself to talk with the Sicilians whom they had encountered. The result was that he spoke the language more hesitantly but more effectively than his comrades. Some of the officers had, because of their superior education, made more progress than he had, but he possessed a native sympathy with the labouring folk among whom they moved that was already enabling him to forge ahead in mastering the colloquial speech. At a fruit stall, where the men went wild and bought great armfuls of grapes, oranges, apples, peaches and prickly pears, he surpassed all his previous efforts when, in the course of a heroic bout of bargaining, he shed his self-consciousness and routed the bewildered vendor. They went on their way eating, laughing, filled with happiness. They had more drinks. They found the ice-cream parlour of which they had heard so much. In a filthy delicatessen shop they gorged themselves on hard-boiled eggs and repulsive-looking sea-food, glad to pay the exorbitant prices because spending money was a pleasure in itself.

At last, when the time for their evening meal drew near, they made their way back to the billet, grubby with sweat and tired out by an afternoon's walking in the sun; and Geoff Jobling spoke for all of them when, passing through the porchway, he said, 'Oh, well, it was a lovely day.'

§§§§

After supper Craddock came out into the street. There was a Sergeants' Mess at Battalion Headquarters at which he might spend the evening, but he was content to lounge in the sunshine, smoking. Children at play were swarming over the air-raid shelter, and their shouts echoed as if among fine glass. From the dark interior of a house came the voice of a woman singing, rising and falling in a savage plaint. In his mind Craddock dismissed the wordless and alien song as 'queer', but as he listened to the hard, flat wail, something more profound in him responded to its changing moods, its sensual waverings and its piercing outcries of woman's misery, and he was stirred.

Two doors away a young woman was sitting with a baby at her breast. He noticed with approval that her legs were clean. Most of the women had by now washed their faces and combed their hair, but their bare legs were still dirty.

It was time to try out his Italian. He pointed to the baby and said, 'How old?

'Two years.'

He thought that he could not have understood her. The baby did not look more than a few months old. He repeated, 'How old?

'Two years.' Her downcast eyes gave a quick, upward flicker, gleamed at him and fell again. She raised her head and looked at him, this time without flinching, and he became aware of her eyes, scared and sombre but with a deep light in them. 'Here,' she touched her breast, 'there is no milk.' She spoke slowly and carefully, choosing simple words, for she realized that this soldier was scarcely able to understand her. 'But the child sucks, and he does not weep.'

'I' – Craddock was rummaging in his mind for the Italian words – 'have baby. Girl. Twelve months old. Her name is Joy.' He did not show her the photograph he had in his pocket. It would have been too cruel a contrast with the pasty face, idiotic with hunger, and the soft, undeveloped limbs of the child she held.

'Ah,' the woman sighed, 'Gioia. È bella.' A quick smile of delight crossed her face; then the gravity returned. 'Married a long time?'

'Two years.'

'You were a soldier when you married? Your wife has not seen you often?'

'Not often.'

'Ah, la poverina!'

'And your husband?'

'A soldier. Missing. All the men from here are away. Missing. Killed. Prisoner. Still fighting. We do not hear any more.'

Craddock said, dutifully, 'It is bad, war.' He did not mean it, but he knew that these people liked to hear it.

'Where do you live?' she asked. 'Town or country?'

'Town. Slough.'

She tried, without success, to repeat the name. They both laughed, and she leaned forward and touched the back of his hand with her fingertips for a moment.

'It is near the countryside,' he added. 'My father,' – he could not find the Italian words, and went through the motions of digging – 'works. Country. My wife, girl from village.'

'And you? Where do you work?'

'Factory. Radio.' He tried to indicate in mime his work on the assembly line, but her dark, heavy face showed only amused bewilderment.

'How old are you?' She was asking all the questions.

'Twenty-six. And you?'

'Twenty-three.'

He had thought of her as older; not because of her face and body, which were young, but because of something

undefinable in her attitude which compelled him all the time
to behave as to a woman older than himself. He studied her
to find what it was; perhaps it was her eyes, charged with
experience. There was something in her eyes which he could
not reach, watching from behind their submissive gaze, cat's
eyes gleaming from the depths of a cave.

She looked up, startled, as a raucous voice came to them
from the street corner, a man's voice singing, 'I was drunk
last night, I was drunk the night before, Oh, I'm gonna get
drunk tonight if I never get drunk no more.' He recognized
the man as one of his platoon, a private named Broom who
had gone off on his own for the afternoon.

Broom came lurching down the street, shouting, 'Vino!
Vino!' He stopped and thumped at a door. 'Vino! Gimme
some vino or I'll come in and cut your hearts out!'

The woman rose in alarm and backed towards the door of
her house. Sergeant Craddock held her arm to restrain her.
He felt her quiver under his grip, and the heat of her arm
came to his hand through her sleeve. 'Stay here,' he said, 'he
will not do you harm.'

Broom approached them. He was a big man with a bad
record. The platoon had tolerated him until an incident
which occurred on their first day in Sicily. They had left
the beach behind them and were following a rutted, white
lane when they came upon their first corpse, a dead Italian
soldier sprawling face downwards by the wayside. The men
had looked curiously, one after another, and gone on their
way. Broom had stopped and plunged his bayonet into the
corpse. In that moment the other men had drawn apart from
him, and hardly a word had been spoken to him since. He
saw the sergeant and halted, a dozen yards away. 'Whoa,
back!' he shouted.

'Well, come on by, if you're going into the billet,' said the sergeant. 'I won't bite.'

'Who's goin' into the billet?'

'I don't care whether you are or not, but cut out the bloody hullabaloo. Get inside or go an' do your drinking somewhere else.'

'Ah-way! I ain't frightened of you or no one else.' Broom belied his words by staggering backwards for a few paces as the sergeant moved towards him. 'We a'n' got ter be in till nine o'clock. See!' He stood swaying for a few moments, daunted, snarling and mumbling to himself in drunken self-consolation. 'Ah-way! I ain't frightened, frightened, me? I'm frightened o' no one!' He turned and went reeling away in retreat.

'To be thus,' the woman said as she watched him go, 'it is dirty. There are many like that. Everywhere in the streets, drunken soldiers, shouting for vino, vino. The women are frightened.'

'Not many,' said Craddock. He was hampered by his lack of fluency. 'They seem many, but out of an army, they are few.' He lapsed into pidgin-Italian. 'Never – before – drink wine. Not know how strong. Drink too much. Wine and sun make – zigzag.'

She shrugged her shoulders. 'Wine, and sun and misery. Ah, fa niente. Poor brutes!' She relaxed in her chair again and settled the baby on her lap. 'You – Catholic?'

'No.'

'In England, Protestant?'

'Not me. My wife.'

'And you?'

'Nothing.'

'Why?' she muttered, shocked.

He made a little gesture, and hesitated as if afraid to reveal himself; then he said, 'Too many bad things in the world. Where is God?'

She sighed, and did not answer.

He stood over her, made shy by the silence that had come between them. His appearance betrayed the contradictions in him. His smiling eyes quarrelled with his bitter, compressed lips; his bearing was a strange amalgam of awkwardness and authority. 'Tomorrow I will bring milk and chocolate for the baby.'

She smiled up at him. 'Grazie. What is your name?'

'Joe.'

'I am Graziella.'

He turned self-consciously away, and as he walked back to the billet he could feel her looking after him.

§§§§

Long after Lights Out it was noisy in the billet. Most of the company were in bed, but latecomers were coming in drunk all the time – Captain Rumbold had told the guard commander not to worry on this first occasion about bringing charges against them as long as they arrived back safely – and were making the night hideous with the clatter of boots on the stone staircases, snatches of maudlin song and soliloquy and the sound of vomiting on the landings.

Craddock's platoon had the top corridor. The men were all in except Broom, and as soon as Sergeant Craddock heard the laggard shouting defiance in the yard below he went to bed.

The men lay on the floors rolled in their blankets and listened to Broom's erratic progress up the stairs. They heard him collapse heavily on the landing and guessed from the shuffling and grunting that he was moving along the corridor on all fours. Using the wall as a support he propped himself up into a walking position and propelled himself headlong through the nearest doorway. There was a thud, curses from Broom, and another man's angry voice, 'Go to your own bloody room!' Again the sound of Broom's steel-shod boots, and of his snarling challenge, 'Gerrup an' I'll fight the lot of you.' There was the minatory crash of a rifle's brass butt-plate on the floor and the words, 'You'll get this if you don't clear out.' Now he was in the corridor again, and the men heard his boots in a kind of drunken dance; they inferred from his mumbled monologue that he was sparring up to his own shadow. Another door swung inward and the men sat up angrily in their blankets as he swayed threateningly over them. A voice, with authority in it, shouted, 'Where's his bloody mates? Why don't they bloody collect him?' Two men of Broom's section reluctantly came out into the corridor in their underpants, took his arms and dragged him to his room. He was still mumbling and singing, and resisting feebly, as they put him to bed.

For five minutes there was a blessed hush, and some of the men fell asleep. Then the drunken voice was audible again, singing discordantly, 'Oh, I painted 'er, I pai-HAINTED 'er.' The song died off into a low monotone, 'Swindling swine, dirty, stinking, Eyetie swindling devils. After your money, that's what they are, after your money, your money, that's all they want.' The voice rose again, thick with indignation, 'Your money. Laughin' at yer, they are, laughin' at yer. Laugh! I'll give 'em laugh.' He shrieked, 'Kill 'em! Kill 'em all! Kill 'a bastards! I'll give 'em laugh!'

There were shouts from all along the corridor of 'Shut 'im up!' 'Shove 'im in the guardroom!' 'Do 'im, someone!' His companions succeeded in subduing him.

There was another hush; then, from all the rooms, groans and curses as Broom's voice was heard again and the thump of his bare feet. 'Lemme alone!' The hiss of a bayonet coming out of its scabbard. 'Ah! That shook yer! Don't like the ol' baynit, do yer? Now gerraway from that door. I'm warnin' yer. Gerraway!' The thick shriek again. 'Gerraway!' He was in the corridor again. He entered another room, and the men shrank back in their blankets as he raised his bayonet above their heads and laughed wildly at them. He staggered across to the French windows that gave on to the balcony and struck at the pane with the hilt of the bayonet. There was the sound of glass breaking and falling, of the bayonet wrenching in the woodwork, of a scuffle between men; a thump, a clatter – he had hurled the bayonet at someone across the room – and a triumphant shout. He was free, and out on the balcony.

Geoff Jobling, in the next room, cried, 'Oh, my God, he's got outside. He'll hurt himself.' He jumped to his feet and hurried barefoot towards the balcony. Harry, struggling out of sleep, sat up and shouted in alarm, 'Get back to bed, you little fool. If he wants to kill himself it's his own business.' He was too late. Geoff was out on the balcony, padding after Broom, remonstrating with him. Harry hurled his blankets away and strode towards the window. He was halfway across the room when there was a loud cracking sound from outside. The clear, boyish voice rose suddenly to a high-pitched shout. There was a rumbling, a cry of alarm echoing distantly up from the sentry in the porch; then a terrible crash, and silence.

The balcony had given way. Broom hung over the balcony rail of the storey below, limp and moaning. The men who pulled him in found that he was unhurt, and in a few moments he opened his eyes, grinned stupidly up at them, bawled a snatch of 'Nellie Dean' and began to curse his rescuers. Geoff Jobling lay on the pavement of the courtyard, and even before the men of the guard had removed the half-ton of rubble that was piled on top of him, they knew that he was dead.

There was the flicker of candles being lit, a babble of voices, the noise of movement in the rooms, a thunder of footsteps on the staircase. The men came crowding out into the courtyard. One group brought Broom with them, holding him imprisoned with his arms twisted savagely behind him. Sergeant Craddock was there, in command, for the officers were away at their quarters. 'Stand back, lads,' he said. He motioned the men back, but he did not interfere with Harry Jobling who stood over the body with a puzzled glint in his eyes. 'Get a stretcher. And get the truck started up.'

There was a loud and derisive belch from Broom, and the men closed in on him, murmuring. There was a shout of 'Murderer!' and another of 'Lynch the bastard!' Harry Jobling raised his head. He looked bewildered. He saw Broom, and heard him singing indistinctly, and his expression changed. The sergeant pushed through the crush. 'That's enough! Get back to bed!' He pushed one man in the chest and sent him reeling back into the crowd. He swung another by his shoulders and flung him away. 'I said, get to bed. I won't tell you again.' He signed to the guard commander and indicated Broom, 'Put this in the bloody guardroom.'

Someone called, 'What'll happen to him?'

'Don't you worry,' replied the sergeant. 'He'll get what's coming to him.'

'Will he?' Everyone was startled by the low voice of Harry Jobling. 'What'll the charge be? Drunk and disorderly? Breakin' a window? They can't do nothing else to him.' He pointed at the body. 'Look!' His voice shook. 'Look at this. After...' Without warning he lunged across at Broom. 'I'll *kill* you!' His hands were on Broom's throat. No one interfered. Two men still held Broom's arms behind his back. Broom uttered terrified, strangling noises. Vomit and saliva trickled from his mouth, and his eyes bulged.

Sergeant Craddock wrenched Jobling away from the other man. 'Leave him to me.' He was holding both of Jobling's arms. He said, more quietly, 'You can't do nothing now, Harry. I'm taking the boy to headquarters. I know it's no use, but the doc's got to see him. You'll want to come along with us, eh? I'll get you a hot cup tea up there. It'll do you good.'

Jobling was shivering now under Craddock's hands. 'Hot cup o' tea! I'll kill him. I'm not a man to threaten, but I swear by Jesus Christ Almighty I'll kill that drunken beast!' He relaxed in the sergeant's grip, then suddenly tore himself free and dived at Broom once more. The sergeant seized his arm. Harry turned and struck at the sergeant. Craddock flickered out of the way of the blow, jabbed his right fist into Jobling's stomach and chopped with the left at his jaw. Jobling sprawled at his feet. The men were quiet. Jobling had done a serious thing. But the sergeant only said, 'Take him away, someone, before he gets into trouble.'

As Jobling was being helped to his feet, the sergeant said to him, 'Listen, Harry, I know it's hard, but try to listen. Don't be a fool. If you can't think of nothing else, think of your old lady. If you was to swing for a piece of filth like that,' – he pointed to Broom – 'it'd be the end of her.'

Jobling said nothing. He allowed his comrades to lead him away. As he was nearing the foot of the staircase he jerked away from them and reached Broom with a leap. He bore the drunkard to the ground, and began to trample with hobnailed boots on his chest and head. This time it took the sergeant and three of the guard to pull Jobling away. He fought with insane obstinacy and smashed the nose of one of the sentries.

'Put him in the guardroom,' ordered the sergeant. 'Better lock him up till the morning. For his own good. We'll see what's to do with him then, when the captain's back. I'll take the other one down to headquarters. Further apart they are, the better. Corporal Honeycombe. I'm going down with the truck. You get the men to bed.'

The body was carried to the truck. Private Broom was flung over the tailboard by the two men who were his escort. The injured sentry climbed aboard, and the sergeant mounted beside the driver.

When the truck had driven away the men dispersed and went to bed. One by one the lights went out. The talking died away, and after a while there was silence.

It was a hot night. The sound of shelling came from the hills inland and from the coast to the north. All night long the bombers passed overhead. But the men were used to the sounds of war, and they slept. Only Harry Jobling remained awake, crouching till the dawn like a caged beast in the corner of his cell.

Chapter Four

ON the way next morning from his sleeping quarters to his company's billet in the Via dei Martiri, Captain Rumbold considered what was to be done with Jobling. He had not expected such depths of anger from so stolid and undemonstrative a man. It all went to show, the quiet ones were the ones you had to watch. Still, Jobling was a good soldier, with a clean conduct sheet. He could hardly be blamed for his behaviour. He would probably be more reasonable this morning; upset, perhaps, now that grief had come to take the place of rage; but ready to listen to sense. The sentry with the broken nose was a decent man; he would be certain to agree if the captain were to let the matter drop. Yes, that was the thing to do. Everybody was entitled to one blow-up. He would talk to Jobling and send him back to duty.

He'd have to write to the mother, too, about the other boy. Pity, it seemed a waste to die so drearily after the dice had come up the right way for twenty-seven successive days of battle. That Chap Up There, whoever he was, with whom the padre professed to be acquainted, ought to leave infantrymen alone when they came out of the line. After all, fair was fair. Nice kid, too. Bit of a boy scout, but a good footballer. Soft on the outside but the right stuff underneath. He had run a message once, from his platoon to the captain, with mortar bombs dropping all round him. He had come scrambling down into the gully where company headquarters was established, gasping, 'Phew, what price Errol Flynn?'

Now, about the letter. 'He was loved by all who knew him.' That was the usual thing. And 'he died instantly, without any pain.' Perhaps, 'he gave his life trying to help a comrade.' That was a laugh. Oh, well, Piggott would help to write it. The first job was to see the brother.

In a couple of hours the sunshine would be white and dazzling, the heat African, but at this time of the morning the light was gay and gentle and English, painting the pavements a daffodil-yellow and filling the air with an awakening warmth. Captain Rumbold experienced a pleasant, after-breakfast feeling as he approached the billet.

But when he turned into the shadowed porchway his plans and his complacency were destroyed. A few minutes ago Harry Jobling, released from his cell so that one of the sentries might take him to the cookhouse for breakfast, had knocked his escort unconscious and escaped.

§§§§

When Craddock was angry or worried his forehead was deeply corrugated, making him look older and more powerful than he was. The men saw this and were subdued in his presence throughout the day. They had many questions to ask him about the Jobling affair, but for the present they restrained themselves. He was bitter against Jobling, for whose escape he would be held responsible; he was depressed, too, at the thought of the man lurking somewhere in the dockside slums, lonely and desperate, being driven by rage and blind grief step by step towards destruction. It was only when he had completed his duties and was washing himself after tea that he remembered his promise to see the woman along the street again.

Her door was closed. He knocked with his knuckles and entered in response to her cry of 'Avanti!' She was just tucking the baby into its cot. She offered him a quick smile of pleasure, drew a chair back from the table for him, and went on talking in rapid Italian with a young girl who stood in the shadow on the other side of the cot. She paused and turned to Craddock again. 'This is my cousin,' she explained, 'Nella.'

The girl grimaced. 'Sebastiana – but Nella is nicer, isn't it?' She was very young, and her slim body moved freely inside her loose dress. She came into the light, and Craddock saw her clearly. Her smooth black hair, piled upon her shoulders, framed a face that was dark and flawless, oval in shape with a pointed chin. The first impression that she gave was one of shyness and childish purity, but when she smiled at him with her head bowed and her eyes half-closed she looked as sly and wicked as the Mona Lisa. She said, 'I must go now. My mamma awaits me.' She scampered without dignity across the room, but at the door she composed herself and smiled at him again. She said, 'Ciao!' and vanished.

Craddock laughed, and jerked his head towards the door. 'How old?'

'Fifteen. My cousin. She lives nearby with her mother. Some nights she stays here with me. People do not think well here of a married woman who lives alone. My husband's mother stayed with me, but she died a month ago, when there were bombardments and no food. Later, perhaps, I will go to live with someone of the family, but for the present Nella keeps me company.'

'She has the,' – he could not think of the word he wanted – 'the look of a woman.'

Graziella laughed. 'She is ardent. But I watch her. She is a virgin. It is necessary to watch her, always. Now, with the soldiers – they will leave her alone, you think, if they know that she is a child? You will watch, too?'

He was embarrassed at the sudden assumption of intimacy, but he said, 'Have no fear.' He took some tins from his pockets and put them on the table. 'Here! Milk, for the baby, another of milk, some chocolate, some biscuits, and for you a tin of beef.'

She clasped her hands. 'Ah, it is good of you. I thank you. My poor little boy, he needs the milk so much.' She gathered up the tins. 'You have no bread?'

He frowned at the impertinence of the request and answered, 'I cannot bring you bread. We do not eat it ourselves. Biscuits are good enough for us.'

'Ah, no. I was not thinking of that. I have a little bread. It is not good bread, but perhaps you would like to eat a piece of it.'

He relaxed. 'No. We eat well. But thank you.'

He moved awkwardly about the room while she arranged the tins on a shelf. He knew what she expected, what all these women expected. Several of his men were already 'fixed up'. He was not wild for it, but it seemed unmanly not to make the next move. He feared, particularly, that she would think him cowardly; and he felt, obscurely, that with her he could rid himself of the strain and depression he had experienced throughout the day. They were looking at each other, and avoiding each other's look. The silence shamed him. He advanced upon her and drove her back to the wall. She looked up at him with fear. He took her by the shoulders and sought her mouth with his. She turned her head away and her full soft cheek was against his lips. He was not sure yet whether this was play or an insult. As soon as he had come within a foot of her he had felt the heat that she radiated, a heat that he had known with no other woman. He could see a palpitation beneath her dress. He tried, with one hand, to force her mouth up to his. She resisted, and repulsed him with a sudden push of her knees. She put her hand up to protect her mouth, and said, 'No! My kisses are for my husband.'

He was about to fall upon her again when he saw the despair in her face. He hesitated, the violence drained out of him, and he moved away, uttering a little grunt of derision at his own defeat.

She said, 'Go now.'

He could not apologize, but he stood his ground as if waiting for an explanation.

She remained leaning against the wall, her head turned away. At last she found the courage to meet his eyes. She had a bruised, sullen air. She said, 'I thought I could have a friend without being a whore.'

He lit a cigarette and held the packet out to her. She shook her head, and suddenly she smiled again. 'Let us go outside. It is better in the street.' She walked to the door, with a silent, animal grace, and he followed.

When they were sitting in the street she said, in a conversational tone, 'I do not know how it is elsewhere. They say in other places it is different, but in this place, among our kind of people, a woman is a virgin, a wife or a whore. I am not a virgin,' – she smiled a little – 'and I do not want to be a whore.'

'I know,' Craddock said, 'forget it. What's your little boy's name?'

'Fifo. It is short for Filippo.'

'How long have you not seen your husband?'

'A year. No letters for four months.'

'You love him?'

'Love?' She shrugged her shoulders. 'My Vincenzo is a good man. He was good to me. He was strong and he worked hard and gave me his money. He bought me little presents, and sometimes we laughed together. Here a wife does not expect all that. Few women are so fortunate.'

'What work did he do?'

'He was a labourer in the port. In the army, an infantry man.'

'We are infantry.'

'I know.'

'That chocolate, you can eat some of it yourself. I will bring more.'

'Thank you.' She paused, as if trying to find a safe topic of conversation. 'Do many of your men desert?'

'No.'

'Why not?'

'If they did, the Germans would win. 'We,' – his resources failed him again – 'like animals – under them.'

'We are like animals now.'

'Finished, all that. It will be different.'

'Rosario says all masters are the same.'

'We think differently. The people can be masters.'

'That is a dream.'

'Many are dreaming.'

Craddock was interrupted by a shout from the direction of the billet. 'Sergeant Craddock! Hey, sergeant!' Piggott came running towards them, his fat body wobbling above his short legs. 'Hey, sarge!' The few seconds' exertion in the sunshine had covered his face with a glistening film of sweat. 'I got news. Bad news.'

They've just sent a message from Headquarters. It's Jobling. He hasn't lost any time, the silly, bloody, crazy idiot. He's just turned up there with a pistol – I suppose he bought it in the town, they're ten a penny in the black market – an' he took a potshot at Broom. Thank heavens he missed. But he got away, and the fat's in the fire now, properly. The redcaps have put out an alarm, and the whole bloody army's after him. God help him when they catch him now.'

'The captain know?'

'Yes. He's in the office. He wants to see you.'

'I'm coming now.' Craddock made his excuses to Graziella and hurried after Piggott.

§§§§

Sergeant Craddock had a room in the billet. The quarters of the rifle companies were scattered about the town, and the colonel had decided that the sergeants should sleep close by their men instead of in their own Mess at Headquarters.

Late that night he was still awake, lying in his blankets listening to Corporal Honeycombe, his room-mate, stirring and muttering in the hot darkness. He could not make up his mind about Graziella. He was not dismayed by her attitude, but he was uneasy. He knew that if he pressed her she would capitulate: he remembered her hunted expression, her heaving breast, the damp heat of her shoulders beneath her thin dress. She was not a woman to play at love and if he forced a decision he might upset her whole life. On the other hand they were both human. How long could they keep up their present relationship without strain and hostility creeping into it? And then, he thought, what did she really want? A man never knew. A woman might repulse him and despise him for not persisting.

He had not much experience with women to guide him. Before his marriage there had been a succession of fumbling episodes with girls at the factory and one night spent with a flashy blonde he had met in a pub, a woman whose cynicism and self-possession had abashed him. He felt deeply affectionate towards his wife but he had never known any depths of passion with her. Their married life had consisted of half a dozen ten-day leaves, during which he had always felt like a visitor in the house rather than its master. She would spend hours absorbed in her housework or with the baby and only at intervals, as if reminded by a sense of duty, would she come to him as a pleasant companion; love was a concession that she granted, not without tenderness, at nights. In the Army he had only been unfaithful to his wife with one woman, a cheerful, sensible bus conductress, herself married to a soldier serving overseas, who had kept him company during his last three months in Plymouth before coming abroad. She had been a good friend and a genial drinking partner. One night, walking home with her, he had pushed her up against a wall and had his will of her. Afterwards she had rearranged her clothing and said, 'That's the last time, Joe, if you want to keep on seeing me.' But when, on the eve of his departure, he had gone to her and said, 'I think we're shovin' off, Bet, in a day or two, for keeps,' she had taken him home to spend the night with her. He remembered her with warmth.

If he hesitated now at the prospect of becoming involved with Graziella, it was not because he was deterred by any principles. He would grin when one of his companions tried to moralize about sex, and would say, 'Dry up, mate, you can't make rules for that game.' Nevertheless there was something that discouraged him.

§§§§

The fact was that Sergeant Craddock had lost track of his future; he was dimly aware of the fact and was disturbed by it. Once he had had plans and ambitions for a life very different from the one he was now leading. He had gone into the radio factory after working for years in useless, errand-boy occupations, in the hope that there he might find an interesting job, a channel for his wasted intelligence. Work on the assembly line had turned out as boring and as futile as any of his previous jobs. Undismayed, he had enrolled for a correspondence course in radio engineering, and for his first two years in the Army he had spent his spare time carrying on with the course. Army life at that time was empty and unexciting, the war was remote and unreal; his marriage in nineteen-forty-one had sharpened his private ambitions and he had worked all the harder. Then, in nineteen-forty-two, he had been sent to one of the new battle schools that were changing the spirit of the Army. A new interest had flooded into the vacuum of his life. His keen mind and sturdy body had responded to the excitement of war. Here was a test, such as he had never known, of quick wits and initiative. Here were trials, each more desperate, that drove the body beyond the last known limits of human endurance and proved to it that it was capable of undreamed-of feats. Here was a sport, the sport of killing, that was more exacting, more breathless, more dangerous than any he had known. There was a wealth of technical knowledge to be mastered, in weapons, explosives, tactics. Promotion came, and with it the new satisfaction of leadership. The future faded out of his consciousness and the past began to blur. His wife still wrote and asked him (for she was still eager about the life they were going to make after the war) how he was getting on with his correspondence course, and he would answer that everything was going well, although he had long since dropped it. Yes, he had lost track of his future.

Now, only four months out of England, he was aware that he had a wife and a baby girl, of whom he was fond and to whom he recognized his responsibilities, but he could no longer visualize them clearly unless he had their pictures in front of him. 'After the war' was something which he no longer talked or thought about. Sometimes he would speculate about the future of the world, for politics interested him, but never about his own. It was somewhere away in the mists, impossible to discern. He did not know it, but he was already convinced subconsciously that he could not possibly survive.

When, sometimes, he managed to wrench his thoughts back to the subject, it was not to make concrete plans for himself, but only to think of his wife and child as the only certainties that awaited him out there in those dark mists, the only entities to which he could anchor himself if he ever wanted to make anything at all of the rest of his life. Thus, although he had no profound scruples about married fidelity, he felt that it would not do to let himself drift too far away from his wife, to increase with woman after woman the distance between them and the difficulty of reunion.

Honeycombe was writhing and thumping about in his blankets, talking to himself rapidly and unintelligibly. He started up, and interrupted the sergeant's thoughts with a shout of 'They're coming through the vines!' He sat up, trembling.

'Hi-aye,' said Craddock. 'Have a fag.'

Honeycombe wiped the sweat from his face and expelled a long, scarcely controlled breath. He added sheepishly, 'I was dreaming about *them* bastards.'

Craddock knew that he meant the Germans.

The corporal lit his cigarette. 'That was a do, wasn't it?'

'The Pink Farmhouse?'

'Ah. Thought it was my lot that time. Them up on the top there, tossing grenades down into the ditch. And that bloody Spandau in the barn. Kep' quiet till we was right on top of it.' He pulled his blankets over him again. 'Queer, I'd forgotten all about it till tonight. You think you never will, but you do.'

'Funny how you forget, isn't it?'

Honeycombe said, 'Ah. Seems a long time already, doesn't it?' But the sergeant did not answer. He was thinking of Graziella.

Honeycombe said, 'Night, Joe.'

Craddock was silent. He lay for a long time watching the red glow of his companion's cigarette, and trying within himself to recapture what he had felt when he was close to the woman.

Chapter Five

THE word 'shop' which, to the soldiers, called up visions of plate-glass windows, awnings and neatly stocked counters, hardly seemed appropriate when they applied it to the den in which Rosario and his mother lived. It was next door to Graziella's dwelling and, like it, consisted of one room opening out on to the street. The only difference was that, while Graziella used the whole of her space as living accommodation, Rosario and his mother only occupied a small strip of floor against the rear wall. In the foreground were trestle benches, with a narrow space to pass between; these and the shelves on the walls were laden with sacks of beans, split peas, dried melon seeds, maize, dried figs, prickly pears, pasta, peppers and other eatables, with casks of wine, drums of paraffin and flagons of olive oil. Ropes of garlic hung on the inside of the door and in the barred window. All of the dwellings in this quarter of the town were of the same size. Most of them had to accommodate large families. Many of them were also shops like Rosario's, or workshops where the bread-winner toiled with his children swarming and screaming in every corner.

At eight o'clock in the morning Rosario opened the door and admitted a little strip of sunshine into the premises. The improvised counters were a barrier that prevented the daylight from ever penetrating to the rear part of the room. The air inside was heavy with the smell of garlic and of human occupation, and Rosario stepped out into the open air with pleasure.

Graziella's front door was still closed. He looked at it with savage yearning. All the strength inside him was urging his body to crash through the flimsy door and to confront her. He could imagine her, startled, in her bed, her hair in a black disorder upon the pillow, her face beautiful with terror. The close warmth of her room was in his nostrils. He had been dogging her for months but he had never done more than glare at her or utter a few inarticulate words. She was careful never to be alone with him and whenever he contrived to come close to her she would daunt him with a glance, her lips compressed, her eyes angry and imperious.

A man was sitting on the low step of Francesca's house across the road. It was the stranger; he was crouched forward over something that he held in his lap. Rosario shouted, 'Buon giorno.' The stranger looked up. He was a small man, with a pale, lean face and smooth, black hair that fell across his forehead. He stared for a moment, and answered, 'Buon giorno,' in a quiet voice that carried as far as Rosario's shout.

Rosario crossed the street, feeling at once sociable and curious. When he came close he saw that the stranger was carving at a block of wood with a black-handled knife. From the wood there was beginning to emerge a figure, about six inches long, of Christ on the Cross. The head, chest and arms were carved in some detail; the legs were only roughly cut out; the cross behind was barely discernible. The stranger was completely absorbed in his task. Seen more closely, his spare body was muscular and his pallor was of the kind that hinted at strength and fanaticism. He handled the dangerous, double-edged blade deftly and, at intervals, his thin fingertips manipulated a piece of sandpaper with a sensitiveness that was fascinating to watch. Without bothering to complete the rest of the figure he was working on the chest and shoulders, bringing out the contours of ribs and muscles and polishing the surface up to a glossy smoothness.

Rosario said, 'It is beautiful.'

The man puffed sawdust away from the block and nodded slightly, without raising his head.

'You make these to sell?'

'No.' The man went on working.

'My cousin is an artist, too. You have seen the posters in the Via Etnea, for the cinemas? It is he who paints them. All day and all night he paints. He is thin and ill. His art devours him. You are a Catanese? I have not seen you before.'

'No.'

'Where do you come from?'

'The North.'

'Where? Piedmont? Tuscany? Liguria?'

The stranger paused in his work and looked up. Rosario

could feel the force and intensity of the man. 'You are a deserter?'

Rosario answered, warily, 'Yes.'

'Then why ask questions?'

Rosario laughed. 'I understand. But I cannot place your accent.' The man spoke a melodious Italian, without the Sicilian harshness or blurring of the consonants: but he sounded his 'r's softly, at the back of his throat, instead of trilling them with his tongue in the familiar way.

Rosario was annoyed by the man's reserve. This was not the way people lived together in the Via dei Martiri. He tried again. 'The English are taking on labourers. There will be work. You will go to work for them?'

The stranger's eyes did not waver. 'Perhaps.'

'I will go. I will fight for no one, but I will work for anyone. There is an English sergeant here who speaks a little Italian. A little only, but he understands. I shall speak to him, for myself. Shall I ask him for you?'

'No.'

Francesca appeared. She was unkempt, still fastening up the neck of her black dress. Her expression was hostile and apprehensive. 'Come inside and eat,' she shrilled.

Without a word to Rosario the stranger heaved himself to his feet, brushed the sawdust from his knees and went indoors. Francesca made as if to shut the door.

'Good morning, Francesca,' said Rosario, mocking her for her discourtesy in not having greeted him.

'Good morning, Rosario.' She looked over his shoulder. 'Ecco! Graziella has come out. She is waiting for you, I am sure.'

Ah, these women knew how to kick a man in the belly! He heard the door close behind him as he hurried back across the street, in a panic to see Graziella for a few seconds before she disappeared again.

§§§§

In the next two days there appeared in every window and on every clothes-line in the street such a flutter of white singlets and khaki tunics that the whole street seemed to be bedecked with flags of conquest. The soldiers had plenty of leisure time. They were mainly occupied with guard duties at dumps, headquarters and other military establishments about the town; small parties marched off every morning and returned twenty-four hours later with twenty-four hours rest to follow, so that there was always a proportion of idle men left in the billet. These employed their spare time in exploring the street and its surroundings, in making friends and – if they were enterprising enough – in installing themselves in hospitable households. A stream of women called daily at the guardroom with bundles of washing or messages; and it was already no uncommon occurrence for a soldier, coming out into the street, to be hailed by a barefoot child with a shrill cry of 'Pappa!'

Of all the men none had become more domesticated than Private Ling. The little man had taken up with a mountainous Sicilian woman. In the evenings, when his friends walked by the house, they could hear the woman's voice everlastingly raised in shrill abuse while Ling sat on a kitchen chair in the doorway, his head averted from her, puffing his pipe stubbornly, wearing the same remote and unhappy expression behind which years of henpecking in civilian life had no doubt taught him to shelter. Yet, sitting there with the woman's half a dozen brats clustering and clambering about him, he looked strangely content at her nagging, and when his comrades questioned him he would assert his fondness for her with a peevish, 'Gah way! Leave us alone, can't yer? She's all right!'

Captain Rumbold was perplexed by all this. He could not confine his men to their billet. He was not the kind of man to curtail their spare time by ordering parades or other extra duties out of spite or as a deterrent. He was a wise enough leader to know that further warnings would have no effect and would only lower his authority. He recognized that there was a process at work which he could not check, and he did nothing.

To Piggott, however, who was his confidant as well as his clerk, he was indignantly eloquent. 'Would you have believed it? Chaps out of decent homes! You'd have thought wild horses wouldn't have dragged them into the kind of pigsties these people live in. Dark, dirty, smelly, bloody holes – that's all they are – holes in the wall – full of flies and bugs and fleas. People in rags, scratching themselves day and night, look as if they've never had a bath in their lives! I can't imagine what's got into the chaps.'

Piggott grinned. 'Can't you? They're a long way from home, you know. It's not the old front parlour they remember nowadays, it's those holes in the ground they slept in out there on the plains. This ol' street may niff a bit, but it don't smell as bad as the water out of polluted wells or those unburied dead rottin' out there in the sun. Besides, from what I've seen, our fellers are makin' a bit of a change already. Quite a bit of spring-cleanin' goin' on in a quiet sort of way, you know. I saw ol' Fooksy across the road beating hell out of a mattress on the pavement. And little Sparrow scrubbing the floor in his place with that big tart of his screaming at him all the time. You can smell the carbolic as you walk down the street.'

'Yes,' said the captain bitterly, 'and it all comes out of the stores!'

'Anyway, it's all in a good cause. Some of these judies aren't bad lookers.'

'What!' exclaimed the captain. 'And you a Salvationist! I'm ashamed of you! Don't tell me you've got one, too?'

Piggott simpered. 'Not what you'd call exclusive. Name of Paloma. Lives across the road. What a dame! It's like a kick from a carthorse when she just slaps you on the back.'

'Sounds like my kind of gal,' said the captain.

Piggott looked ingratiating. 'Want to make an appointment?'

'Away, you little ponce! Back to your typewriter! Do I look as if I need your leavings?'

It was not, the captain thought, as he went off to inspect the billet, that he objected to the men having a bit of relaxation. He just didn't like the way they were taking a nose-dive over the whole thing, and getting so thoroughly mixed up with this crowd of foreigners. There was no need to make such a business of it. Take your fun and forget it, that was the soldier's way. After all, a soldier had to keep in condition; and to keep in condition he needed plenty of good food, when he could get it, plenty of sleep, when he could get it, and – when he could get it – a little bit of cuddle to loosen him up. But no strings. Anyway, it was about time he looked around for himself. He'd been busy up to now, getting the company settled in, seeing that they made a decent home of their billet, scrounging a little bit more than their allotted rations for them and seeing that the cooks turned it into something tasty. He could do with a bit of a bender now, to keep in trim. He'd have to see about it. He was not a man for beating about the bush. There was no time like the present. He'd have a look-see in the next couple of nights. Of course, he could do what a lot of the officers at HQ were doing, and go visiting among the local bigwigs, in search of a nice contessa or a bonny baroness. This island was lousy with titles. But that might take time, and while the tedious pursuit was going on among the coffee-cups and the small-talk, the battalion might be whisked off. No, there was time for the social whirl later. To start with he'd take what was going nearer home. Not too near, for his men were vigilant; and nothing would entice him into one of those verminous beds. No, he knew the drill: the utility truck, a nice girl, and a nice, quiet lane somewhere outside the town. The old civvie technique, that had enlivened his insurance round. He found a cobweb behind a door, roared an angry command and grinned indulgently as men scuttled to obey.

§§§§

Craddock and Graziella spent both evenings together. Neither of them referred to the incident in her house, and both treated their friendship as a matter of course. Graziella accepted Craddock's presence as a protection from the attentions of other men, and because he was the source of the food which was already bringing life into her baby's eyes. She was grateful, too, for the company of a man, even though this incomplete relationship sometimes stirred her painfully, after months of loneliness. Craddock was also feeling the strain. She behaved without reserve in his presence, leaning towards him and placing her hot hand on his when she became excited in conversation, or letting her thick hair brush close against his face so that soon, even when he was apart from her, he felt himself alive in response to the warmth that she radiated. Nevertheless the time passed pleasantly with her. It was fascinating to grapple with the language, and somehow easier to talk with a woman. Fluency seemed to come as much by listening as by talking and his confidence increased almost hourly. Her personality, too, puzzled and attracted him; he watched her intently, pondering about her, all the time they were together. She was illiterate, but she often displayed an instinctive wisdom. There was pride in her every attitude, and at the same time submission. She had, like all these women, no apparent interests of her own in life; her whole being seemed designed to complement that of a man; yet there was always something secret and independent in her manner. While he was talking Craddock would suddenly notice her and the other women listening, as still as a group of statuary, their heads inclined to one side, no trace of comment in their eyes or in the set of their dark faces. They would sit or stand thus, utterly without motion, for minutes on end. Then the moment and the mood would break up, like light on water, and they were all movement, violence, laughter and shrill voices again.

For the sake of propriety the two of them remained outdoors, on the pavement. A noisy group of neighbours would gather to join in the conversation, always around the same nucleus; at the centre, seated, Craddock and Graziella; nearby, lounging in his doorway and occasionally addressing Craddock with great familiarity, Rosario, who had already accosted Craddock in the street, elicited a promise of any odd jobs that might occur about the billet, and in general laid the foundations of what might become a very profitable and interesting friendship; cowering at Craddock's elbow,

Old Buonocorso, peering at Craddock out of the wreck of a once-intelligent face and chain-smoking the sergeant's cigarettes; and behind the old man, his ten-year-old son Aldo, standing with an arm round the neck of the huge Sicilian mastiff that always accompanied him.

'That old man,' said Graziella – the boy was out of the way at the time, but she spoke quite brutally in front of the father – 'how old do you think he is?'

Craddock was embarrassed, but Old Buonocorso only grinned waterily at him and mumbled, 'Una sigaretta, signor sergente? Craddock gave him a cigarette and answered, 'I don't know. In his sixties, perhaps.'

'Forty-four,' said Graziella, 'eh, old man?'

Buonocorso showed his broken teeth in a grin of confirmation.

'Three years ago,' she said, 'he lived among us. A fine man, a lion. Others were frightened, of the militia, of the secret police, but never he. He brought secret newspapers, he read to us the truth. Everywhere in the town today you will meet men who say they were always anti-fascists inside. This one was an anti-fascist outside. He fought against our misery.' She laughed. 'See what happens to those who fight against our misery. They took him away, and a few weeks ago, after the fascist government had fallen and the prisons were opened, this,' – she indicated the old man – 'came back to us. He crawls, he whines, he begs, he is not a man any more.'

Rosario said, 'The spirit is dead. He is like the rest of us now.'

'Worse,' said a woman who stood behind Graziella's chair, 'he is humiliated. Better to be dead and buried than living and dead.'

Craddock asked, 'How does he live?'

'I told you,' said Graziella, 'he begs. Everyone gives. I do not know how, but everyone finds something to give. And the boy looks after him. The boy looks for work. He is a fine boy. The father brought him up in his own image, and now the boy is what the father was. For three years the child waited to see his father again. His father was a hero. Aldo boasted to the other boys about his father, and sang to them the "Bandiera Rossa", and he said, "see, that is the forbidden song. People fear to sing it, but my father taught it to me." Now the father has come back and the son is broken-hearted. But he is loyal. He is a good boy.'

The old man was nodding incessantly and grinning up at Craddock with a wild, horrible eagerness. 'It is true. I am finished. You cannot imagine what it is like in those places. They degrade, they defile. They make a man insult his own soul. They make him trample on others. After that it is useless. But my boy is good.' He extended a shaky hand, 'Ancora una sigaretta, eh, signor sergente?'

Aldo had come back, and he tugged at his father's sleeve and said in agony, 'Not from the sergeant, pappa, the sergeant is our friend.'

Craddock said, 'Here, take a packet and be quiet.' To the boy he said, 'What is your dog's name, Aldo?'

'Vittorio.'

'He's a fine dog. Bring him here.' He patted the dog, and drew Aldo down to sit on his knee. 'Do you like to listen to the radio? You can come into our billet and listen to the radio if you want. Bring Vittorio. The soldiers will like him. They will give him plenty to eat. I think he needs plenty, eh?'

'You have a radio?' asked the woman behind Graziella. 'What is the news?'

'The fighting on this island will soon be over. The Germans are going back to Messina. You see our bombers going over all day, hundreds of them, all the time. Noise, brrr, brrr, all the time, eh? They go to bomb the German evacuation beaches.'

'Good,' said Rosario, 'magnificent. The Allied aviation is magnificent. It is enormous. It is incredible. Your soldiers are all heroes. They have liberated our Sicily. Tell me, sergeant, what then?'

'Then, Italy.'

'Ah, magnificent. What courage! You will follow the Germans to Italy. You will fight them from one end of Italy to the other? Your bombs, your shells will fall on every metre of Italy to defeat the Germans, yes? You will destroy them and every house that shelters them, even if they shelter in every house in Italy, yes?'

'Yes.'

Graziella whispered, 'Ah, poor Italy!'

Craddock said stolidly, 'Already the Germans are coming into Italy. Many new troops, from France, from Austria. You do not want that.'

Rosario cried, 'No, no! What could be worse? We want to be liberated. And already, your airmen are starting to liberate us. The last three nights, they have bombed the Germans in Northern Italy. I, too, listen to the radio. In Milan they have destroyed the Brera Art Gallery, the Fata Bene Fratelli Hospital, the Sforza Castle, the Natural Science Museum, the Church of Santa Croce, and they have damaged the Scala. In Turin are destroyed the Carignano Palace, many churches, the Balo Theatre, the City Library and many dwellings in the workers' quarters. In Genoa are destroyed the Palazzo della Rinascente, the Church of San Stefano and the Palazzo Rosso. Everywhere in Italy they are bombarding the Germans. It is magnificent!'

'It is war. In nineteen-forty the finest cities in England were bombed. In one week, all the workers' quarters around the docks in London. In one night, all the ancient churches in London. In one night a whole town, Coventry. Italian airmen came, too.'

'For the love of God!' Graziella cried. 'I am frightened by you men. There is war even in your voices!'

'But what have I said?' Rosario protested. 'I am a friend of the English. I am full of admiration. I am admiring them now. I am the friend of the sergeant. You have all seen me walking in the street with him. I am going to work for the English. The sergeant has promised me. Is it not true, sergeant? Are we not friends?'

'Sure,' said Sergeant Craddock.

Chapter Six

PALOMA is a word that comes across the water from Spain. It means 'dove'. It was a nickname. She had been christened Teresa; and the newcomer to the street who protested that the nickname seemed as demure – and therefore as inappropriate – as her baptismal name would be referred, in reply, not only to her dove-like sleekness and to the shape of the bosom which strained at her black dress, but to the throaty cooing with which she was in the habit of announcing her amorous triumphs.

Most of the housewives of the Via dei Martiri were sternly virtuous; at least, each strove to maintain in public the appearance of virtue; and Paloma's exuberances were loudly condemned. However, she lived on excellent terms with her neighbours. She was a popular guest in every house. Her descriptions, minutely detailed, of her adventures were eagerly sought after, and if the other women often abused her to her face, she recognized the vein of good nature in their invective and accepted it with genial indifference. She knew that most of them envied her, not for her way of living but for her independence.

It was exactly a week since the soldiers had come to the street. It was just past midday and the billet was quiet; the soldiers, after their lunch, were resting in their rooms, sheltering from the sun's white radiance. Craddock could hear the cackle of women from the street and, from the window, he saw Paloma standing outside her house, her back arched against the wall and her face turned blissfully up to the sun, while her neighbours clustered about her. Her eyes were half-closed, but she was evidently talking to them, for they screamed ribaldries and encouragement, and she would raise her voice from time to time to reply with vigour. Perhaps she was telling them about her latest lover; or perhaps – since she had already, with some justification, acquired reputation as an authority on the doings of the military – she was answering their questions on the past, present and future of the battalion and of the British Army in general.

Corporal Honeycombe, stooping in front of a fragment of mirror, finished brushing his smooth fair hair. 'I'm going out,' he announced, 'I feel like a bit of hunting. That one down there,' – he indicated Paloma – 'looks a bit of all right.'

The sergeant grinned. The idea of anyone 'hunting' Paloma appealed to him, but he kept his thoughts to himself.

'Well!' Honeycombe smote his hands together. 'Just sit by the window and have a dekko, Joe, if you want to see how it's done.'

'I wouldn't miss it for a pension.'

Honeycombe went downstairs. He was a little taller than the sergeant, and more finely built. The sergeant followed him, and stopped in the shade of the porch to watch from a convenient distance.

Honeycombe walked across the street, with a slight roll to his gait. The women looked at him, appreciatively, and at Paloma, expectantly. Their conversation became subdued. He sauntered past them and stopped close to Paloma. 'Buon giorno, girls.'

There was a chorus of buongiornos, a pause, and an explosive giggle from Nella.

'Hot today, a'n' it?' He spoke in English. The initial greeting had exhausted his Italian, and besides, as he often pointed out in the billet, a bloke could get on with dames in any language.

There was an interrogative twitter from among the women.

He leaned against the wall with one hand, at arm's length, and looked down at Paloma: the masterful pose. At length he said, 'Hallo, ducks.' A simple opening, but one which as a ladies' man he could certify to be effective. It had worked on a hundred street corners in Blighty.

Paloma raised herself from the wall on one elbow and looked him up and down. She took her time. She said to the women, 'What do you think of this one?'

The women clamoured advice like a farmyard let loose. 'Va ben',' said Paloma, 'we shall play.'

Honeycombe was not deterred. He knew all about the coy ones, who liked a tussle, and the sly ones, who made it a battle of wits. 'What you doing this afternoon, honey?' To underline his meaning, he gave a doggish twitch of his eyebrows towards the door of the house. She answered in a man's strong voice – he could not understand what she was saying – and with a man's hearty chuckle. He seemed to be making progress. He asked, 'Aren't you going to ask me in, sweetheart?' The great thing was to get away from this crowd of sniggering, cackling women. Paloma's only response was to feel his biceps and to prod experimentally about his body. Her lips were compressed and she was frowning studiously. She began to speak, over her shoulder, to the other women, in the tone of a pathologist reporting on a post-mortem. The women were clapping their hands, screaming with mirth, pushing each other ecstatically in the ribs and uttering shrill comments.

For once, Honeycombe began to feel uneasy in the presence of a woman. This was no giggling little imitation film star who would listen admiringly to his blandishments, hang confidingly on his arm and afterwards write him adoring letters. What was the use, when she could not understand him, of uttering those time-proven and magical incantations, 'Where have you been all my life?' or 'I could go for you in a big way, kid,' or 'Don't tell me, I bet your name's Gloria'; or of those accustomed references to beautiful, big, brown eyes, and going places and doing things. This woman was looking him over and poking at him as if he were a good meal on a plate.

The grin on his face became frozen and ghastly. He sweated, and was dizzy in the sunlight. He would have sweated more if he had understood what was being said about him.

Craddock, coming closer, heard Paloma say, throatily, 'Well armed, this soldier!'

There was more shrieking from the women, more spluttering laughter. Lucrezia Chiulemi wiped her streaming eyes and pointed at Honeycombe, who had backed up against the wall looking nonplussed and defensive. She howled, 'How fierce he is! How bold! How ardent! How aggressive!'

'A devil!' gasped Nella, choking and thumping her chest.

'An impetuous one!' screeched Tina di Spirito.

Paloma clasped her hands to her bosom and muttered humbly, 'And he loves me!' She looked up at Honeycombe in a transport of ardour and humility. 'Ah, my love, my pigeon, my dear one!' She stroked his arm and caressed him; she pouted her rich lips at him; she overwhelmed him, amid shrieks of appreciative laughter, with such outrageous endearments that his nerve suddenly broke and he tried to sidle away, mumbling excuses in English and keeping his crimson face averted from Sergeant Craddock's interested gaze.

But Paloma flung her arms about his neck, sank upon his breast and bore him back to the wall, moaning, 'No, no, do not desert me, my darling, my hero!' Her audience was growing. Windows and doorways were crowded all along the street. Soldiers were swarming out of the billet. Paloma released her victim for a moment and drew back, admiringly. 'See!' she cried. 'See how impatient is my lover!' – as he tried to bolt and she clasped him again.

She pushed her street door open with her right foot and, with a sudden violent thrust, sent Honeycombe reeling into the house. 'I cannot keep him waiting,' she explained, as she blocked the doorway with her strapping body just in time to prevent his escape. She held out her hands towards the women. 'See,' she said modestly. 'See how I am trembling, like a bride!'

Honeycombe's terrified face appeared behind her shoulder.

'Don't break the bed,' shrieked Lucrezia Chillemi, who was doubled up with her hands clasped across her waist.

'We shall tell the soldiers,' called Fat Lina, 'to wait here with a stretcher!'

Paloma favoured her audience with a conspiratorial wink. 'Kurroo, kurroo!' she cooed wickedly, and slammed the door in their faces.

§§§§

It was evening, and Nella was playing with her two boy friends, Ciccio, aged thirteen, and Tiger, aged nineteen. Craddock, watching them, felt that it had been a brilliant idea on his part to introduce the young soldier to the other two. Tiger, who had received his nickname because he was puny and pale, was one of a batch of young conscripts who had joined the battalion in the spring. When the time had come to embark, all those who were less than nineteen-and-a-half years old had been left behind; a few, including Tiger, who were a few weeks over the required age, had come abroad. Tiger was the only one of these who had survived, and the sergeant felt a special responsibility for him. Here, with Nella, he would be kept out of the way of bad women, while Nella would be safe in his company, for he had promised the sergeant – whom he worshipped – not to interfere with her.

When the three youngsters had first come together, yesterday, it had seemed as if the experiment might fail. They had looked at each other with reserve and suspicion. Soon they had lost their self-consciousness; the boy soldier had shed his assumed swagger, Ciccio his assumed cynicism, Nella her assumed solemnity, and they had played together like children, shouting, shrieking and wrestling, unaware of anything but their sport.

Their play, however, was always on a fine edge. Once, yesterday evening, Craddock had caught Nella squirming on top of Tiger on the pavement by the air-raid shelter. He pulled her away and said to Tiger, 'Time you come up for air, son.' Tiger, wiping his face, gasped, 'Lucky I promised, sergeant.' Now, in play, she had scratched Tiger's face deeply. Tiger stood sullenly in front of the sergeant, dabbing at his face with his handkerchief. Nella was unabashed, and lurked behind him, squealing with wicked laughter. Ciccio had fled.

'You go to the medical room and get that dressed,' the sergeant said. In this climate, any break in the skin might turn to a purulent heat sore. Tiger obeyed. To calm Nella, who was still flushed and exultant, Craddock took an English newspaper from his pocket and showed her a picture of ATS girls on parade. She asked, 'They are women of the army?'

'Yes.'

'They are for the soldiers?'

'No.'

For the officers'

'No.'

'What then?'

'They are soldiers, real soldiers, like the men.'

She paused, then clasped her hands. 'Oh, beautiful, beautiful.' She studied the picture. 'How nice they look, in their uniforms. And those caps!' She asked, 'Is it true that women in England can work, like the men?'

'Yes.'

'They keep the money?'

'Yes.'

'They spend it as they wish?'

'As they wish.'

'They walk in the streets, alone, and go where they like?'

'Of course.'

'Even when they are married?'

'Yes.'

'Even dancing?'

'Yes.'

'I would like to go to England. Can I go to England?'

Graziella said, roughly, 'Take the baby inside, little fool, and put him to bed.' Nella hoisted the child against her shoulder and took him into the house. She was a capable little housewife, who loved minding the baby and who scrubbed and ironed as if it were a game. When Nella was gone Graziella asked, 'Was that the truth?'

'What?'

'Are women in England truly free, like men?'

'Yes.'

She sighed. 'Here it is different. It is very different.' She sat and dreamed, far, far away from him.

Nella went home, and Craddock and Graziella were alone. Craddock brooded, empty of words. Graziella tapped at the pavement with her feet, looking down at her shoes. What pettinesses were there left to talk about? The prospect of more futile conversation awoke an anger in Craddock.

He leaned forward and rested his hand lightly on her arm. The legs of her chair scraped on the pavement as she squirmed quickly back out of reach and hissed, 'No!'

He knew from the urgency of the movement and of her voice that she was near to breaking. The trust that she had placed in him stood between them. He rose to his feet, feeling cheated and infuriated. He said curtly, 'Good night.'

He turned to leave, but she seized his wrist, and drew him into the house.

Chapter Seven

ROSARIO presented himself at the guardroom at eight o'clock on Saturday morning, as he had been told to do, and asked the sentry for 'Il sergente C'rah-dock.' The sentry answered, 'Aspett' and called another man who went off, unhurriedly, in search of the sergeant.

The east side of the inner courtyard was still shady, the rest flooded with sunlight. Strong voices drifted down from the windows, snatches of song, and the clatter of buckets. A party of men were swilling water across the pavement and sweeping it to the drain with big brooms. Others were scrubbing the stone staircase. Some, stripped to the waist, were washing themselves at the ablution benches, their wet bodies gleaming in the sunlight. Fatigue men were sitting outside the cookhouse scouring pans. They were mad for cleanliness, these English. This sunlit spotlessness, these floods of water smelling faintly of dust and disinfectant, made the whole place more like a hospital than a house where men dwelt. Clearly there was no comfort here.

On the shady side of the yard the big captain – Il Rosso, the Red One – was inspecting a squad of soldiers. They were drawn up in three perfect ranks, dressed in shorts and tunics that were newly washed and pressed, and wearing webbing equipment pipe-clayed to a dazzling whiteness. They were strange men, these English. Rosario could not see on their faces the doglike sullenness that Italian conscripts would have felt under inspection. They faced their officer with alertness; they were almost vibrant as they waited for the next word of command. A sergeant spoke sharply and their boots crashed on the pavement as they came to attention and the front and rear ranks, each like a single unit, moved out into open order. There was another command, all the rifles came up together, in a single movement, and each man smacked his left foot forward, at the same time swinging the barrel of his rifle forward so that the muzzle was presented, at eye level, for the officer's scrutiny. The officer moved down the ranks, inspecting the rifles.

There were two aspects to these men, Rosario thought. In the street he had seen them lounging about, or sitting humbly in the houses of their civilian friends, and he had said, 'These men are without force. Look at them! The victors! They do not even know how to behave!' Now he said to himself – for he had a child's capacity for levelling inconsistent accusations against people and then hating them doubly – 'These are conquerors. They are men of war. What chance had we Italian soldiers, men of peace, against them? They deride us as cowards. What right have they to deride us as cowards when we had no chance against them? Why do they swagger among us, and oppress us, these men of war?'

He drew back as they marched past him, and watched them swinging away down the street. They looked straight to their front, without a glance or a shout for their civilian friends. Hypocrites! Conquerors!

Sergeant Craddock came across the courtyard, smiling a greeting. Rosario smiled expansively back, and his heart swelled with pride. The mood of a moment before was forgotten. He was their friend, the friend of the victors. All the people had seen him walk into their billets as if he belonged there. He would be an important man in the street, a source of information, an intermediary even, through whom others – if they were wise enough to please him – might apply for favours. He would be working for the English, for the victors; a public functionary under the new regime. A thought pierced him: perhaps *she*, perhaps even she might think again. His legs trembled.

Sergeant Craddock said, 'Hallo!'

Rosario seized Craddock's hand in a two-handed clasp and shook it vigorously. 'Buon giorno, signor sergente,' he cried joyfully, and loudly enough for the people in the street to hear him, 'you see I have come to help you, as I promised.'

'Good. Come and see the captain.'

They approached the officer. Rosario said, 'Buon giorno, signor capitano,' with even more emphasis than before, and assumed his most ingratiating smile. The captain did not look at him, and began to talk with the sergeant. Rosario could not follow the conversation, but once he caught an English word that sounded like the Italian 'disertore', and he guessed what it was. He saw, too, the brief glance of disgust that the captain turned on him, and he was possessed by a great hatred of the man. What a brute this was, what a picture of haughty insolence! They thought themselves above all others, these enormous men with their pink, smooth skins, full of blood and good food. No wonder they won the battles, with their strength and their food and their equipment. They had everything. They behaved as if everything was for them. If a man like this were to cast his eyes on *her*..!

The captain left them, and the sergeant said, 'He says you can work for us. A pound a week. Four hundred lire in your money.'

'Magnificent. My heart is full. I thank you, sergeant.' He touched the sergeant's sleeve. 'I shall not forget you, sergeant. Every week I shall repay you, for your goodness, out of my wages.'

The sergeant looked puzzled for a moment; then he made an angry remark in English.

'What is that, signor sergente?'

'The next time you say a thing like that – out! Finished!'

It was Rosario's turn to look puzzled. He began to gabble apologies. The sergeant cut him short. 'Come and have a cup of tea. Then I will show you your work.'

Rosario took the big mug which the sergeant offered him and sipped at the thick, sweet beverage. It was not unpleasant, but its strength furred the mouth and its sweetness cloyed. It was a drink to rob a man of his appetite and his thirst. He longed for a glass of rough, dry wine with which to cleanse his mouth. He still felt hurt. He said, 'And now, Signor sergente, where is the work?'

'Every morning at eight o'clock, you will come here and take the latrine buckets in a cart, and empty them into the sea. You will wash them, bring them back and scrub the seats. At seven o'clock in the evening you will come again, this time to empty the rubbish from the cookhouse. Then you will scrub the cookhouse floor. That is all.'

Rosario was silent. They must have plotted, these Englishmen, they must have planned among themselves to find the best way to humiliate a man! They had thought of this, and they had laughed. He saw them laughing. They had said, this was a good way to humiliate a man before the women. They would sit and laugh with the women while he went past with the cart and the filth. This sergeant, he sat every day with Graziella. He had planned it, for her. Perhaps she knew! Perhaps she had already laughed!

'It is only two hours work a day,' said the sergeant.

Rosario looked at the shelves of the cookhouse, stacked high with tins of food, and the stores, full of crates and bundles. These people had everything. It had not been a fair fight against them. Through the office door he could see the captain, perched on the edge of a table, laughing and joking with a clerk. Look at him, a man without dignity! – Rosario had already forgotten his own contrary reaction of a few moments before – without pride! He had never seen an Italian officer demeaning himself like this!

'And each time you come,' said the sergeant, 'you can eat at the cookhouse.'

'But my mother,' said Rosario, 'my mother is poor, and old, and sick. How can I eat, here, when my mother is at home, hungry?'

'All right, the cooks will give you food for your mother, too.'

'Ah!' Rosario clasped the sergeant's hand again. 'You are a noble man. I am fortunate to have such a good friend. My mother will pray for you.' He was filled with goodwill, and with the desire to show his worth. "Where is the cart, signor sergente, I shall start at once. Without losing a second I shall start.'

§§§§

Graziella was ironing a shirt of Craddock's when he appeared in the doorway of her house that afternoon. She paused, brushed the hair back from her eyes and said, 'Come in. It will soon be ready.'

Craddock walked round the table towards her, expecting a kiss, but she was intent on her ironing again. He sat down, and leaned on the table with folded arms. He asked, 'Are you glad to see me?'

She looked up at him, and a smile flickered in the depths of her eyes; then the expression returned which he had seen in her eyes last night when he had left her, an expression which might have been hostility. She set a tumbler on the table before him, filled it with wine and said, 'Drink.'

'Not you?'

She shook her head. She folded his shirt with quick, skilled movements, set it aside and sat down, well back from the table, with her hands in her lap.

Craddock emptied the glass. 'This is good wine.'

'It is the wine of Etna. In my village they make it. You want more?'

'No.' Even when they had been together last night she had been as remote as this, and their conversation as insignificant. Her agonies and her satisfaction had been entirely private.

'I have some pasta cooked, and cheese. You want to eat?'

'No. We have eaten in the barracks.'

She smiled, and pointed to the cot. 'Fifo sleeps. He sleeps much now, and he hardly weeps. It is the milk.'

'And the chocolate, eh? His face is covered with chocolate. You should wash him.'

She laughed. 'Why? It tastes nice when I kiss him.'

'You must put chocolate on your face.'

She uttered a scornful noise, but she smiled at him with more warmth. 'You must change your clothes again before you go. I will wash them.'

'After only one day?'

She pushed back the dark mass of hair that fell across her eyes each time she moved her head. 'You have two sets. Each day I shall wash one of them. Each day you shall wear a clean one. You will look good, and you will feel good. And I shall be proud of you.'

He leaned back in his chair and said, 'Come here, Graziella.'

She did not move. She brooded for a moment, and said, 'I have thought much. I do not know what to do. One sins once, one sins twice, one sins always. But perhaps it is too late to think.'

'You do not want?'

She laughed, and made a little movement of her head. She came to him, and sank on to her heels at his feet. 'Your boots are heavy. Let me unlace them. You will feel cooler.'

Her cheek was against his knee, and he touched her hair with his fingers. She asked, 'Does your wife do this?'

'No. But in the morning she brings me a cup of tea in bed.'

'Do you think often of your wife?'

He shrugged his shoulders. 'You are not afraid anymore of what people will say? If someone comes now and sees us?'

She went to the door, shut it and bolted it. 'Now no one will come.'

The room was in shadow. The barred and grimy window was in a recess containing a charcoal stove and a lava sink, and what little light came in was lost among the dishrags that hung above the sink. The white-washed walls, bare except for some shelves on the window side, some garish holy pictures and a porcelain Madonna on a bracket, glimmered palely. The only furniture consisted of the huge marriage bed, the small table, four plain chairs, the baby's cot, a wall cupboard for clothes and a two-tiered corner stand bearing an accumulation of ornaments and family photographs. Graziella sat on the bed, and her wooden-soled sandals fell with a clatter on the tiled floor. She pulled off her shabby dress, and said, 'Ecco!' She looked at him through her hair. In her dress she looked slender, but now the soft amplitude of her bosom was revealed, her broad hips and her strong, thick calves. Her dark, broad cheeks fell away to a pointed chin that, with the gleam in her dark eyes, gave a hint of mockery to her face even in the tenderest moments.

Lying with his arm about her shoulders, Craddock said, 'Speak the truth. You are glad to be with a man again.'

She pouted. 'Half and half. Without a man it is bad sometimes. But it is peaceful. A woman can be content thus, having lived only to serve a man for years.'

'You never thought of other men? You never wanted?'

'Never. There was one man who wanted me. He did nothing. He only looked at me. Sometimes he touched me, or said a few words, but no more. But he made me feel hunted, like a beast desired by a beast. If he made me feel like a woman, it was only the more for my husband. For this one I felt only disgust.'

'And for me, what do you feel?'

'I do not know. What do you want me to feel?'

'Love?'

'Love? That is a word for girls, not for people like us. Perhaps a friendship, a friendship of the body.' She squeezed his hand. 'But this is not the time to talk.'

'It is the best time to talk.' He stared in a long silence at the fly-specked ceiling. 'You know about the Simeto? There were dead in the river, and dead in the fields, everywhere. We could not move, in the daytime, to bury them, because of the enemy guns above in the hills. They rotted. It was very hot.'

She held his hand and let him talk.

After a while she said, 'I will bring you more wine.'

'No. Stay still.'

'No, wine is good now. Then you can close your eyes, and sleep.'

He raised his head to watch her padding about the room. The sight of her, clumsy-haunched but graceful, gave him a sense of comfort, of belonging.

There were footsteps in the street. Other footsteps had gone by occasionally, sounding as if they were in another world, but this time she looked up in alarm and said, 'Silence!'

There was a rattling at the door, and Nella's voice, 'Graziella! Graziella!'

Graziella signed to him to remain still.

Graziella!' Nella tugged and thumped at the door. The baby stirred at the noise, and moaned. Graziella hurried to the cot and soothed the child. Nella must have heard its whimpering. She cried, 'Graziella! What is the matter? I can hear you.'

Graziella shouted, frantically, 'Be quiet, fool, you will wake the baby. I am washing. I am all wet. I cannot open the door. Come back later.'

'You can open the door,' Nella shrilled. 'I will come in and shut it quickly.'

'I tell you I cannot come!'

'I shall wait. Do not be long.'

Graziella looked about her, distracted. She fumbled at her purse, took out some paper money and pushed it under the door. 'There! While you are waiting, run and get me some fish, some sardines to fry.'

'You did not buy this morning?' There was a quaver of suspicion in Nella's voice.

'No. Go now, quickly.'

They heard Nella scampering away. Graziella sighed, and began to dress. 'It was ugly, non è vero?' she said.

Craddock nodded. He, too, felt depressed. 'This will happen again.'

'Yes, it will be difficult. Perhaps I shall tell her. I do not know yet. Now you must go.'

He was already buttoning his bush shirt. 'Listen, Graziella,' he said, 'it cannot be like this every time. I will not hide in the dark with you every time. I would like to walk with you, in the street. They are opening cinemas. I want to take you. I want to go to the shops with you. That is friendship, too. This was good, but that is good, too, outside in the sunshine.'

'Ba?' She was incredulous. 'You do not understand our life here! I must live here when you are gone. I cannot walk in the street with you.

'All right, not in this street, but we can meet somewhere.'

'Non si fa così. This is not a big town. Listen, tomorrow morning I shall go to Mass. You want to come?'

'Where?'

'The cathedral. You know the cathedral? The people of this street do not go there. We go to a little church, near here.

But tomorrow I shall go to the cathedral, at ten o'clock. You will be there?'

'Yes.'

'Good. Now go.'

He was blinded for a moment by the sunlight as he stepped out into the street. He raised his head to face the light, and saw Rosario standing in the entrance of the shop next door. Rosario's deep-set eyes gleamed. A smile distorted his face; he inclined his head in a movement so exaggerated that it was almost a bow, and said with great courtesy, 'Buongiorno, signor sergente, buongiorno.'

§§§§

The evening was cool and sweet. Nella, hot and flushed with running, paused and rested against the low sea wall. She was tired, not only by her exertions but by the waning of the hysteria that had possessed her. It was two hours since Graziella had driven her away from the door. She had lurked, trembling and suspicious, at the street corner to see what would happen next – had Graziella thought she was a fool, not to suspect? – and she had seen the Englishman coming out. She had wandered off in a daze, hardly knowing what she was doing as she went to the market, bought the fish and took it back to Graziella. Graziella had looked at her, and she had looked sullenly at Graziella; and she had burst into tears. There had been a little spell of comfort while Graziella held her, and stroked her hair, and murmured to her. 'We are women,' Graziella had whispered, 'we are sinners, we are weak,' and, crying a little herself, 'what else have we?'

'You will say nothing?' Graziella had asked, embracing her as she left; and Nella, feeling suddenly flattered at being the possessor of a secret, at being treated as an older woman, had kissed Graziella and consoled her, and had promised.

Afterwards, when she was alone on the waterfront, and the warm comfort of shared sorrows had worn off, she felt tricked and disillusioned. If she had been capable of calm thought she would not have blamed Graziella. Her life in these swarming streets, as well as the impatience of her own young body, had taught her all about the needs and impulses of the flesh. But jealousy took possession of her; jealousy of the man who had come between her and her beloved Graziella.

It had been wonderful with Graziella; helping her to keep house, and being trusted by her as an equal, as a fellow-housewife; sharing secrets and confidences and whispered, ribald jokes with her. At home with mamma life was always uneasy and strained. Mamma was silent, or querulous, or mumbling, but never of her own world, an old woman, shrivelled like a dead fruit; Graziella was young, with blood that ran like her own, thoughts and curiosities that surged like her own. Together in that manless house they had embraced each other, mingled tears, known and consoled each other's hunger. Oh, the beauty of being women together!

The jealousy, working in her immature and tormented mind, bred new resentments. To think that Graziella was the woman who had lectured her, who had protected her, who had implored her to be good! Good! Only children were good. Women said these things, but they went their own way. Her feverish imagination dwelt on what must have been happening behind that bolted door. She felt hot and weak at the thought of the forbidden pleasures.

She believed herself spurned now, shut out by Graziella,

the strange and secret intimacy for ever lost. Heartbroken, she had wandered away along the waterfront, in flight from this new and terrible loneliness and from the incomprehensible longings of her body.

She had come a long way, past the railway station, through the tangle of streets beyond, out into the northern suburbs of the town. She had not known where she was going, and for a second she was frightened. Graziella had never permitted her to go so far on her own – scorn and anger returned – a fine one Graziella was to protect her!

It was pleasant here, on the dusty, white road through Ognina. On her left, with the foothills rising in terraces beyond, were villas and peasant cottages, white walls and dark walls of heaped lava, groves of orange trees and olives and almonds, infusing the evening breeze with their scent; on her right, the bay, with the tranquil sea shaded from cobalt to purple, gaily coloured fishing boats drawn up on the beach and the Rocks of the Cyclops rearing in the distance. The far-off rumble of artillery and the mutter of aircraft overhead did not disturb. British army cars swished quietly along the road. A car crawled past – a tiny, square-bodied truck with a canvas hood; she looked idly, felt an impulse of recognition and looked again. She knew the driver, the fine, big man with the bold face and the red-gold hair. It was Il Rosso, the English captain about whom all the women whispered.

A peremptory whistle roused her from her thoughts. The car had stopped on the other side of the road. The captain looked out through the open window and beckoned. Nella left the wall and took a few paces towards the car. She stopped; the first quiver of curiosity was gone, and her instincts took hold of her, conflicting instincts of fear and desire. The captain gestured again; his face was unsmiling. Still Nella hesitated. She was in a panic. Thought was impossible, and the violent thumping of her heart made her feel sick. The captain turned away from the window and she heard the engine of the car snarl again. Nella cried. 'Wait!' as the vehicle trembled on the verge of movement. She was confused with defiance, despair, passion, tears. The captain called out to her in an impatient voice, and she scurried across to the car. 'Just think,' she told herself ecstatically, as she settled herself in the warmth of the cab, trying to ignore the beating of her heart, with the man at her side apparently quite indifferent to her presence as he looked out over the bonnet, 'Just think, I am going for a ride in a car!'

Chapter Eight

THE piazza in front of the cathedral was gay in the sunshine, its pavements crowded with Sunday morning strollers whose summer suits and white dresses enhanced the brilliance of the light. The air itself seemed to be astir with a million flashing fragments of noise and light and colour. Watching the scene from the cathedral steps, Craddock experienced the same sensations of clarion and gaiety, of sharing in a universal lightheartedness, that in another existence he had known on bright summer days at the seaside or on the towpath at Richmond.

The building, from the outside, was less attractive, its ornate front dirty and decaying, its left wall disfigured by bomb damage. Entering, however, he was immediately subdued by the contained vastness of the interior, the hushed gloom of the nave and the white dazzle within the roof where all the furtive noises of the congregation seemed to gather.

People moved like shadows among the great piers and the gilt and marble tombs, some tiptoeing to a side chapel where a priest was preparing for the next Mass, some making their way towards the High Altar, others going down the aisle towards a chapel where tall candles glimmered in front of a draped image of the Virgin; today was a Catholic feast and many had come to make their devotions to the Madonna.

He could not see Graziella anywhere. He walked round the fringes of the group of people who were assembling for the Mass, feeling self-conscious as his footsteps provoked an occasional glance of annoyance. She was not there. He stood behind the congregation, leaning on a pillar, and watched the Mass. Within the vast, whispering quietness the chanting of the choir at the High Altar mingled with the beehive mumble of the Mass. The ceaseless, unarticulated drone and the quivering purity of the candle-flames before his eyes were hypnotic. Scepticism was dulled and he submitted to his surroundings, enjoying the contrasts of dimness and white light and the sad, sensuous sounds of worship.

Graziella came hurrying past from somewhere within the building. There was scarcely any recognition in her glance as she saw him, before she joined in the Mass.

The congregation dispersed and he lost sight of her among the swirl of people. He followed – some instinct seemed to enable him to distinguish the tapping of her sandals on the mosaic floor among all the slap and shuffle of shoes – and caught sight of her again. She was waiting for him on the steps as he emerged into the sunlight.

She smiled faintly, and kept a little apart from him. People were clattering past them into the street. On the pavement below two nuns were marshalling a duster of tiny, black-frocked orphans into a procession.

'I did not see you come in,' Craddock said. 'Where were you before the Mass?'

She was looking down on the children and the passing crowds, her lips slightly parted as if she were enjoying an unaccustomed pleasure. She did not turn her head towards him as she answered, 'At confession.'

'You confessed?

'Yes.'

'About us?'

She nodded, and he laughed brutally.

She turned to him angrily, 'You have no right to laugh. I have told you, you do not know our life. A woman is shut up in darkness all her life. All her sins, all her sorrows, all her suffering, gather within her own soul. It is good to confess, to confess everything, not only the truth, but everything. It unburdens the heart. One can breathe again for a little while.' She smiled at him, sadly but with more tolerance. 'There are even some women who find comfort because only here may they talk to another man beside their husbands. Their lives are lonely and dark, and here they sit, with no one to see their faces, and they can talk, and talk, and empty their hearts, and know that behind the screen a man is listening. You smile? You think that it is foolish? But I cannot believe it is evil, even when the priest is weak and he holds their hands.'

'Does he?'

'Not here. It is not a thing that a priest should do. But in our church, ours does it. I think he likes a pretty girl. Well,' she said, angry again as she saw him grin, 'why not? When I was a young girl, in our village, I was very shocked because the priest used to push a pram about in the street with his two children. They were twins, and we all knew the mother. She was not a bad woman. Everybody used to stop, and talk to him, and tell him how beautiful the twins were, and he was proud. I cried to my mother, "How can you go to a priest who has bastards?" My mother looked puzzled, and she said, "But if the priest may not marry, he must have bastards." I was very young, and my blood was not yet hot, and so I said again, "But it is bad, bad!" And my mother laid her hand on mine, and she said, "He is good to us. Why should not a woman be good to him?"'

Craddock said, 'I think you do not really believe in God. You women choose to deceive yourselves. It is foolish. There is no need. There is a better way.'

'Whether I am foolish or not I do not know,' Graziella cried. 'I am only a poor woman. But I need God, and I will not give Him up. It is all mystery for us, all sin, all suffering, all misery. Si sbaglia sempre nella vita. What is our life but one blunder after another? What do we know? Where can we go? Who will guide us? What else is there?'

He did not answer, and she repeated, 'What else is there?'

He made a furtive gesture towards the procession of children that was bobbing across the street, and looked away, as if ashamed to have betrayed himself. Graziella was silent, then she smiled and touched his arm, 'You see, you, too, need a dream. Let us go.'

He followed her down the steps, keeping at a little distance. He said, 'Let us not go straight back. Let us walk for a while. The sun is good.'

She smiled at him over her shoulder. It was the first time he had seen her look so youthful and coquettish. She smiled with her lips parted wide, and there was no care in her face. They walked to the left, through an arch into a park. The trees were tired and their leaves dusty, but their shadows dappled the golden pathway with changing patterns that shifted and trembled like the surface of water. Here there was sunlight, and coolness, too. Children squealed and chattered. It was peace. Craddock and Graziella strolled, still apart, not speaking, but both utterly happy and utterly absorbed in each other. They came out into a street behind the dock gates and turned homewards.

A convoy of ambulances was drawn up in the kerb, and wounded were being taken through the dock gates to a hospital ship. Craddock paid no attention; he was habituated to not noticing such sights. Graziella was wrapped in her own happiness. They paused to let a squad of stretcher-bearers go by. The stretcher-bearers, too, showed no concern for their burdens. They were sweating and disgruntled, and as they passed they talked loudly to each other of their hardships.

The door of an ambulance opened, and two attendants led a man down the steps on to the pavement before Craddock and Graziella could pass. The man had a huge, splendid body and a fine head. He wore an officer's uniform. He stood on the pavement as if unaware of his own actions, without will or intelligence. His body seemed strangely collapsed, without tension, with no nerves to command or muscles to obey. The attendants tried to lead him, like a shambling bear, across the pavement, but after a couple of paces he halted and would not budge, uttering senseless grunts with his mouth wide and slavering. His arms dangled at his sides, his legs sagged as if at any moment they might cave in under the body's weight. His head was sunk into stooped shoulders, his cheeks were cavernous and his eyes were lost in deep, black pits, so that he looked like some monster uninhabited by a human soul.

Craddock felt a sickness in his stomach. To him the sight was a reminder of something that he tried always not to see. Graziella looked at the madman, and then she looked up with horror into Craddock's face, as if comparing the two. Craddock said huskily, 'Come, quickly,' and hurried her past.

She pressed herself to his side. Her face was set and, heedless any longer of her good name, she gripped his arm fiercely all the way home.

§§§§

A bathing party – the first, for the beach was only now being cleared of mines – was spending the afternoon by the sea.

Pink bodies, brown bodies, sprawled on the beach, scattered like the dead, arms and legs rigidly outflung, eyes closed, faces frowning against the glare that clenched eyelids could not keep out; bodies inert, each sunk in a white mould of hot sand, the sunlight prickling like sleet at every inch of exposed skin; drugged with sunshine.

Within the head each felt the numbing pressure of heat; the mind spurned thought. Before the eyes, shifting veils of blood-red and black, and fantastic patterns in every colour. The world was vast, all sea, all sky, with only a fringe of white sand and drunken red-roofed houses heaped on a hillside to soak in the sun. The heat imposed a vast silence in which all sounds remained as tiny and isolated as the insects that crawled in the rippled whiteness of the sand. Voices filtered into the consciousness without awakening the intelligence.

'You should never of led diamonds...'

'...not a stitch on, under her dress...'

'...take a tram from the Elephant and get off at Hawthorn Street, by the chapel...'

'The trouble with vermouth, it's too sweet.'

From far away, the hollow thump of men somersaulting off the breakwater into the sea; curtains of brilliant spray upflung against the sun; a hubbub of boyish shouting. The voices murmured.

'...you don't want to stuff your garden up with bushes or fruit if you want to grow good vegetables... '

'... a lovely voice but she wouldn't look after it...'

'Do all my own repairs. I wouldn't let a builder into the house if he paid me for it.'

Beyond the mutter of voices, the nervous buzz of insects, and beyond that, a deeper drone impregnated the air; the insects flitted like little specks of light as their transparent wings caught the sun; and beyond, again, high up in the blue, moved more specks of light, always in orderly patterns, always going northwards, cluster after cluster, without end. The mind did not associate the sight with the sound, was not conscious of the carnage beyond the distant hills, was shut tight against words like 'bombs', 'friend', 'foe', 'retreat', 'evacuation'. It was open only to immediate sensation and to the bludgeoning heat.

'...we was teaching the kiddies musical chairs. They nearly went mad laughing. I was having a good time myself...'

Lazy eyes admired the sea and sky, passed over the ugly and irrelevant litter that disfigured the beach; for instance, the anti-aircraft gun on the sea wall; for instance, the mines stacked below the wall; for instance, the ripped-up tangle of barbed wire; for instance, the two soldiers' graves in the sand.

Sprawled in the sand were the naked bodies of men. Whose were the uniforms that hung like scarecrows on the barbed wire?

'...her skin is as soft as milk, and when she kisses me...'

Thought and memory were stilled. There was no past, no future, no war; only the sun, the sand, and the sea, all fused in one white glare.

'It's tea-time, lads. Dress yourselves and get fell in.'

Movement was a burden. The vision was still obscured, the mind stupid, the limbs leaden. Why not have stayed for ever in this trance.

A voice, 'No kidding, Fred, I've never had a holiday like this before. Have you?'

§§§§

Doors and shutters were closed against the sun. Everyone slept but the children, who wandered, undaunted, in the streets.

Ten days ago Ciccio Martinelli had looked like a little brown-skinned old man, with a flat, small-peaked workman's cap pushing the ragged hair down over his puckered face, a pair of long trousers rolled up at the ankles above unshod, dirty feet, and a torn black jacket to cover his bare chest. Now his hair was cropped, and he wore a British soldier's fore-and-aft cap with the flaps buttoned under his chin, a British battle blouse, and on his feet a pair of soldiers' canvas slippers. He was squatting on his haunches, on the scorching pavement, playing cards with Aldo Buonocorso. Aldo also had cropped hair, with a straight fringe. He wore a man's collarless striped shirt, which he had cut down and washed himself, and a pair of shorts that barely reached below his thighs. The dog Vittorio sat behind him, studying the cards over his shoulder. Both the boys smoked cigarettes, like grave old men.

Aldo said, 'Nella,' – Nella was leaning against the wall, with her hands behind her back, dreaming up at the sun –

'tomorrow I am going with my father into the country. Would you like to come?'

Nella did not answer.

'We are going to San Martino. Many friends of my father are there, from the village, to gather the grapes. There will be much to eat, and dancing. It will be good. I am going to bring back a lizard in a box. Nella?'

'Leave me alone, child!'

'My father once told me that one can tame lizards, and play with them. Graziella will let you come.'

Nella snapped, 'It is no affair of Graziella's.'

'Ciccio, you come!'

'I am at work.' Ciccio was employed in the officer's mess at a British stores depot, as a waiter and handyman. 'Besides, I do not like the country.'

'I like the country. I would like to live in the country. In the country there is much to do.'

'Crazy! One can earn more in a day here than in a month in the country. I go for ice cream for the officers, they give me fifty lire. A colonel, he asked for a signorina. I brought a girl to him. He gave me a hundred lire. And after, I told the girl he had given me nothing, and she gave me another fifty lire.'

'That which you do, it is not work. It is not good. Is it, Nella?'

Nella said, 'You are too young to know.'

'I am not too young. My father has told me. My father has said that we need to work, for ourselves and for our country. My father has said that the evil years have corrupted us, and that we must work to change our life.'

Ciccio uttered a screeching laugh and slapped his knee. 'Your father! Your fine father! And when did he tell you that?'

'A long time ago.' There were tears and defiance in Aldo's voice. 'But I have remembered!'

'Your father does not remember.'

'He remembers. He is sick. He will be well again.'

'Your father is a beggar.'

'No!'

'Your father creeps about like a filthy old dog. He is weak and cowardly, and he should die, like a filthy old dog.'

Aldo screamed, 'No!' He said, his voice trembling, 'I tell you he is not well. He will be better. In the country he will begin to feel better. You will see, after tomorrow!'

A British soldier came towards them. Vittorio turned his head and bared his teeth in a growl of welcome. Ciccio cried, 'Ciao.' It was the soldier called Tiger.

Tiger stooped over them, with his hands on his knees, looking down at the game like a grown-up.

Ciccio was anxious to show off to his friends the English that he had acquired. He held up his hand of cards. 'Carrd-ass, yess?'

'Cards,' said Tiger, in a voice like the schoolteacher's.

'Speak-a good, yess? One two free carrd-ass. Win all caramelle from Aldo.'

Tiger asked him something in English.

'Game-a si chiama scopa. Play scopa. Not inglese. Game-a italiana.'

Tiger pointed to himself. 'Noi different. No play scopa. Cards molto different.' He pointed at the gaily coloured medieval playing cards. 'Nostro cards – different.'

Ciccio nodded proudly. 'Si, si. Play Nap-a, Brag-a, Solo, huh?'

'Not for caramelle. For money – dinaro.'

'Si chiama gamble, yess? Noi gamble, polizia come. Capisc' polizia?'

'Police?'

'Pollis, yess. Pollis stop gamble. Take to calaboso. Prison. Gamble al-aways in house.' He mimed concealment. 'I know all house. Bad house. Know Piazza Stesicoro? Market?'

Tiger nodded. 'Piazza Stesicoro bad. All streets there out of bounds. Military polizia – capeesh? – stop soldati.'

'Si, si! Red-a-cahps! Ciccio know house. Many house for men. Carrd-ass. Vino. Bigliardo. Signorinas. You want go? Ciccio take.'

'No. Houses no buono.'

'Mi, all-a soldati go. Ciccio take all-a. You go, only see. No go house, only street, see. Red-a-cahps no see.'

Tiger hesitated, and said, 'Okay.'

'Okay, Okay.' To Aldo Ciccio said, 'You can come, too. And you, Nella.'

Nella answered sullenly, 'No. I shall not come.'

The boys went off with the soldier. Nella was left alone in the street. She looked around her, and seemed to feel her loneliness. She stood with her head lowered for a moment. Vittorio shook himself, looked back at her and trotted after the boys. Nella cried, 'I am coming,' and ran after them.

§§§§

Tiger sought out Sergeant Craddock that evening in a state of great excitement. 'Here, sarge,' he gasped, 'guess what?'

'You aren't half in a state. Where you been? Robbin' a bank?'

Tiger brushed white streaks of plaster from his shirt and wiped his sweating face. 'Here, guess who I saw?'

'Who?'

'Jobling.' Tiger tried to steady his breath.

'Who?'

'Harry Jobling.'

The sergeant looked round and signed him to go into the empty guardroom. 'Now, sit down and get your breath, and take it easy. Now then, where you been?'

Tiger sat for a few seconds until the trembling in his legs had stopped. 'Up the Casbah.' This was the name that the men had given to the honeycomb of streets and alleys behind the Piazzo Stesicoro. The quarter was out of bounds, because of its bad reputation, and was always surrounded by military police.

'Bright little feller, aren't you? How'd you get in there'

'Well, like, I was with my tart – you know, that kid Nella. She's not a bad-looker, is she? I think she's a bit sweet on me. Well, like, we was going for a bit of a walk round, a couple of kids out o' the street come with us, and we went down that way. Just for a look, sarge. I only wanted to see what it was like. They don't half know their way around, these kids. We went into a house, an' through back yards, and up stairs, and over the roofs. Dead easy. We didn't have to go past the redcaps at all, an' we come out right in the middle of it. Here, sarge, what a gaff! You ought to see! Bloody streets so narrow, you can touch both sides at once. Just a drain down the middle, runnin' with I don't know what. Smells like a public lavatory, no kidding! Stinkin' fish, rubbish everywhere. You can't see for the washing hangin' out. Dark doorways, courtyards, it wouldn't take you long to get lost there, I can tell you.'

'Get on with it!'

'I am. Well, there's all tarts everywhere. In the windows, on balconies. They aren' half cheeky. I mean, I was with a girl, an' they didn't care. Smilin' at me, they were, and waving, and calling out. There was one up on a balcony, she held her dressing-gown open. You oughta seen! Right in front of Nella.'

'Where did you see him?'

'Well, like, I was looking up at the windows...'

'I bet you were!'

'...and all of a sudden there was Harry Jobling looking down at me.'

'Where was it?'

'I don't know. It was one of them high houses, all yellowy and peeling, with like all curly iron bars in front of the windows. Proper gaff, it was.'

'I said, where was it?'

'How do I know?' said Tiger desperately. 'I took another look and he was gone.'

'Didn't you go in?

'How could I? The door was shut. They wouldn't let me.'

'Who wouldn't let you?'

'Well, I mean, I had a tart with me. Look, sarge, I couldn't make them understand. I tried to explain, and they jabbered away, and they were all laughing at me, and then the dog started barking, and they said, come on, there was a redcap coming, and we all run like muck.'

'Ah, you little nit. Why didn't you get the address?'

'They got no addresses there. The streets got no names. No numbers on the houses. They all look the same. It's all twisted up, like.' Tiger was in a panic. He confessed, 'I tell you, sarge, I was all in a doo-dah.'

'Was he in uniform?'

'How do I know? I only see him a second.'

'Sure it was him?'

'Well, I...'

'All right. Thanks for telling me. You go in and get washed now. And don't go up the Casbah again, or I'll pulverize you.'

'Okay, sarge.'

'And, Tiger?'

'Yes, sarge.'

'Remember, mum's the word.'

Chapter Nine

THE plain was vast, so vast that the whole of Catania, lying behind Aldo and his father, was only a spatter of white in a corner of the picture; but the plain itself was as tiny as a doormat at the foot of the infinite sky. Sky and plain met in an endless line so far away that even the thrusting hills scarcely spoiled its flatness. In the soft, milky light of early morning, when they had started out on their sixteen-kilometre journey, it had been frightening enough to emerge from the sheltering streets into this limitlessness, but now that the sun had risen and filled the world with its glare, the unbounded became twice as big and doubly terrifying.

A giant had unrolled a ribbon of white road across the plain, and it stretched before them like a lifetime. Aldo had often watched ants toiling for hours to cross a pavement, and now he felt as if he and his father had been bewitched

into two tiny ants, black specks crawling across the face of
the earth. The giant was Etna, towering out of its foothills
to half the height of the sky.

'Father, how far have we come?'

'Coraggio, coraggio! We have already come six kilometres, and soon we shall leave the main highway. You want
to rest?'

'Oh, no, pappa. Look at Vittorio! He is not tired. He likes
the country. He has never been so gay before.'

Vittorio had abandoned his usual pose of sullen dignity
and was bounding ahead of them, rushing into ditches,
exploring farmyards, leaping easily to and fro across the
dry-stone walls.

'It is not good for a dog to live all his life in streets. Look,
he is bringing us a stone. I hope he does not decide to bring
us back a hand grenade. There are many in the ditches here.'

'Is it here that the soldiers fought, pappa?'

'Here, yes, but principally to the south. Soon you will see.'

Aldo was filled with joy at the strength in his father's
voice. Everything was happening as he had foreseen. At the
outset of their journey, Aldo had been fearful and doubting
at the sight of the familiar, hopeless droop of his father's
shoulders and at the weary pace at which they had moved;
but, with the town behind them and the sun on their faces,
pappa had already straightened his back, was swinging his
arms and stepping out more briskly, and was speaking as if
the world about him once again held some interest for him.

'The plain is rich, is it not, Aldo?'

'How?'

'Look about you. Those wide, brown fields have borne
wheat. There, as far as you can see, are groves of olives.
There, and there, and there, are plantations of oranges, figs,

peaches, lemons, almonds. From the hills comes sulphur, to the factory by the railway. Those fat, yellow melons that you love are grown here. Do you see the vineyards? They are too many to count, are they not? And the maize. The earth is rich – but the people are poor.'

'Why are they poor?'

'I am ashamed that you ask, Aldo. Have I not told you? Men and women raise all these riches, but not for themselves, nor for their children, nor for us. The land is owned by a few, and the riches are taken by a few. Those who work gain nothing but the food for their next day's labour, and little enough food at that. There is no difference between them and the oxen they employ. They live together with their oxen, and it is fitting that they should live thus, for they are all the oxen of their masters.'

'Why do they not work the land for themselves?'

'The masters are too strong.'

'But you said that the masters are few.'

'The masters have police and soldiers.'

'But the police and soldiers are from the people.'

'They obey. Look! Vittorio! Hey, Vittorio, here Vittorio! Why does he obey? Too many men are dogs.'

Aldo trotted at his father's heels, feeling crushed at his inability to answer this argument and offended at the slighting reference to Vittorio. He was disturbed by vague memories of a time when his father had spoken differently, but the memories were elusive and he could not take hold of them. He tried to work out for himself the differences between dogs and men, but he could not make his protest articulate. 'There are no birds in the sky,' he said. 'An hour ago the sky was full of birds. I could hear them singing everywhere, even when I could not see them.'

'The heat is too great for the birds. They are all in hiding. It is not good to be in the heat. That is why we started early. The birds rest, but not the peasants.' He pointed to the tiny figures of people working in the distant fields.'

'Nor the soldiers.'

'Nor the soldiers. Nor those...' he pointed to the slender green lizards darting to and fro on the white walls.

'Nor the mosquitoes, pappa,' said Aldo, excitedly, making a game of it, 'nor the cicadas.' The silence thrummed with the sound of insects.

A British lorry rushed down upon them, its tailboard clattering, and dwindled along the road, leaving a long plume of white dust spreading behind it. Aldo felt the dust settle on his face and licked the metallic taste from his lips. For seconds after the lorry had vanished the puny sumach trees at the roadside trembled, their leaves in a silvery disarray. The dusty leaves of the olive trees caught the sunlight like tinsel. There was a sound like a battle and a motor cycle hurtled past, and again a cloud of dust wreathed out towards the ditches. Aldo's heart banged with excitement at the glimpse he had caught of the rider crouched over the handlebars in goggles, gauntlets and grim, smooth helmet. The heat beat down on the road, the routed silence crept back and time slowed down again.

They turned off into a side road whose rutted and flinty surface made walking an ordeal. The dust lay so thick that the sound of their footsteps was muffled and a little white smoke followed at their heels. There was a rattle of wheels and a peasant cart overtook them. The cart was painted all over in brightly coloured pictures of local legends, and it was pulled by a reproachful-looking donkey which wore a collar of silver bells and tall plumes of red and green. The driver's seat was empty and the donkey's master lay fast asleep among the sacks in the back of the cart. Aldo hoped that his father would ask for a lift, but his father said, 'Let him sleep.'

They were alone again, but Aldo was no longer bored or timid, for there was much to look at. The ditches now were cluttered with the rubbish of war: cartridge cases, helmets, articles of clothing, tins and cartons with English and German labels on them. Little trenches were cut, neatly as slots, into the banks, and dugouts burrowed like rabbit-runs. Beneath a huge cactus that raised its spiky leaves like warning hands against the sky. Aldo found a rounded sap in which rows of little bombs nested in holes cut in a wooden shelf. He would have taken one, but his father called, 'Come away from there. There are mines buried in those ditches.'

Now the fields were pitted with round holes, each hole with a rim of yellow-burned earth. Here and there were to be seen untidy little clumps of graves, mounds of brown earth each surmounted by a crude wooden cross, a broken rifle and a heap of soldier's equipment that was usually covered with a black gum of sun-dried blood.

The farmhouses that were outlined against the blue sky were burned and ruined. Tanks lay, blackened and half-sunk in the soft earth. Aldo could not imagine that they had ever moved; they looked as if they had been here as long as the squat oak trees.

It was all very interesting; but disappointing, too, for there was nothing here in this empty desolation which Aldo could associate with the highly coloured pictures of war and glory that he had seen so often in illustrated magazines. He looked for the dramatic, and instead he saw these occasional patches of untidiness around which the vines and the maize were already closing again, screening the marks of destruction with their fruitfulness, and amongst which the peasants moved slowly at their work, driving their oxen and tending their crops as if the rhythm of the seasons had never been interrupted. Families were living in the smashed farmhouses, and from the gaping walls he could faintly hear across the fields the sounds of work, of altercation and of screaming children.

He felt a little happier when Vittorio came leaping at him to lead him to a discovery; something more like what he had expected. A corpse lay on its back under a cactus hedge. He went close up to it and studied it with great interest. Under the German helmet was something that looked like a mouldering black pudding. The tunic was filled out by the ribs, but the stomach had fallen away so that the waist of the trousers lay as if empty on the ground. The arms were outflung, but instead of hands there emerged at the wrist only shining white bones, the fingers driven in a death-grip into the crumbling earth. Vittorio sat on his haunches and growled with distaste, but Aldo looked round him for a stick with which to poke at this strange object. He was curious to find what it was that swarmed out of the blood-blackened holes in the tunic like rice from a bursting sack. His father explained, 'Maggots,' and drew him away.

He ran on to inspect an abandoned machine gun, and it was only later, when they were near to their destination and the vineyards around them were filled with the noise and movement of people, that he remembered the dead man and pitied him for lying all alone and forgotten in that great emptiness.

The world shrank again as they followed the path through the vineyards, and he forgot the dead man and the bare, brown plain. On either side the vines loomed above him, leaning on their sticks under the weight of the black bunches of grapes, shaking and whispering at the ceaseless attentions of the harvesters. Behind the pattern of writhing vine-stems and shrivelled foliage, Aldo could see a ceaseless, busy movement of people, and every few seconds a woman would come out on to the path and walk proudly away with a big basket of grapes on her head.

They were welcomed by Turi the overseer, his father's friend, a man like a great tree, with a face as dark and knobbly as the face of a tree, who moved from place to place as massively and as deliberately as if he had to drag up his roots each time he stirred. Aldo was fascinated by his leather waistcoat, with its rows of cartridge-pouches. Aldo was ill with heat and exhaustion. Great, burning hands seemed to be pressing down on his head and shoulders. The sweat made his eyes smart and blurred his vision, and his skin was chafed by his dusty, sodden clothing, but delight revived him as he saw the two men above him clasping each other powerfully and exchanging news and greetings in deep, strong voices. It was as if Turi were conferring something on his father.

Turi led them out of the dust and the glare, and they rested on a cool stone bench in the shade, while he brought them water with which to bathe their faces, wine, and bread and hard-boiled eggs. Later, while the men talked and smoked, Aldo went off with Vittorio to inspect his surroundings.

The rest of the day passed in a delirium of exploration. The faint headache with which the heat had left him only served to augment his excitement. He crept among the men who bustled to and fro in the yard of the wine-factory, looking up with wonder at their size, their strength, their faces so dark and leathery that they might have been brother-mastiffs of Vittorio's, and the thick, black clothes with which they muffled themselves against the sun. He went into the big, gloomy barn where the wine was being pressed, enjoying the sickly, intoxicating smell and envying the men and boys who stood with their trousers rolled up to their knees trampling the heaped grapes while the dark juice filmed the sloping floors and gurgled away along the gutters. He wandered among the vines, eating grapes until his hands and clothes were sticky with juice, lingering to help fill a basket until impatience or an outburst of distant laughter sent him on his travels again, bragging to the women, telling them importantly what was happening in the town, inexplicably warmed by their sad, kindly glances and by the touch of their warm, rough hands. He met almost-forgotten uncles and aunts who laughed and wept over him, and a horde of cousins who, with the other boys and girls of his own age, paused to pelt him with grapes and draw him into screaming, joyful battles that lasted until a grown-up arrived to drive them back to work. He watched, wide-eyed, while two men killed a big, black snake with sticks, dodging and beating at it while it lashed about with incredible speed and strength. They chopped it in two with a spade, and the pieces still writhed. Long after they had shovelled it into a fire, Aldo crouched and watched the white, coiled skeleton glowing in the heat.

In the evening the people gathered in the courtyard, the old men wearing their black coats like cloaks and puffing at long pipes, the children as tireless and noisy as ever, the young men and women in separate groups. Aldo found his father sitting among a group of friends who were listening with respect as he told them how things were going in Catania.

'Do you think the war will come back?' they asked him anxiously, and they were happy when he assured them that the Germans had been driven back almost to Messina and would soon be gone.

'And the English?'

'The English, too. They will follow to fight in Italy.'

'Here,' said Turi, 'it is as it has always been. As soon as the soldiers went the people came down from the hills. There are mines in the vineyards, but we gather, and there will be wine. There are mines in the fields, but we sow, and there will be crops. The roads and the bridges will be repaired. We shall rebuild our houses. There will be wars again as there will be storms. But next time let it be somewhere else.'

Afterwards there was singing and drinking. When it was dark the people ignored the law that the soldiers had made and lit a big fire. There was more music, and some of the men danced. They grew hot as they danced, and they took their shirts off and danced bare to the waist. They made a trial of endurance of it, keeping up the furious step interminably. One man swung a child on to his shoulders; others snatched up children; the first man took up a second child; and they danced, with their burdens, while one after another dropped out, the people clapping and stamping all the time until only one man was left, to be acclaimed like a hero.

Young men and women were talking to each other on the outskirts of the crowd, shyly, watched by their parents. One lad seized a girl by the arm and tried to draw her away into the dark. The girl screamed, and Aldo jumped for joy as one of her brothers leaped forward and there was a clash of knives in the firelight. The combatants were separated as soon as blood was drawn, and for minutes afterwards there was a tremendous hubbub of screaming and quarrelling between the two families and their supporters, with the women outdoing the men.

'Pappa,' Aldo asked fearfully, 'what will happen?'

'Nothing,' his father chuckled, 'but I think that he will marry her.'

'But the other one might have killed him!'

'Then he would not have married her,' replied his father, and all the men around roared with laughter as if his father were a great humorist.

The fire died down and people drifted away to bed, the families to the stables or ruined hovels which they occupied, the unmarried men to a big barn.

Aldo lingered for a while in the darkness, enjoying the cool air and pretending, in the starlight, that he was a lone adventurer in a strange, ghostly land. Lizards scuttled in the cactus hedges, not the delicate, beautiful little creatures that he had seen in the sunlight, but ugly monsters, a foot long, with slug-like white bellies, rough backs and bulging eyes. He squatted on his haunches close to them and imagined that they were as big as crocodiles. Far away in the darkness white flashes flickered like lightning, and coloured lights rose and died mysteriously in the night. The olive trees were like witches dancing. He shivered, and assured himself that Vittorio was near.

He went back to the barn and was glad of the thick, smelly warmth. A hurricane lamp near the door cast a little splash of light that was just enough to make all the darkness flicker and the shadows dance. The sleeping men were like great black bundles heaped about the floor. He crept under his father's blanket and took Vittorio in beside him, in a grateful embrace. Between the warmth of his father and the heat of the dog he lay for a while in a happy dizziness of fatigue, remembering confusedly the endless white road, the fierce sunlight, the stir and clamour of the vineyards, his father's face lit from within by manhood, the gleam of steel in the firelight, the red glow on the skins of the dancers, the hideous eyes of the lizards; then he slept.

His father woke him early in the morning. They took the bundles of food with which their friends had provided them, and the box in which Aldo had two little green lizards, and climbed up on to a cart that was going in the direction of Catania. The cart was stacked high with barrels and Aldo sat on top with his father, holding on to the binding ropes to keep his balance and looking proudly down from what seemed an immense height on the people who were waving and shouting goodbye to them.

All the way back Aldo was beside himself with pride and happiness. He could hardly wait to see his father come face to face once more with Nella, and Ciccio, and all those people in the street. He talked incessantly, shouting to every passer-by, bawling songs, banging with his fists on a barrel as if it were a drum, playing king-of-the-castle on his perch, day-dreaming a dozen adventures as the sun rose in the sky and the parched fields crept by.

The carter set them down at the cross-roads outside the town and they continued on foot along the straggling Via Acquicella, past the outlying huddle of alleys and shanties, to the town gate. They made their way through the streets, and the nearer they came to home the more impatiently Vittorio bounded on ahead, while Aldo, also prickling with impatience, tugged at his father's hand and tried to hasten his step.

His father, although the effort had been so much less than yesterday's, resisted and slowed down his pace, hesitating to look vaguely at shop windows, mopping his brow and saying in a gruff voice, 'There is no hurry, the sun is up.'

They turned at last into their own street. Aldo, who, unable to contain himself, had raced on ahead with Vittorio, halted and looked round. He was surprised to see his father so far behind. He waited, his heart thudding with breathlessness and with a strange, cold premonition. He seemed to be waiting for ever. He cried, 'Pappa!' His voice was still bright, feigning a childish impatience, but he was stricken with panic and disbelief. 'Pappa!' His father hardly seemed to be coming nearer, and the sick thumping of his heart measured out an eternity of time. He tried not to hear the tell-tale, melancholy footsteps, or to see the too familiar shuffle, the sagging shoulders. He ran back, smiling eagerly up at his father and taking hold of his sleeve. The English sergeant came by and Aldo smiled at him, too, blinking back the unbidden tears.

His father half-turned, as the sergeant passed them, and extended a hand. Aldo cried, 'No!' and pulled at his father's sleeve. His father ignored him, and whined, 'Buon giomo, signor sergente. Una sigaretta, per favore? He plucked his sleeve away from Aldo's grasp, and as he took the cigarette he muttered peevishly to his son, 'Leave me alone, I am tired after that journey. I need a cigarette.'

Aldo did not answer. He walked beside his father, trembling a little. The tears were gone; his eyes were hot and dry, and he felt as if he would never cry again.

Chapter Ten

ALL day long the black flocks of aircraft swung across the sky, and the nights trembled with their roar. Phosphorescent gun-flashes made the mountain peaks leap in and out of the darkness. Lorries rumbled northward, and ambulances came lurching back along the deep-worn roads. Ragged mobs of prisoners swarmed into the compounds. Then, one day, the last echo died among the hills. The last stains of shell smoke drifted away from over the straits and left the sky serene. The last Germans slipped aboard their ferries and Messina was empty and silent, a desert of white ruins. There were no more aircraft in the sky and no more convoys on the roads. The war was gone from Sicily. This was on the seventeenth day of August.

In the Via dei Martiri, the days were tranquil, and human life flourished like a garden. Every mind was closed to the carnage that continued across the face of the earth; soldiers and civilians alike told each other, 'La guerra è finita.' They nourished themselves on this illusion, 'The war is over,' disowning, as is the way of men, all the world outside themselves, all time but the present.

The aspect of the street had changed. At one end, outside the billet, the road and pavements were spotlessly dean, and even the rest of the street, by force of example, was tidier, the rubbish being piled in a few great heaps against the walls of the air-raid shelter. It was unusual, now, to see groups of soldiers hanging about outside their habitation, for most of the men had found homes for themselves. Only a minority had women of their own, but many more had been adopted into families and spent their spare time helping the old folk or playing with the children. The street might have been a village, leading a life of its own in the midst of the greater life of the town. The children were all looking well after two weeks of feeding on British rations, and many of them were neatly dressed in clothes whose material bore a suspicious resemblance to khaki drill or army blankets. There were fewer of them playing in the street, for the priest – with money given to him by some Catholic soldiers – had bought pencils and paper and had started a little school. The company's medical corporal had established an unofficial dispensary to which women and children streamed every day to have their ailments treated. Curtains, never seen before in the street, had appeared in a few windows, and one domesticated soldier had even knocked up a window-box. A new language had come into being, which not only served for intercourse between English and Sicilians, but which was in common use within each group. Thus a soldier complaining at the cookhouse would grumble, 'This munjah-ree's no bloody bonna,' to which the cooks would probably reply,

'Fangola!' – while a Sicilian housewife, expressing approval of a neighbour's latest purchase, would tell her that it was 'jus'-the-bloody-job'.

Captain Rumbold, helpless in the face of this process, did not know whether to laugh or to be angry. He was having a good time himself; in the Mess, he described the girl he had picked up as 'a fiery little bitch'. It was not greatly displeasing, when he walked down the street, to see his men sitting quietly at the street doors, passing their time soberly, often singing quietly and harmoniously with their women and their friends the songs of the moment, 'Piccola Santa', 'Amo Pola', or the banal and heartbreaking 'Lili Marlene'. He had laughed loud and long on the Sunday morning when Ling had come to him for a pass out of billets 'to take the kids to church'. 'Why?' he had asked. 'You're not a Catholic, are you?' Ling had stood for a moment frantically corrugating his bald head in search of an answer before he had replied, 'No, but you got to bring 'em up decent, like, 'aven't you, sir?' The captain had granted the pass. But he had been furious when a Sicilian woman had called out to Sergeant Craddock, in his presence, 'Ciao, Pippo!' 'Pippo?' queried the captain. 'Who's that?' 'Me,' admitted Sergeant Craddock, a little unhappily. 'Well!' exclaimed the captain, staring at the solid, ruddy face of his favourite sergeant. 'If you're going native that's the bloody limit!'

§§§§

On the day after the fighting ended Craddock drew three months' back pay, went to the market and bought an old portable gramophone, some records, a bottle of good wine and a Spanish comb.

'What are these things for?' asked Graziella as he unloaded his gifts on to her table.

'The comb is to wear, the wine is to drink, and the gramophone is to play.'

'But for me?' She wrung her hands, in a harassed way, and smiled wonderingly. 'Why?'

Craddock set out two tumblers and filled them with wine. 'No more questions. Drink.'

She emptied the glass, looked at him shyly, and laughed. He refilled her glass. 'Go on,' he said, 'all of it.'

'Ah, no, you will make me drunk.'

'A little. Come!' He sat beside her, with one arm round her shoulders, and with his free hand raised the glass to her lips. She sipped obediently, like a child, looked at him again in inquiry and broke into uncontrollable laughter. He squeezed her shoulders and said, 'There, that's better.'

She calmed herself and asked, still gasping a little with laughter, 'What are you doing, madman?'

Craddock left her and began to wind up the gramophone. He placed a record on the turntable. 'Your cheeks are flushed and your smile is without a shadow. I have waited a long time to see that.' He pressed the switch. 'Do you know this waltz? "The Blue Danube". Now we shall dance.'

Graziella made a noise of derision. 'I do not dance. I am a married woman with a child. My time for dancing is finished.'

'When it was your time for dancing, did you dance?'

'No.'

'Then you will learn now.'

'It is too difficult.'

'No, it is easy. Let me confess. I have only danced three times since my wedding, and rarely before. But I will teach you. I have watched you. You will learn easily.'

She rose to her feet, but hesitated, holding the back of the chair.

'Come. To please me.'

'Do I not please you now?'

'You please me much. But I am not satisfied.'

'Why?' Her hesitance was a sham; she was excited and pouting already.

'You are too wise. And all your wisdom is a bitter wisdom. You are like a woman older than me, but you are only young. I want to be able to see that you are young. You must learn to be young, and to laugh more.'

'It is not easy to laugh in this life,' – but she was laughing again. She came into his arms, and he guided her round the table in a waltz step. Their movement was clumsy, and they faltered, and laughed, and clung to each other. Craddock broke off and gave her some more wine. She giggled and shook her hair free. She moved lightly, humming the tune against his ear. Soon it was Craddock who felt clumsy and she at ease, and when she glided into the turns it was he who was the burden. The record shrieked to a stop, and she clapped her hands and cried. 'Make it play again!' They played the waltz twice more, and at the second playing she cast him off, snatched up the baby from the cot and whirled round the room holding the child high, laughing and singing. Craddock sat on the edge of the table by the gramophone, glorying to see her so wild and youthful. 'Tomorrow I shall ask my friend, the Corporal Honeycombe, to come and dance with you. He dances well. He is good for all things with women. You deserve a good partner.'

She came and sat beside him, with the baby on her lap, giving the child sips of wine from her glass. 'You are not serious?'

'Yes, I am serious. Why not?'

'But I must not dance with another man. It is not decent.'

'Why?'

'It is not permitted. He is not my man.'

'No one permits. You are a free woman. You may do what pleases you. You must learn that.'

'Perhaps you want me to kiss him, too? Her voice was hostile and she looked sulky, but he saw the tell-tale gleam of laughter in her eyes.

'If you kiss him I shall break your neck. But not if you wish to dance with him.'

'I am a free woman. I may do what pleases me. Perhaps it will please me to kiss him!'

'Perhaps. But, speaking purely as a friend, I advise you not to.'

'Ah!' She buried her face exultantly in the child's neck, and her body shook with laughter. 'Englishmen are jealous, too!'

They danced and drank, and played the other records. When the bottle was empty Graziella ran out, not troubling to arrange her disordered hair, and came back with a jug of cheap wine. She could not stop talking. 'When I said that I had never danced, it was not true. When I was a child I always danced. The day I came back from my first Communion, I was wearing a beautiful white dress, and I was walking so nicely in the street, and I heard an old man playing the violin. I danced and danced, and the old man saw me and played always more, always faster, and I danced always faster. I forgot my good behaviour and I danced until I was hot, and my beautiful dress was all disarranged and covered with dust from the street, and still I danced. My uncle saw me, and shouted to my mother. He was angry, for the sake of the family. My mother came and dragged me into the house, and scolded me, but when we were inside the house she embraced me, and she wept over me and told me that when I was dancing I was as beautiful as a bird, and that I reminded her of her own childhood. She cried, "Oh, that you might always remain my child and never become a woman!" My mother was good.' She rested her head tipsily on his shoulder. 'But if I had never become a woman I would never have been with you.' She looked solemnly at him, and went off suddenly into a volley of laughter, leaning across his lap. 'Ecco! Now I laugh even without knowing why.'

'Be careful with the baby,' said Craddock, 'and do not give him any more to drink, or you will make him drunk, too.' He added, after a little pause, 'How long before he is asleep?

Graziella raised her eyes. 'That is why I am giving him wine,' she said.

§§§§

It was night, and Graziella was alone, except for the baby sleeping in its cot. She moved about the room barefoot, humming to herself, still flushed with wine and pleasure. Half the room was weakly lit by a paraffin lamp, the rest in shadow. She looked at her mirror, twirled across the room, softly singing 'The Blue Danube', and came waltzing back to the mirror with the lamp in her hand. She stooped in front of the glass and held her hair back with both hands. 'I must have it thus,' she said aloud, 'and I must brush it more so that it will shine like Paloma's hair. And I will put the comb in,' – she reached for the Spanish comb – 'thus.' She blushed at the image that confronted her. 'I did not look as young as this, or as beautiful, on my wedding day!'

The words were a reminder. She drew back from the mirror and looked with dismay at the photograph on the shelf, from which Vincenzo's face, square and strong and framed in black hair, stared at her sullenly. She looked at the photograph, and at the Madonna above her bed, and again at the photograph.

'Oh, Madonna,' she cried to the image. 'Oh, darling Mary! You understand. I know you understand. What can I do?' Her face softened, and she smiled again. 'You are a mother. That is why all the women pray first of all to you. You are a woman,' she said tenderly. 'Do you think I believe that story about you? You will not be harsh. I know you will forgive!'

She took the comb from her hair, and turned down the lamp. She was still humming the song to herself as she climbed into bed.

Chapter Eleven

THESE were dream days, a time of sunlight and languor, lived under a glass bell of unreality.

It took a fragment of a second, on a quiet Sunday morning, to shatter the peaceful dream.

At a little after ten o'clock Craddock threw back the blanket and heaved himself reluctantly up from the warmth of his palliasse. The tiled floor was cool to his feet. The window was open and the room was pleasant with fresh air and sunlight. He drained the last drop of tea from his mug – Honeycombe had brought his breakfast to him in bed – and dressed. There was a bowl of water on a chair, and he washed and shaved, enjoying the touch of the cold water against his skin.

There were no voices of command to be heard from the courtyard; only the unhurried footsteps and the idle murmur of a day without a timetable. Men lounged on the landings, sat in the sun writing letters, or strolled into the latrines with newspapers under their arms. A party clattered away to church parade. A few civilians appeared in the street neatly dressed for church, but most of the doors were still shut. Even the children who played around the air-raid shelter were quieter than usual.

Craddock stretched his arms and wondered what to –

The explosion made him flinch. It was loud and sharp, not blurred by distance. The whiplashing echoes died away into a profound silence.

He was stunned. A woman uttered a fearful, penetrating scream. He went to the window. All along the street doors were crashing open. There was a stampeding convergence of bodies, and the white roadway disappeared as the mass of people heaved and spread like a dark flood in every direction. A deafening clamour ascended, agitated voices, the bestial screaming of women, the shouts and the clattering boots of soldiers who poured out of the billet. The crowd flowed and swirled, and broke up into mad patterns of light and dark as little groups formed, coalesced and dissolved in a bellowing, gesticulating frenzy.

Craddock was already on the landing when the mob of men in the courtyard parted and the guard commander came bounding up the staircase. In his arms, pressed tightly against his body, was a big bundle, shapeless and darkly sodden. He plunged past Craddock without a word and hurried to the medical room along the corridor. Craddock was still staring at the thick splashes of bright red that bespattered the staircase when another soldier came racing up towards him, with a screaming child flung over his shoulder; and then, with long, thundering strides, Captain Rumbold, his face dark with fury and his uniform soaked with blood, bearing a silent and stupefied Aldo. Aldo stared without recognition at Craddock as he was carried past, and looked helplessly at the horrible, bloodied masses of meat where his hands had been.

The captain shouted, as he went by, 'Get the truck out!' He vanished into the medical room and reappeared, without his burden but still dripping with blood, before Craddock had reached the foot of the stairs. 'Sergeant!' Craddock paused. 'It was up by the shelter. Get along there and find out what happened.'

The brilliant light in the courtyard confused the sergeant and deepened the sense of nightmare that oppressed him. He was enraged by the gaping indecision of the men who pressed around him.

'Corporal Honeycombe, stand by with six men and stretchers! Larkin, get that bloody truck started up! No, I don't know what's happened. Don't stand there yawping. You, you and you, come with me!'

Civilians thronged into the porchway. 'Corporal of the guard,' the sergeant shouted, 'clear this lot back!' The crowd retreated. Rosario stood his ground, supporting a frantic, howling woman. 'Chi è? La madre? Let this one in, corporal, it's one of the mothers. Don't let her in to the medical room till the captain tells you.'

Craddock pushed through the crowd, with his three men following him. The women were making hideous demonstrations of grief, puffing their hair down over their faces, beating their breasts, blubbering, shrieking themselves hoarse, or, with glazed eyes, bobbing and mumbling ave marias. Voices gabbled questions and explanations at the sergeant, and hands reached out to detain him. He found himself face to face with Graziella. Her cheeks were smudged with tears, puffed and ugly. She clutched at him, and cried, 'Pippo, what is it? What has happened? He put her angrily aside, without answering, and went on his way. He reached the shelter, and his men began to press the crowd back. The clamour increased as the people were squeezed back towards the pavement. Craddock ignored the noise and turned to his task.

One of the rubbish heaps had been disrupted into an uneven litter of rags, waste paper, chickens' guts, dirt and decaying fruit skins. Amid the scattered filth lay the body of Aldo's dog, stretched in a hideous neatness, its entrails spilled in a fluid, many-coloured heap between its crossed paws. He could not recognize in this limp heap of bedraggled fur, from which arose a hot, horrible smell, and upon whose wounds buzzed a black crust of flies, the strong and living creature whose muscular beauty he had admired.

He ignored the stench and went on with his search. The shelter above the rubbish heap was scarred by the explosion and splashed with blood. There was more blood among the refuse. He stooped over the nauseating heap, probing gently with his fingers. He searched patiently among the rubbish until, close to the wall, he came on a blackened end of wire. He groped along the wire to a staple in the wall. The crowd was subdued now; the hysteria had petered out and there was a low chatter of comment, broken by sudden shrill-nesses, as the people watched Craddock at work. He called two more soldiers out of the crowd and told them to search the pavement for metal fragments. He went on working through the rubbish heap.

A low, human moan attracted his attention. He looked up. The dog's flank was rising and falling feebly, and its eyes were moving above the shattered muzzle. He called to one of the soldiers, 'Go and get a rifle.'

'It's all right, sergeant.' Captain Rumbold appeared. He took his pistol from his holster. 'Poor old feller,' he said gently, and pulled the trigger.

The shot echoed deafeningly between the shelter and the houses. There was a fresh swirl of movement from the people, as if the shot had been fired among them. Craddock felt that he was losing his grip on reality. He became aware of the smell. The sunlight bewildered him, increasing his nausea and unsteadying his vision. His head was still ringing with the reverberations of the shot, and the voices around him only came to him faintly. Into what dream world had he descended, with the trail of blood along the white pavement, the captain standing tall and terrible in a blood-soaked uniform at his side? He heard the captain saying, 'What was it?'

Craddock straightened up. 'Jerry booby-trap. Pretty straightforward. They must have left it behind in this rubbish heap when they pulled out of the town. It's the kind of thing they do. A couple of potato-masher grenades lashed together,' – he showed the captain a charred cylinder of wood and a thin piece of metal – 'probably with one-second detonators shoved into the handles. There was a pull wire from the grenades to this staple in the wall. They probably figured that whoever cleared the rubbish away would catch it. These poor kids got to it first. They must have been playing mud-pies, or something, on the heap, and dug down on the wire.'

There was a babble of inquiry from the pavements. The captain said, 'Tell 'em!'

Craddock raised his arms and shouted, 'Silenzio!' He was seized with an inexplicable revulsion against these people as he looked at them. A moment ago they had been mad with fear; now they were yelping with curiosity, their faces white and greedy in the sunshine. 'Silence!' The noise subsided sufficiently for him to speak. 'Your children were wounded by a German bomb.' There was no reaction in the faces before him; the same gaping callousness. He became angry. 'A bomb hidden in your street by the Germans, by the Fascists. They left it there to do you harm.' No reaction. 'They have spilled the blood of your children. The Germans. The enemy. Do not forget.' He shouted again, 'Do not forget.'

'All right,' said the captain, 'break it up. Come on, you chaps, get these bastards moving.' The soldiers began to disperse the crowd. Craddock walked back to the billet with the captain. Little groups of people lingered everywhere, waving their hands at each other and arguing noisily.

'What about the kids? Craddock asked.

'One of 'em's done for. There's another not badly hurt. You saw the third, the one I had...'

'Aldo?

'Is that his name? They'll probably have to take both of those hands of his off. It'll be touch and go whether they save him.'

'Pity, he's a good kid.'

'Ah, what's the odds? They breed like flies and die like flies here. They're not worth a toss, anyway. I'd sooner it happened to them than to a couple of our chaps.'

'I suppose so,' said Craddock gloomily. 'Still,' – he fell silent for a few paces until at last he exclaimed violently – 'those bastard Germans!'

In the courtyard the men surrounded him, with questions. 'It was a Jerry booby-trap,' he explained. 'One kid's dying and the other two'll probably be crippled for life. You might like to remember that, lads. For later on.' He looked up at the staircase. 'You two, get a bucket and wash that blood away. It's a fine state for a billet to be in on a Sunday morning.'

He went to wash the filth from his hands and to change his clothes. After a while the street was quiet again. But the quietness had changed. It was not calm, but unease, that lay upon the street.

Chapter Twelve

BY the next morning the incident was apparently forgotten. The billet was crowded and full of activity. Reinforcements had arrived to bring the company up to war strength. The new men had to be absorbed and a training programme had been started which, with their normal guard duties, robbed the men of much of their former leisure.

Among the reinforcements was a new officer who had come to replace the dead commander of Craddock's platoon. Mr Perkington was small and dapper. He had come straight from an officers' pool to take up his first appointment on active service. He had only been in Sicily for a few days, and his journey, up from the base at Syracuse through this strange island had served more to unsettle him than to prepare him for his new duties. He was still confused by the heat, and by the contrast between the savage splendour of the country and the desolation that inhabited it. There were too many impressions. The ancient towns spilled in heaps in the white sunshine, the famished people swarming among the ruins, had left him with a sense of loss and despair. The sunburned soldiers, branded with experience, to whom he had come, seemed to look patronizingly upon him, and he felt inadequate in their presence. He would have to assert his authority.

His platoon was on parade when he arrived. The sergeant came up to him and saluted. He returned the sergeant's salute.

'Sergeant Craddock, isn't it?

'Yes, sir.'

'My name's Perkington. I'm sure we shall get on together. You play ball with me, and you'll find that I'll play ball with you. Okay?

'Yes, sir.'

'What's your first period?'

'I was going to give them a bit of a talk. For the new men. About some of the tricks the Jerry infantry get up to. We've picked up quite a bit since we've been here.'

'Hm. Well, we can have that later, sergeant. Start them off with a spot of arms drill.'

'Arms drill.' A slight pause. 'Yes, sir.'

Mr Perkington watched the platoon march out. The sergeant was a clumsy fellow, with a queer, uninspiring gait. The men carried their rifles slung, instead of at the slope, and they swung their arms carelessly, talking on the march. A few hundred yards along the waterfront they halted. They went through a little arms drill. The movements were ragged, and the sergeant made no attempt to correct them. They stood easy after a while, and the sergeant walked up and down in front of them telling them about their faults in a conversational tone. No snap, Mr Perkington noted, no standing well back in the proper manner and keeping them wide awake. More arms drill followed, a little better this time, but again the sergeant showed no concern at the mistakes that were made. Captain Rumbold had come out of the billet and was watching, without comment. The sergeant gave an order quietly, and the men broke ranks and trooped across to the sea wall where they made themselves comfortable and lit cigarettes. The captain gave no sign of interest. Evidently he was waiting to see how the new officer took his platoon in hand.

Mr Perkington went across to Craddock. 'What's up, sergeant?

'Giving them a breather, sir.'

'Rather early, isn't it? You didn't come to Sicily for a holiday, you know.'

'I know, sir.'

'Well, give them another minute and fall them in again. I'll take them myself. I don't know which was the sloppier, their "slope" or their "present". Is there anything they do well?'

'They don't fight badly, sir.'

'Good drill is the foundation of efficient soldiering, sergeant. We'll start off with the "slope", counting the time, and we'll carry on till they've got it right. That'll do to begin with.' He was annoyed by the frown that flickered across the sergeant's face. 'I see I shall have to make a few changes here, sergeant.'

'Yes, sir.' The sergeant was expressionless again.

'I'm not too satisfied with the turnout, either. You chaps are supposed to be soldiers. It's my intention to see that you look like soldiers.'

Craddock's gaze wavered as Captain Rumbold approached. He checked himself and looked straight at Mr Perkington again. 'Yes, sir.'

'Perkington,' said the captain, as he came near. 'I shall be in the company office. Look in and see me when you've finished, will you?'

The men fell in again and Mr Perkington began to drill them. He ordered them to slope arms, shouting the time, and a terrible muddle followed, with some men bawling and others mumbling and the rifles wavering in every direction.

'That'll do, lads,' said the sergeant quietly.

'I'll see to that, sergeant,' said Mr Perkington. 'You go to the rear and check the movements.'

The next attempt was more orderly and soon the platoon was drilling smartly. Mr Perkington felt triumphant. He had been vaguely uneasy after the captain's intervention, but he felt that he could face Rumbold now. 'Take over, sergeant. And keep them up to the mark.'

'Yes, sir.'

He found Rumbold in the company office. The captain told him to be seated. 'Well, what do you think of them?'

'Oh, they're all right, sir. How long have they been without a platoon officer?'

'Three weeks.'

'I thought so. I'll soon have them in hand.'

'You will?

'Oh, yes, sir.'

Rumbold walked away to the window, and turned suddenly. 'I suppose they gave you lectures when you were learning to be an officer – what do they call it? – Man Management?'

'Yes, sir. I've still got my notes.'

'I bet you have. Get a hold of 'em from the start, eh? Show 'em who's boss? That sort of thing?'

'Yes, sir.'

Rumbold said, as if to himself, in a tone of deep disgust, 'Man Management! I don't know!'

Perkington looked up at him in alarm. The captain swiped violently at a fly. He relaxed, and sat on the edge of the table. 'You married?'

'Yes, sir,' answered Perkington, startled.

'Good looker?'

Perkington blushed and produced a photograph.

'Hm. Lucky feller.'

'Aren't you married, sir?'

'Me? I've been loving 'em and leaving 'em so long I can't get out of the habit.' Rumbold grinned. 'I suppose you're one of these moral birds? True and faithful, eh?'

'Well, I...'

'I know. Pity. There's so much crumpet walking around here it's a shame to see it wasted. I've picked up a nice bit myself. Sweet fifteen, fresh and lovely. You can have her if you like. It's about time I had a change.'

'I...' Perkington was shocked and speechless. He feared that he would never understand this man, nor any of those others. 'I don't...'

'All right, don't swallow your tonsils. I was only trying to be matey. What's mine is yours. That's the way of it here. Listen,' the captain said earnestly, 'you may live to a ripe old age. I don't know, it's always possible. But if you do, you'll never meet a better man than Sergeant Craddock. My advice to you for the next month is to feed 'em, clothe 'em, and leave the rest to Craddock. And don't be afraid to treat him with respect. After that, if you're still in one piece – and if you are, you'll probably have him to thank for it – he'll be only too glad to hand you the platoon on a plate.'

Perkington's blush deepened. 'Yes, sir. I understand.'

'And don't worry. He won't rub it in. The men won't play you up while you've got Craddock. Okay?'

'Yes, sir.'

'Right, you'd better get outside and have another look at them. And, Perks?'

The lieutenant turned in the doorway.

'Sure you don't want my baby doll?'

Mr Perkington fled.

§§§§

Late in the afternoon two German fighter aircraft flew over the town. They were very high, hardly visible against the sun, and they crept here and there across the sky as if they did not know where they were going. Anti-aircraft fire pursued them and, at last, on the far outskirts of the town, they dropped a couple of small bombs.

In the Via dei Martiri the sound of engines did not attract any attention at first. When the guns began to fire the people came to their doors, and there was a murmur of surprise and hesitation. The wavering drone continued to filter down from the sky; the paralysis of doubt was broken, and the people rushed to the air-raid shelter.

Craddock, coming down the street without haste, saw Graziella hesitating on the pavement. People streamed past her, shrieking, and scrambled in the doorway of the shelter. She was staring after them and clutching her baby against her, but Craddock had told her to expect him at this time of the day and perhaps this was what kept her from following the mob. She looked about her, and the hunted expression on her face changed to one of relief as she saw him coming.

As he came near she stretched out her hand to him and cried, 'Quickly, to the shelter!'

Craddock smiled, took her hand and led her into the house. She was trembling slightly. They stood in the room without speaking. Her head was averted, and she kept her body still, but he could guess from the desperate pressure of her hand at the panic inside her. He said, 'No wine?

She released his hand, carried Fifo to the cot, went to the table and poured wine. Her movements were careful, painfully controlled. She pushed the glass across the table and smiled guiltily at him. The ornaments on the shelf danced to the anti-aircraft fire. He let her see that he was laughing at her. Her face cleared, and she said in a little girl's voice, 'My stomach hurts from fright.'

'Come here, and you will feel better.'

She came and sat on his lap; he did silly things with her hair, and soon they were both laughing. She moved her lips against his cheek, kissing him softly. 'Do you know,' he said, 'you are changing? Now it is you who are making love to me. It is the first time.'

'I am a lost woman. I am in love.'

'I, too. With your wine. Give me some more.'

She leaned across to the table and poured wine. 'Only with my wine? Not with me?'

'All right, with you, too.'

'Always?'

'Always.'

'You will stay with me?'

'I will stay with you.'

'You will not stay. You will go away.'

'Yes, I will go away.'

'Why did you say that you would stay?'

'Why did you ask? There is a war.'

'And that you love, is that true?'

'You ask too many questions, dear one. Questions are not good.'

'But is it the truth?'

'In war, nothing is the truth but war.'

'War! War! You are here and the war is far away!'

'The war is over our heads. Listen to it. Yesterday, we discovered the war in a heap of rubbish. You know, I and my comrades did not come to Sicily for a holiday.'

Two bombs exploded in the distance. Graziella looked in agony at the cot. 'For the baby, we should have gone to the shelter.'

'It is nothing. It is finished now. They will go. There!' The gunfire had stopped and the sound of the aircraft was fading away. 'You hear?'

'Since yesterday,' Graziella said, 'I have hated the war so much. If only we could try to forget it!'

'Since yesterday I have known that I must not forget it.'

'A man speaks, and a woman speaks,' she said bitterly. 'See the difference? But I beg you to tell me, is it the truth that you love me?'

'I love you. That is the truth.' She was holding him in a hard, quivering embrace. He was embarrassed. Now she was as he had wanted her to be, yet he could no longer feel as he had hoped to feel. 'They say that in wine there is truth, too. Let us find out.'

She kissed him. 'This is the last glass for you. You are beginning to drink too much.' She looked into his face anxiously. 'You are tired. Have I made you tired?'

'No.' He went across to the cot; his limbs were heavy. 'At least I am a little tired.' He hoisted the baby out on to the floor. 'There, Fifo, walk, come, walk to me.' The baby staggered forward for a couple of paces and collapsed into his arms. 'You see, Graziella, he walks. Again, Fifo, come, come, again!' He made encouraging noises and caught the baby a second time. 'His legs are growing stronger. It is the milk.'

The baby was uttering pleased, explosive sounds between his lips. 'Pi-pi-pa! Pi-pa!'

'What is he saying? Pippo, or pappa?'

Graziella laughed. 'Perhaps both. Here, let me take him. You are so tired. Is there much work, with the soldiers?'

'Yes, there is much to do again.' He lay down on the bed and sighed with contentment. 'Ah, that is better!' He muttered, 'There is a new officer, he makes me sick.'

'He is harsh?'

'Harsh?' Craddock laughed. 'No, he is a boy. I could eat him. But he is foolish, and he makes things more difficult. We have many new men. There is not much time to teach them to fight, and he is wasting it.'

Graziella muttered something, bending low over the child, and Craddock asked, 'What is that?'

'Nothing.' A little later she said, 'You know that one of those children is dead?'

'Yes. The other two will live. We telephoned to the hospital, today.'

She spat on a cloth and wiped Fifo's face.

'Put water in a bowl,' said Craddock from the bed, 'and wash him properly. You have no lack of soap now.'

'You sleep, and leave a mother to her own business.' She wiped Fifo's face so vigorously that he began to cry. She soothed the child, and the room was quiet. 'Pippo,' she said softly, 'are you asleep?'

'No,' he mumbled.

'I would like to have a little money from you.'

He sat up. 'Now you are talking like a real wife.' Until now she had refused to take money from him, except to buy a bottle of wine or some food for their meals together.

'Stupid, it is not for me. In the street, we are making a little collection.'

'For the children in hospital?'

'No, for Lucrezia, the mother of the dead boy. She must take her child from the hospital, and she must bury him. To bury the child like a Christian costs money. Otherwise they will throw the body away like a dead cat. That is how it is in this town today, there are so many dying. And Lucrezia weeps, for she has not even the money to burn one poor little candle in the church for her dead child, let alone to bury him.'

'Why do you not also collect for the other two children? They will need more food if they are to live and get well. That is more important than a funeral.'

'You do not understand. Her misery is the greatest. We cannot collect for all. We have little money. Each family will give a few lire, and even that will cause them hardship. After we shall try to help the others, but first we must give comfort to Lucrezia.'

Craddock reached for his wallet. He counted out some notes, then hesitated. 'Listen. I shall not give you money now. This evening, in the barracks, I shall tell the soldiers, and they will give money. From them there will be much more money than from all the people in the street, enough for Lucrezia, and enough for the children in hospital.'

'They will not be angry, to have to give money to us?'

'They will not have to give. They will give freely. They will want to give.'

'I have not known such soldiers before,' she said. 'They will be blessed.'

'That will be useful,' said Craddock with a touch of mockery. 'They will need your blessings one fine day.'

He did not know what impulse of cruelty had made him answer thus, and he waited for her reply. She did not speak. He lay back on the pillow, unable to face her sombre, steadfast gaze. There were points of light in her shadowed eyes that might have been pain or pity. 'Sleep now,' she said gently. 'Sleep.'

§§§§

Wally Fooks was in a bar on the waterfront when the Messerschmitts flew over the town. He heard the thin, uneven engine beat, drained his glass of vermouth and said to two sappers who were sitting at another table, 'I'll lay yer a quid that's Jerry, tosh.'

'Ah,' said one of the sappers thoughtfully, 'it's 'im all right.'

'He wants to get shagged,' said the other soldier, 'muckin' up a nice quiet gaff like this. Here!' He waved to the barman. 'Another vermutty, capeesh?'

Anti-aircraft shells coughed in the sky and the civilians in the bar realized for the first time what was happening. A couple vanished into the street; the rest crowded in the doorway in a state of agitation. There was an increasing clatter of footsteps in the street.

The ripping, thudding sound of gunfire was continuous. The din of footsteps on the pavements grew. Shouts echoed between the tall buildings. One of the men in the doorway shouted, 'Al ricovero!' and bolted. The barman rushed to the door, looked apprehensively at the soldiers, took a few hesitant paces back towards the counter and halted in indecision.

A battery on the docks opened fire with an ear-splitting series of detonations. The whole room rocked. There was another scream of 'Al ricovero!' and everyone but the barman and the soldiers poured out into the street and joined in the stampede.

'They say them shells cost fifty quid each,' mused one of the sappers.

'What's this ricovero lark they're shoutin' about?' asked Fooks.

'Al ricovero – to the shelter,' the sapper explained. 'Listen to 'em!' The frantic voices of men and women could be heard amid the uproar in the street, 'Al ricovero!' 'Al ricovero!'

'F— a duck!' exclaimed Wally Fooks. 'What we waiting for?'

He jumped to his feet and shouted, 'Al ricovero! Al ricovero!'

'Ol' bleed'n' windy all of a sudden,' said one of the sappers in disgust.

'Oo's windy?' shouted Fooks. 'Al ricovero! Al ricovero!' He seized the bewildered barman by the arm and hustled him towards the door. The barman, more out of confusion than courage, resisted. 'Al ricovero!' Fooks put his mouth to the barman's ear and bellowed, 'Bang! Bang!' He forced the trembling Italian out through the doorway, 'Come on mate, quick! Bang! Bang! Al ricovero!'

Fooks and the barman rushed away along the street. Fooks stopped, and watched his companion, caught up in the panic, borne away in the streaming, heaving, human surge. He pushed his way back to the bar. 'Al ricovero!' he roared from the doorway. 'Ol' rags and lumber! Apples a pahnd pears! Star, News an' Standard!' He urged the mob on with heroic gestures. 'Come on, the Spurs! Chamberlain Must Go! Al ricovero!'

He crossed to the bar counter, selected a bottle of vermouth, and filled three glasses. 'The ol' 'elpin' 'and,' he explained. 'One good deed every day. They learn you that in the Boy Scouts.' He leaned over the cash register and pressed keys. A bell rang and the drawer flew open. 'Jus' like the ol' pin table, eh?' He held up a handful of lire notes. 'The ol' 'elpin' 'and. See what I mean? The Lord Will Reward.' He counted the notes. 'Three thousand, one 'undred, two 'undred – four 'undred an' sixty. Talk about a one-'orse joint! Never mind!' He found a bottle of brandy and presented it ceremoniously to the sappers. 'Compliments of Littlewoods Pools. You don't deserve it, you dozy sods. Proper bloody sappers, no initiative. I'm orf now. Ta-ta.' He paused on his way out. 'If I was you blokes, I'd skedaddle before the ol' geezer comes back. God looks after the righteous, but 'e's got no time for mugs.'

There was a crowd of soldiers in the courtyard when Wally Fooks arrived back at the billet. Sergeant Craddock was talking.

'What's up?' Fooks asked a man on the fringe of the group.

'Bloody collection for that Eyetie kid that died,' the man explained. 'We've got about twenty-six hundred lire. The sergeant's trying to get it up to a round three thousand.'

The sergeant, who had noticed him, called, 'How about it, Fooksy? You haven't given anything yet.'

Fooks fumbled with the notes in his pocket. His vainglory took hold of him, and he passed up four five-hundred lire notes. 'Joe 'unt,' he mourned, 'that's me. Softest 'eart in Shadwell. Always good for a touch.'

'Two thousand!' the sergeant exclaimed. 'You been gambling again?'

'Garn!' said Fooks. 'Chickenfeed. Don't you know me? You wanna look me up in "Oo's Oo". Baron Fooks of Mile End, the millionaire docker. Made 'is fortune out o' Navigation Wharf an' the Stepney Labour Exchange. Noted philamfrerpist. Family motta, "Spit in yer beer an' no one'll drink it." 'Obbies, polo, solo an' crumpet. Anyway,' he added, as much to console himself as to impress his comrades, 'there's plenty more where that come from. It's all done by mirrors.'

Chapter Thirteen

THERE were many funerals to be seen in the town in these days, little groups of red-eyed men and women straggling through the streets carrying coffins that were as crude as packing-cases; few of the processions were as long as that which formed up in the Via dei Martiri to accompany Rico, the dead boy, to his grave. Some of the soldiers were there, and all of the civilians except for Francesca and her man, who held themselves unaccountably aloof and who watched from their doorstep without heeding the hostile glances and comments that were flung in their direction.

The mumbling of the crowd had the tone and rhythm of a chanted chorus. From out of it there rose a cry from the mother, a cat's wail that faded away into breathless little screams. An old man took up the shafts of the hearse – a little handbarrow with a canopy supported by spiral columns, painted and ornate as a hokey-pokey cart – and began to trudge along in the roadway like a tired horse. In front of the hearse a nun led a troop of little children. Some of them were proud, some looked mischievous, some self-conscious, some unnaturally solemn, but although they told their beads and chanted ave marias like multiplication tables, it was clear that all of them had given up trying to understand what connection their vanished friend Rico had with the little box on the hearse. Behind the hearse two women supported the mother, who panted noisily as she dragged her feet over the cobblestones. The neighbours shuffled behind, a bobbing procession of black in the sunlight. Their heads were bowed and they frowned fiercely as if each was pondering on the problem of mortality, but the reverent murmuring and the funereal pace could not conceal the pride, even the shameful pleasure that the occasion gave them. With sorrow there are no half measures. Real grief cannot be put on like a garment. Those who are not felled by it are passed by. The people wore the clothes appropriate to the event, they composed their faces into the expressions proper to the event, and they commanded themselves inwardly to feel as they ought; but all three actions made them equally uncomfortable. To them this was a day apart from the lifelong succession of dreary, ordinary days. It was a day of ceremony; and they loved, they needed ceremony; throughout their lives they looked forward to it; it was a fire to light their darkness. It was a day of importance when they, the humble, the disregarded, trod the streets in solemn procession while the well-dressed people on the pavements looked at them with dread and respect. It was a day when they walked, without anxiety, in the sun. Their hearts were heavy for the mother; she still bore the burden of life which they all knew, and for her the burden had become even heavier; but, when they had overcome the first impulse of terror for themselves with which the death had struck them, they forgot the child. Among these people, death was the least of misfortunes.

§§§§

Paloma and Tina di Spirito were walking together. They talked in sidelong whispers.

'I do not know how you can walk so far in those high heels,' said Tina.

'It is easy when one carries the body gracefully.'

'I have never worn such shoes. I would fall over if I tried to wear them. Perhaps one day you will let me try them on, just for a little while?'

'You would not be able to wear these shoes.'

'Why not? I am not fat like you.'

'I know you are not fat, shrivelled one. Nor am I fat, but strong-bodied. You are smaller than me, but your feet are bigger. My legs are not thin, to disgust men, but my feet are small and beautiful. Many people have seen them, and can tell you.'

'Many men!'

'I am not ashamed that men admire me.'

It is not because of your feet that they give you shoes!'

'Your eyes are too big, Tina, and also your tongue!'

'I would not wear, at the funeral of an innocent child, shoes and a dress that I had bought with my body!'

'Ha! You have nothing to sell!'

'No? Let me tell you that many soldiers have come to my door, but I have never opened it to them. I have my virtue, and I do not sell it.'

'I sell nothing. I ask nothing of men but pleasure. I cannot help it if they bring me gifts to show their love. I live as you others fear to live!'

'You ought to live in a house!'

'Do not call me a whore!'

'The truth hurts?'

'Malignant one!'

'Stinking one!'

There were indignant whispers from behind them. They lowered their heads and held handkerchiefs to their eyes, two mourners walking in silence and sorrow.

§§§§

The mother's head hung as if her neck had been broken, and although her feet, beneath her long black skirts, crept in agony over the cobbles, her body was a dead weight on the arms of her companions.

'He was so good,' she moaned, 'so gentle, so young. His smile was as fresh as the dawn over the sea and his laugh was as sweet and as delicate as the little goat-bells. His heart was full of love for his mother. Always he wanted to help. He was without sin, a saint, an angel.'

Her head lolled back and she raised her swollen eyelids like a blind woman whom the sun's glare could not hurt. 'For whose sins was he taken? For whose sins do I suffer? For whose sins did the storm arise and drown my husband in the sea? What have I done that all my children should die? Lord, why did you strike them down with fever, with hunger and with war?

'He was my last born, my last hope. Who will care for me when I am sick? To whose house shall I creep when I am old and helpless? Why has God left me alone in this evil world?

'Who sins, and who is punished? All my life I have been a pious woman, and my children were good children. I see the wicked flourish, I see them gather riches, I see them drive the poor from their path, I see them take the good food from the mouths of our children, but I see them flourish, I see them laugh, I see their children dance and sing. The innocent are punished for their innocence. The suffering are punished for their suffering. From we who have little, all is taken away.'

She uttered a long, trembling cry, and raised herself on the arms of her companions. 'The Lord is good! The Lord has taken them from this dolorous life! May the Lord in His mercy take me, too!'

Her body sagged again, and her neighbours dragged her along, behind the hearse, as if to her own grave.

§§§§

Nella whispered, 'That Francesca! Did you see her?'

'Be quiet!' muttered Graziella.

'But did you see her?'

'Do not look so sprightly. Walk more slowly. This is a funeral, not a wedding.'

'You walk like a bride yourself. All the time you walk like a bride, not only today. You are happy, aren't you?'

'This is not the time to talk of such things. Be quiet!'

'She did not even come across the road. She is afraid even to stir out of the house with that man of hers. That man, I am sure he is a thief, or a murderer. He is afraid of people. Honest men are not afraid of people.'

'She has good reason.'

'Why?'

'I tell you, she has good reason. I have spoken with her. Now be quiet!'

But why? What has she told you?'

'Walk with respect. Everyone is looking at you.'

'Tell me!'

Graziella frowned and walked on in silence.

'Now you have secrets. Before, we did not keep secrets from each other. All right, you are not the only one who can have secrets.' She said, self-consciously, in English, 'Mum's the word, gel.'

'What is that?'

'That is English. You are not the only one who learns English words.'

'Where are you learning these words?'

'That is my business. I know more words.'

'I have told you to keep away from the soldiers. If I find that you are going with the soldiers...' the anxiety faded from Graziella's voice, and she smiled. 'It is that boy, isn't it, that Tiger?'

'That one!' Nella laughed, a harsh, woman's laugh. 'He is enamoured of me, I know that. He trots about after me, and he looks at me like a sick dog. But that one is not for a woman. He put his hand on my breast once, and he ran away as if I had burned him.'

'Listen to the woman talking! Well, play with your Tiger. With him you will come to no harm. Pippo watches him.'

'Pippo had better watch well, then.'

'Watch yourself, child. For the love of God, be careful, and think of the future.'

'What future?'

'Your future. How will you ever find a husband if you are not a good girl?'

'Why do you not think of your own future?'

'Of that I dare not think. I do not know what will become of me. What is already done is done. God will deal with me, and I am content to leave it to Him, without thinking any more. It is not kind of you to remind me. But with a girl who has not yet begun to suffer, it is different. I see girls every day who have been foolish with soldiers, and there are many others, many, many, who have to lead that life for bread. Poor things, it is not their fault, they are driven to live thus by the hunger of their families. While the English are here it is not so bad for them, but what will happen to them when our men come back? No man will take one of them for a wife. They will have to lead bad lives till they die.'

'Their lives will be no worse than those of other women. I do not intend to live like them, and I do not intend to marry here and be a slave for the rest of my life. I shall go to England.'

'Ha! Shall I laugh or weep for you?'

'You can laugh if it pleases you. What you do not know, you do not know! I am young and beautiful, and I shall marry an Englishman and go away from here, and live a free and wonderful life, with a big house, and money, and a motor car, and dancing.'

'Dear child, how you dream! In your house, when your mother talks to you, you dream. In bed, you dream. Every night you sit on a bench at the cinema and dream. You walk in the streets dreaming. Well, if that is your dream, enjoy it. Every woman has her dreams to sustain her. I would not rob you of yours. But keep your dreams in their place or they will break your heart.'

Nella walked on in silence, letting her dreams take possession of her. She knew them for fantasies. He had offered
her no promises or encouragement. He used her briefly and
cruelly, and sent her away from him each time as if he were
dismissing one of his own soldiers. Each time she would
get out of the truck; he would grin at her, say curtly, 'Same
time, same place, tomorrow,' and would drive off without
any farewell gesture; and she would stand looking after
him, her hands clasped behind her back, her feet crossed
childishly, her head inclined and her eyes alight with secret
thoughts. She forbade herself to recognize the truth. He
was so big and handsome, he had chosen her out of all
the women in this city, she did so much to please him, he
was a man from those magic lands which a hundred films
had revealed to her. She saw the future as if on a flickering
screen in the smoke-filled darkness of a cinema; he was
struggling with himself, that was why he was so brusque
– it was an old story – and on the eve of parting he would
surrender to his love, he would come to her and confess, he
would carry her away.

Triumph uplifted her. She acted inwardly the scene when
she received his homage. She could no longer see the hearse
behind which she walked, nor feel the cobbles beneath her
feet.

§§§§

Rosario nudged Craddock. 'You believe in this nonsense?'

'No. I have buried too many friends without all this.'

'Then why did you encourage it? It was you and your
soldiers who paid for the funeral, it was your men who
paid to have candles burned in every church in the town,

even in the cathedral, and to have masses sung everywhere. Such a funeral is for a prince, not for a brat from the docks. It was very good of your men. But why did you trouble yourselves?'

'One does these things for the living. There is the mother. And there are the two children in hospital. Most of the money we collected we are using to send them toys and food, to help them get well. We even bought Aldo a puppy and persuaded the people at the hospital to let it stay there with him. He will make friends with it, and it will not be so bad for him when he realizes that Vittorio is dead.'

'I admire you. Yet I think it is a waste of time. Everything you do, including your war, is a waste of time.'

'I do not think so. Fascism is the strongest support of an evil system...'

'Do not lecture me about systems. I know all about them. Old Buonocorso used to be an expert on the subject.'

'...a system that denies the world to the people who live in it. When we have destroyed Fascism, men will be more free to create the world as they wish it to be.'

'You have a touching faith in their ability to understand what they wish it to be. You believe in man. Others believe in God. I cannot believe in either, for I am cursed with the capacity to think.'

'I believe as I do because I think. I can prove to you...'

'Please do not try. You will not convince me, and I have no desire to create doubt in you. It would make your life very unpleasant.'

'Speak freely, I am not frightened to listen.'

'No. On my side, too, it would be a waste of breath. When one is upheld by faith, no reasoning can weaken it, nor even experience. The more your experiences belie your faith, the greater your need for that faith becomes, and the more you cling to it. Every blow only serves to strengthen it. The tragedy is that experience stores up within you, and one day, when some crisis forces you to think, everything is revealed to you in a terrible flash. Faith crumbles, and you are left adrift.'

'How do you know?'

'I had a faith once. I was a Fascist. You are angry?'

'No.'

'Do not worry. I am not a problem for the authorities. It was a long time ago. I was not unhappy then. Life made a clear picture. There was the feeling of strength when the bands played in the packed stadium, there was the illusion of grandeur when the great shout went up in the square, there was the pride of having something to serve and the joy of having something to hate. There was the illusion that one could compel respect.'

'I do not think that a defeat could change me so easily.'

'It was not defeat, it was what defeat revealed. Everything that should have seemed tragic seemed only ridiculous. I despised myself when I saw the shabbiness of the things which had dazzled me. If I believe in nothing, it is because I have seen everything. I have not even...' he could not avoid seeing Graziella walking in front, and his glance lingered like kisses on her smooth calves, hesitated, cheated, at the hem of her skirt, and moved on to discern the sway of buttocks and shoulders beneath her black dress. His entrails hurt...'I have not even the energy to hate.' He drew a long breath. The road was steep. 'Nevertheless you are an intelligent man. It pleases me to speak with you.'

'Me, too. I do not often have a chance to talk about these things. It is one of the things I miss.'

'Yes. Do you know, one of my greatest pleasures used to be to talk, every evening, with the men in the street, and with my friends at the café? I had many friends. It is very lonely now, living among a crowd of empty women. One cannot talk with women. That is why I value your friendship so much. You do not mind if I consider myself your friend?'

'No, it pleases me very much. I cannot see the priest in this procession. Where is he?'

'He will be waiting for us at the cemetery. He has many burials to perform.'

'Do you enjoy football? We are going to Acireale on Saturday to play against another battalion. I am in the team. We are going in lorries, and you will be welcome if you wish to come.'

Among all the black shapes swaying in front of him he tried not to see Graziella's. 'I shall be proud to come.'

§§§§

All the whispers mingled and the mother heard them, a devout undertone that surrounded her and comforted her.

She was emptied of her grief, weak and dizzy, as if after vomiting. Her mind was numbed and freed of the weight of affliction. She consoled herself that her child was at peace. 'May the angels lead thee into Paradise,' the priest was chanting.

On each side of the narrow flight of steps that led up into the cemetery vaults lay open, their thick stone walls torn apart by bombardment. In some of them lay heaped unconfined bodies, the cadavers of the poor cast here like refuse, shrunken by hunger, mangled by wounds, or bloated with decay, made loathsome by the heat and the flies. The stench was horrible. Behind, a soldier lurched out of the procession and stumbled down the steps to the gate, retching loudly, his eyes streaming, a handkerchief clasped against his nose. The pallbearers did not notice the smell as they grunted up the steps, their faces red and dazzling with sweat. The children did not notice it, watching the priest with big eyes. The priest did not notice, chanting mindlessly the too-familiar prayers. The mother did not notice, walking up the steps with the light tread of the dazed.

Soon the black pit would yawn before her. She would gather all her strength for a last performance. She would rave, shriek, tear her clothes, struggle to cast herself down into the grave. She would move all the women to a wailing chorus and the men to a mumble of pitying admiration. But now she was uplifted by her visions. She could see the hundreds of candles in the dim churches, tall and slim in their white purity. The soft radiance of their flames shimmered in her eyes like tears. She could see the priests, all those priests in all those churches, bowing before their altars and plying the saints with prayers on her behalf. She could hear the intonations of their requiems. It was all for her child. It was glory. The angels were bearing him up to Paradise like a little prince. They were lifting him up; their robes shone white against the sunlit vastness of the heavens; their wings beat with slow, soft power as they went upwards, infinitely upwards.

It was she who was being raised up, she from whose womb had come this glory, she of whom all would speak. She walked lightly; her head was proud; there was a blind radiance in her eyes. Not at her marriage had she walked like this. No bride could ever walk like this. She was ascending the steps of heaven.

Chapter Fourteen

CORPORAL Honeycombe fastened his belt, gave the gleaming brass buckle a last wipe with his cuff, and said, 'Well, I'm ready when you are.'

'I just want to finish these letters,' said Craddock. 'There's no hurry.'

'Getting a proper family man, aren't you, inviting your friends for supper?'

'You won't get no supper. I told her to get some nuts and wine in, that's all. We'll have a bit of a chinwag and play the gramophone. It ought to make a nice evening.'

'Ah, it makes a change, in this sort of life, doesn't it? You're a lucky bloke, Joe, getting your feet under the table like that.'

Craddock went on writing. 'Oh, I don't know.'

'Be funny if they forgot about us, wouldn't it, and left us here for the duration? I've heard of things like that.'

'You've heard wrong, mate. They don't forget. Do you really want them to?'

'Well, it's a cushy enough billet, isn't it? It ought to suit you, anyhow, the way you're fixed up.'

'It suits me all right. I can't help thinking sometimes, though, it's not the life. Not for us.'

Honeycombe brooded. 'You get fed up with everything, I reckon.'

'Hand us over that box,' said Craddock. 'It's some almonds for the missus, and a doll for the kid. Just these last couple of days I've been feeling it. I can't keep my mind off it. Those poor kids. It's as if the old war had suddenly popped up out of that rubbish heap, right in the middle of us, and said, "Hi! Remember me? Thought you'd forget me, eh? Well, here I am, and I've been here all the time, see!"'

'You don't half get some queer ideas.'

'Me? You look at the blokes on parade in the morning. There's not one of 'em wouldn't swear blind, if you asked him, that he was willing to stay here till doomsday, yet you can see the difference already. These last few days, they're taking an interest in their training again. They don't know it, but something's given 'em a shot in the arm. They're restless. And I know why. It's a laugh, though, old Perkington thinks he's the one that's done it. "They're looking brighter, sergeant," he says, "definitely brighter." Oh, well, if it makes him happy!'

Honeycombe asked, 'Everything all right at home?'

'Yes, the baby's fine. She's having a photo taken. I'll be getting one soon. Kid's trying to walk already. She's very playful, too, she likes banging saucers on the floor. She's broke four of the willow-pattern set my in-laws bought us when we were married. Writes a nice letter, my missus. I didn't hear from her for weeks, then a whole heap of 'em came, all at once.'

He laid his hand fondly on the pile of letters. He knew what an effort it was for his wife to write a long letter. These letters were cheerful, full of news, affectionate. She must be missing him more than he had thought possible. She was trying, in her own way, to tell him for the first time what he meant to her, and to fortify him against ordeals which she could only dimly comprehend. At the sight of the envelopes he had felt a stab of resentment; it was a fresh blow from the outside world at the sealed, timeless life he was leading. But the letters touched his heart and aroused a sense of guilt. He tried to remember home. After all, he told himself, it ought not to be so hard. It was only – how long was it – Good Lord, it was only four months since they had sailed.

It had been easy to remember home on the warm decks on the troopship. Home in those days had been something of which to talk and sing sentimentally. It had been easy to remember home in the first days ashore, on the white, wandering roads, passing through the deserted ruins of towns, lying among the olive trees in the green hills. Every letter had brought a beautiful pang. Where had it all died? On the plains, yes, on the parched, wide plains where so many men had died. The heat had killed it; the stink had killed it; the noise had killed it; the endlessness of the whole thing, the twitching, fear-burdened, obsessed endlessness, the days when men were afraid to move from their oven holes and the nights when the sky had been lit with great jagged flashes and flares had winked like traffic lights in the darkness. Home – he tried, clenching his fists, to remember. Yes, there was something there, at the back of his consciousness, as disturbing and elusive as a recurrent dream. He fought to recall it, so that he might answer her kindness with kindness and send her, with the gifts, a letter as sincere as her own. He said, 'She sent me a poem. She cut it out of a newspaper.'

'Show us.'

Craddock read it, not mocking it, but gently:

> *The room is quiet, your empty chair*
> *Reminds me of my heart's desire.*
> *I sit for lonely hours and stare*
> *Into the dream world of the fire.*
>
> *But then I put my thoughts away*
> *And set to work with might and main,*
> *To help bring near that radiant day*
> *When you, my love, come home again.*

They were both silent for a little while.

'You got a good wife there,' said Honeycombe.

'I know.'

'Here,' said Honeycombe, breaking the silence again, 'give me that parcel. I'll wrap it up while you finish your letter.'

§§§§

Graziella had drawn the table back to the rear wall of her room and the tiled floor, cleared for dancing, was freshly scrubbed. She had covered the bed with a gaily patterned counterpane, and a curtain had been hung across the window recess to make a little scullery. Paloma beamed at the men as they came in. 'I am invited, too,' she said. 'Now the corporal will have someone to dance with.'

'Where is the baby? Craddock asked.

'I took him to my aunt's,' Graziella said. 'I do not want him to be kept awake all the evening. Nella will look after him there.' She ran to pull a chair out for Craddock, and when he put a cigarette between his lips she hastened to light a match for him.

'We have guests,' Craddock said. 'Look after them. I am not a baby.'

'Let them look after themselves. A woman's first duty is to her husband.'

She would never let him do a thing for himself. She washed his clothes, helped him on with his jacket when he was dressing, cleaned his boots for him; she had even wanted to scrub his webbing equipment and polish the brass, so that he might be the smartest-looking soldier in the street, but his pride had revolted at this. She had been brought up to believe that it was the duty of a wife to wait on her man in this way, and she would not listen to his protests. In the last day or two she had redoubled her attentions. Craddock suspected that she sensed a change in him and was trying the harder to bind him to her. He was grateful, but uncomfortable. The more she tried to please him, the more aware he became of an intangible barrier between them. That was one of the reasons why he had arranged this party.

'I thought your eyes would still be red,' he said, 'you wept so much last night.'

'Why?' asked Paloma. 'Did you beat her?'

'No, we went to the cinema. It was a sad film, *Wuthering Heights...*'

'An English film,' interrupted Graziella, 'but they spoke in Italian. And he has never beaten me.'

'My husband never used to beat me,' said Paloma. 'Few wives can say that. But then, there are few wives like me.'

She laid Honeycombe's hand on her biceps, flexed her arm, and winked. 'If you beat her,' she said to Craddock, 'she will love you more.'

'I will try to remember that. I have never heard women weeping like last night at the cinema. It was worse than Rico's funeral. Sometimes I could not hear the words of the actors, all the women in the hall were wailing so loudly.'

'There were few who wept like me,' said Graziella proudly. 'Ah, that poor girl. How she suffered! It made me so sad. I have been sad for her all day.'

Honeycombe was sitting uncomfortably forward on his chair, showing by his look of strained attention that he could not understand a word.

'Wine?' Graziella asked him. She imitated the raising of a glass to her lips.

His expression brightened. 'Vino,' he said, 'I know that word. Vino...' he struggled to summon up more words. 'Molto buono, eh?'

'Ha!' Paloma thumped him on the back. 'You are learning. You know amore?'

'Sure. Amore buono, too.'

'Give him his wine! He knows all that he needs to know!'

They drank, and danced to the music of the gramophone. Paloma had brought a song sheet and they crowded round it to sing together. Graziella went behind the curtain and returned with a dish of torrone. 'Do not eat too much,' she warned them, as they took the lumps of sticky almond toffee.

Craddock said, 'Why not?'

'Wait and see. We have a surprise.'

'Now,' she said a little later. 'You two men go to the door and look at the street for a little. Do not look round till I tell you.'

Craddock and Honeycombe stood in the doorway. From behind them came the scuffling of the women's feet, whispering and giggling and the clatter of plates.

'Now!' Graziella commanded, and they turned round. The table was covered with dishes, and the two women were still hurrying backward and forward with more plates of food.

Craddock stared at the display. 'Where did all this come from?'

'All food comes from God.'

'Unfortunately we still have to pay the middleman. Where did it come from? I only gave you enough money...'

'To talk of money now is not polite. We have guests. Remember? Look after them.'

Paloma and Honeycombe were already at the table and Craddock took his place, frowning. They began with crispelli, oily fritters stuffed with cream cheese or lumps of half-cooked fish. The men did not like them but forced themselves to finish one each. The women ate enormously, tearing at the fritters with their fingers and stuffing great lumps into their mouths. Then Graziella set before them plates heaped with spaghetti. 'Here,' protested Honeycombe. 'Tell her that's too much for me!'

'Are you men or babies?' jeered Paloma.

'Perhaps they have worms,' suggested Graziella.

The women attacked their food with the boundless appetites of those who know hunger. Graziella was bending low over her plate, grinning up at Craddock like a greedy child. Her chin was smeared with tomato sauce. He could not get used to some of her habits; the way she ate, the physical frank-nesses in which she indulged in his presence, her bawling at his side at the cinema, her lack of concern when the baby was dirty. When he tried to discuss these things with her she would look at him with big eyes of incomprehension, or would make a scornful reply, or dismiss his suggestion with a shrill, hostile laugh. He felt able to look at her critically now.

After the pasta came big plates of soup with eggs beaten up in it. Craddock finished his soup and said, 'Well, that's the biggest meal I've had for a long time.'

Honeycombe groaned. 'Don't talk too soon. Look what's coming up now. Oh, my guts. Where do those women put it all?'

The men eyed in misery the hard-boiled eggs rolled in strips of meat which Graziella placed before them, and the mounds of fried potatoes with which she heaped their plates. 'There,' she said contentedly. 'Eat and be happy.'

They ate what they could, and leaned back in their chairs, gasping and heavy with food. The women laughed and chattered, and rounded off their meal with plates of fried sprats, which they ate with their fingers.

'I reckon,' said Honeycombe as he lit a cigarette, 'I reckon we ought to get mentioned in dispatches after that, Joe. It was a smashing dinner, but I'd sooner take on a tank with a tommy-gun than face another lot like that.'

'Oh I don't know,' said Craddock. 'It makes a smoke taste good afterwards, anyway.'

The men could not move, but the women were busy clearing away the dishes. 'I am sorry there was no bread,' Graziella said. 'I tried to get some but it cost too much.'

Craddock took her hand and squeezed it. 'Thank Heaven for that, love. Another mouthful and I would have burst all over your nice clean floor.'

Paloma shrilled from the scullery. 'That bread, it is a disgrace. There are supposed to be rations for all, but it all goes into the black market. If the women in this street were not such cowards I would take them all with me and teach some of these shopkeepers a lesson.'

'Brave talk!' cried Graziella. 'What would you do when the carabinieri came?'

'Men!' Paloma shouted. 'When a man is alone in the house with his wife he is brave. But face a thousand men with a thousand wives and see what happens then! We would change a few things, I can tell you!' She came out from behind the curtain. 'Men! Look at them! There is only one thing we need from them, and they never even have enough of that. Wake up, you!' She prodded Honeycombe with her foot. 'I have not finished feeding you yet, baby.'

The women brought out fruit, nuts, torrone and more wine. 'It is time for some more dancing,' Paloma said. 'Come.'

'Go away,' mumbled Craddock. 'Let a man rest.'

They drank wine, and the men lolled in their chairs struggling against sleep while the women ate and talked. At last, Paloma stretched herself and uttered a long, satisfied grunt. 'Well,' she said, 'there are two things that make life beautiful, and I have just had one of them.' She shook Honeycombe. 'Have I ever shown you my wedding photographs, corporal? I am sure you would like to see them.'

Honeycombe made a face of resignation and rose to his feet. 'The end of a perfect day,' he said to Craddock.

Paloma followed him out of the house. She turned in the doorway and chucked, 'Kurroo, kurroo. Sleep well, my little turtle doves.'

§§§§

'That was a good evening,' said Graziella when they were alone. 'Are you pleased with me?'

'Now,' Craddock came and sat on the bed beside her. 'Where did you get the money?'

'Are you not pleased? I was so proud. I thought you would be happy to entertain your friend as if in your own home.'

'I have asked you a question.'

She lay back on the bed and stretched her body. 'Stay the night, dear. You have never stayed the whole night. As long as you go away after an hour, we are still strangers.'

'Tell me where you got the money.'

'I had no money.'

'Where did the food come from?'

'Now, after this beautiful evening, you start a quarrel. Why? Paloma brought some of it. She wanted to help.'

'And the rest?'

Graziella was silent.

'And the rest?'

Graziella cried, 'Look at my feet!'

'What are you talking about?'

'Go on, look at my feet!' She drew her legs up and placed them across his lap. He looked at her feet. The soles were covered with cuts and blisters.

'How did this happen?'

'For you. I did that for you, to please you.' Her voice was unsteady. 'I had no money. I walked to the farm where my uncle lives. It is near Misterbianco. It is fifteen kilometres there and back. The road is steep and stony, and the heat was great. I told him I wanted food, and he gave me meat, and eggs, and cheese, and fruit. He put it in a big bag and I carried the bag all the way here on my back. I had to start very early, and I did not arrive home until an hour before you came.' She looked at him expectantly, through tears.

Craddock looked away, frowning. 'Aren't you tired? he said at last.

'What does it matter?' she cried.

He sighed, and looked down at her in perplexity. 'You must never do this again.'

'Why not?' she said defiantly. 'For you I would do it every day.'

Craddock said, with an edge of anger in his voice, 'I am serious. You must listen to me, or it will be finished between us.'

She stared at him. Her face was taut with incredulity; muscles quivered beneath the skin, and her full cheeks went slack and ugly with grief. There was an empty second, then a sudden vomit of sobbing burst up from deep inside her. She wailed, in a cracked voice that forced itself through the thickness in her throat, 'I wanted to please you!' She rolled away from him, sobbing in great spasms that seized her whole body.

Craddock felt helpless, at once weary and contrite. 'Don't cry!' he muttered awkwardly. He reached out and put his hand on her quivering shoulder. 'It is only that you do too much for me.'

The sobbing subsided. She sat up, with a bubbling sniff and wiped the back of her hand across her cheeks. 'You are not truly angry?'

He stroked her feet gently with his fingertips. 'Poor Graziella! Your poor feet!' He reached out and brushed her hair back from her forehead. 'Do you really want me to stay with you all night?'

She took his hand before he could withdraw it, and held it tight. 'He says I do too much for him,' she said dreamily. 'Oh, the stupid man! Too much!' – and she began to laugh.

Chapter Fifteen

A FAT colonel stopped Captain Rumbold in the street. Rumbold was hardly aware at first that someone was calling him. The streets which had confronted him like a maze of white buildings on the morning, exactly three weeks ago, when he had marched in, were now as familiar to him as if he had lived here for years; and his legs took him wherever he wished to go without making any demands on his mind, which at this moment was occupied with planning the day's training.

'Here, you!'

Rumbold paused. 'Are you talking to me?'

The colonel's red cheeks were inflated with anger, and his little eyes glittered. 'Yes, you! You're an officer, aren't you?'

Rumbold touched the captain's insignia on his shoulder straps. 'Can't you see these?' The colonel only stood chest-high to him. 'I'll bend over.'

The colonel's flush darkened. 'Blasted insolence! Don't you know how to speak to a superior officer? What do you mean by gadding about the streets dressed up like that?'

Rumbold was wearing brown corduroy trousers, a blue shirt that he had taken from an Italian officer and a yellow silk sweat-rag. He was going to take the men on an exercise among some ruined houses, and there was no sense in dressing uncomfortably or in spoiling a clean uniform. 'You're behind the times,' he said agreeably. 'It's what the well-dressed man is wearing this season. Didn't you know?'

The colonel's cheeks quivered with rage. 'I've a good mind to have you arrested. What's your unit?'

'Tenth Kents. What's yours?' Rumbold studied ostentatiously the supply service badge in the colonel's cap. 'Lord's Day Observance Society?'

The colonel fumbled in his pocket and produced a notebook. 'You'll be hearing more of this. Your name?'

'Goldberg. You can call me Basil.'

'Tenth Kents,' repeated the colonel as he wrote in his notebook. He glared up at Rumbold. 'You'll be laughing out of the other side of your face in a day or two. I shall insist that you're made an example of. I shall report this personally to your commanding officer.'

Rumbold brought his heels together and jerked his arm up in a monstrously correct salute. 'You'll really have to excuse me now,' he said politely. 'It's been so nice!'

He marched away like a Guardsman; but, when he had turned the corner and relaxed into his normal pace, he felt less cheerful. He was not worried about the consequences of this encounter. It was the new atmosphere which it betokened in the town that made him uncomfortable. A couple of weeks ago the town had been just behind the fighting line.

Now it was – he hated the words, they made him ashamed of his presence here – the Base. A couple of weeks ago there had been nothing but comradeship, a sense of recognition, among the men who swarmed in the streets. There had still been the sound of artillery in the distance, mingling with their cheerful hubbub, to unite them; a salute had been a greeting freely offered. Now the men walked about in the streets with a grudging constraint. The lorry convoys were on the move again, more and more offices, depots, hospitals, were springing up, in readiness for the next phase of operations. A horde of administrators had moved in to wind up the machine again while the soldiers waited uneasily. Provosts, staff officers, middle-aged martinets of every kind, continuing on their plush-lined odyssey from Cairo and Algiers, lurked everywhere, issued regulations, dispensed punishments and reprimands, the masters of this new order. Rumbold believed in discipline. He exacted it from his own men and he did not grudge it among his fellow-officers of the fighting army. But it irked him to see these newcomers putting up 'OFFICERS ONLY' signs outside every good restaurant, over the front seats in the theatres, even in the windows of the best of the barbers' shops. This was not his idea of discipline.

'By God!' he said to Perkington when he arrived at the billet. 'It's time we were getting out of here!'

'Yes,' said Perkington, 'I feel rather creepy waiting about here and wondering what's going to happen next.'

'Oh, Lord! You don't want to start mooning about that. Time enough when the muck starts flying past your ears. Eh, Porky?'

Piggott looked up from his typewriter. 'You! You don't know when you're on to a good thing. I'd sooner put up with a few brass hats, any day, than have those bastard eighty-eights plonking down all round.'

'You're getting soft in your old age, Porky. You'd better not get too comfortable. Something tells me it won't be long now.'

'I know,' groaned Piggott. 'I've got eyes.'

'Why didn't you come to the party last night?' the captain asked Perkington.

Perkington blushed. 'Oh, I had some reading to do.'

'You ought to come out of your shell a bit, Perks,' the captain said. 'Then you won't have so much time to worry about how you'll make out.' He smiled. 'No need to be shy, you know. There's another binge tonight. Why don't you come?'

'Oh.' Gratitude flickered in Perkington's eyes. 'Thanks, I'd like to.'

'I'll show you my countess. First time I've ever copulated with the aristocracy. Now I know what they mean by a democratic war.'

'Hi-aye,' said Piggott, 'off with the old and on with the new!'

'She's what Porky here would call a peach. Tall, slender, honey blonde hair, golden skin. She thinks the Germans were horrid, but some of their parachute officers were rather nice. She thinks I'm nice, too. There she was on one side of the room, and there was I on the other. About two hundred people in between. She takes a look round and comes sailing across to me with a cocktail. A little bit of backchat, and the whole thing's in the bag. I will say this for the nobility, they're as smooth as silk. What a woman,' he said reminiscently. 'She could pinch a beggar's last crust and he'd feel flattered. You know, she introduced me to her husband, a poor little man like a monkey perched all alone on a settee. There he was, in a beautiful grey suit, he looked up at me with big, mournful eyes. He knew what I was there for, all right. And all the time she stood on the other side of him, looking at me over his head. He spoke perfect English, in a sad, polite kind of voice, inviting me to come and stay with them in their villa at Taormina, and all the time she was giving me the old eye. It was obvious why she'd showed him to me. It was her way of telling me the coast was clear. And, by God, it was, too! I stayed there till this morning and I never got another glimpse of him.'

Piggott asked, 'What about Little Nell?'

'Oh, her! Have a heart, there's a limit to what a man can do. It's time for her to run along and play.'

'You're a baby-snatching old bastard, aren't you?' said Piggott. 'Did he tell you,' he asked Perkington, 'she's only fifteen?'

'Away with you,' said the captain. 'She loves it, the little bitch. They're all the same here. Early ripe, early fade. They're a randy lot.'

Piggott asked, 'Did that Nella cost you much?'

'Not a penny. All she wanted was my own sweet self. Quiet, like a little girl with a doll. Queer kid. I suppose I ought to give her a present, or something. What d'you reckon? Five thousand do?'

Perkington said, 'I wouldn't know.'

Piggott exclaimed, 'Save your money, you silly old sod.'

Perkington was looking at Piggott in surprise. 'It's all right,' said the captain. 'He's a privileged person. He's my privy counsellor. What do you recommend, Porky?'

'You can get the pick of the bunch for fifty lire. Give her five hundred and tell her she's lucky to get it.'

'That's your job,' said Rumbold. 'Here's two thousand. You can give her my love and tell her to go and blow bubbles.'

'Me?'

'Why not, I'm doing you a favour. You can try your own luck while you're about it. It's vacant possession. Girls like that don't stay long to let. Now beat it, I'm busy.' He turned to Perkington.

'Don't try so hard not to look shocked, old son. You've got a face like a slab of frozen cod. We've got a busy day in front of us. We're going to give the troops a taste of rough stuff for a change. They won't like it, but it'll get their blood up. I know my men. You watch 'em!'

The two officers busied themselves with their plans.

§§§§

Wally Fooks counted the roll of notes, stowed it safely in his pocket and sauntered out of the café into the sunlit confusion of the Piazza Stesicoro.

A handsome woman, with the bleached hair and short skirts of a prostitute, crossed his path, and his bowels leaped. The sunshine struck through her light frock to reveal the whiteness and the sumptuous outlines of her body. She walked with a sway that maddened him, towards the narrow, forbidden streets at whose corners the military policemen paced. She looked back at him and mocked him with a smile, and he turned to follow her.

Today's training among the ruins, with the thunder of grenades echoing among the broken walls, had awakened a dismal thought in him. In its first four weeks in action the company had lost nearly half its strength through death, wounds or malaria. How many of the men would be alive in four weeks' time? Or four weeks after that? He had dismissed the thought, for no soldier likes to let his imagination roam backwards or forwards in time or to dwell on what is happening to his companions; but it had, working in the obscure depths of his consciousness, awakened Private Fooks to the futility of laying up earthly possessions. He was an audacious and industrious pilferer. It was a habit that many of the men had brought with them from civilian life, where their employers were their natural enemies. Even Sergeant Craddock would risk his rank, when on a visit to the technical stores, by winding fifty yards of copper wire round his waist and smuggling it out to sell for a few hundred lire. Most of the men stole rations or stores to sell or to give to their sweethearts. Wally Fooks was more ambitious. He had received his training on London Docks, in a daily battle of wits with the port police. He already had stowed in his kit thirty watches, packed in grease in flat tobacco tins. Today he had enriched himself to the extent of three thousand lire, by the sale of a German pistol, a pair of boots and six typewriter ribbons and suddenly, at the sight of woman's flesh, he was overcome by the urge to enjoy while he might all the good things of life.

The woman walked past the redcaps, turned and looked back at him in inquiry. He made a furtive sign to her to wait. He looked around him. In the middle of the square was a rank of horse-drawn carriages. He went over to one, climbed into it, and explained to the driver, with much gesticulation and pidgin Italian, what he wanted to do. The cabby drew off the great black overcoat which he wore against the sun. Wally curled himself up on the floor, beneath the hood, and the cabby flung the coat over him. The cab swayed and jolted over the cobbles while Fooks huddled, sweating, in

suffocating darkness. The smell was acrid and overpowering, and he felt the fiery bites of fleas on his skin. He slid
to one side as the cab lurched round a corner; then he was
free again, in the blinding daylight.

The woman was not in sight. He walked down the narrow
street in search of her, avoiding the refuse that stank in the
gutters. She must be somewhere ahead; or perhaps she was
waiting for him in a doorway. She was nowhere to be seen.
Other women beckoned to him, but they were drab and
slack-bodied. The insolence of the woman he had followed
burned inside him; he wanted what her flimsy frock had
hidden, and he hunted for her.

He searched in streets, alleys and dank courtyards, until
black patches of sweat stained his collar and the armpits of
his khaki shirt. He turned into a street of silent, shuttered
houses. No women stood in the doorways, no children
screamed in the gutters. The clamour of the town came
faintly to him as if through blankets. He heard his own
footsteps, loud on the cobbles; and footsteps behind him.
He turned and saw a Sicilian following him, loping along
on short, thin legs to keep up with his own long stride. The
Sicilian hesitated as Fooks confronted him, then came on.
The man wore a creased and dirty suit of white duck and a
Panama hat; his haggard face twisted itself, around his beak
of a nose, into an ingratiating smile, but his eyes, feverish
and intent, followed every movement that Fooks made.

'Tommy want signorina?'

Fooks relaxed; he had been on guard; soldiers had been
knifed in these streets. 'Looking for a blondie. Big here.
White dress. Capeesh? Know her?'

'Sure,' – the man had an organ-grinder-American accent –
'I get you a fine blondie. Blondie, red hair, dark hair, French

girl, Polish girl, any damn thing you want. I guess you like a drink, too, eh, Tommy? You come along with me. I show you a swell house.'

Fooks grinned. 'House no bonna. I'm looking for someone. Beat it!' He turned and walked on.

The Sicilian scurried after him. He plucked at the sleeve of Fooks's shirt. 'Aw, come on, fella. You wanna good time. I show you everything.'

Fooks shook the man off and struck threateningly at him with the back of his hand. 'Ah-way, you shower! I don't want no pimp pawin' at me!' The man continued to trot after him. Fooks halted, at the street corner. 'Listen, useless, how d'you get out of here?'

'Sure, you come with me, I show you. Ala-ways glad to help Tommy.' He led Fooks down an alley and indicated an archway. 'T'rough here, you come-a quick to water-front.' Fooks followed, and found himself in a dark, paved courtyard. He could see no other exit. 'Here!' he exclaimed. 'What's the idea?'

The man had backed away and was behind him in the archway.

Fooks started towards him and stopped. Two other men had come silently out of the shadows. Fooks saw the gleam of steel and understood. He moved instinctively to place his back against a wall and took stock of his surroundings. The doors and windows facing on to the courtyard were all barred. The houses had shut their eyes against any plea for help; the blank slats of wood were like closed lids. The three men came warily into the yard; one of them in a well-cut grey suit and a broad-brimmed trilby, the jowls of his face fat and purple; a second, enormous and stooping, in ragged black trousers and a collarless shirt; the man in white lurking behind them. Far away, beyond the thick silence in the yard, Fooks could hear the murmur of the town.

The men came nearer. Fooks could feel the blood beating in his temples. He heard a child's playful shriek in the distance; the sound of water being emptied; more faintly, from within a house, the tinkle of breaking glass and the laughter of men. He breathed deeply, and clenched his fists. There was more laughter. It was full and strong, English laughter.

He threw back his head and shouted, into the enveloping silence, 'Hi-aye! Any British about?'

His shout died among the walls. The deep little bursts of laughter continued to come to him, girls' voices, the sound of a piano. He could hear the men and the girls laughing and singing 'Lili Marlene'.

He gathered his breath again and lifted up his head. He shouted, 'Bundle!' He drew the word out into long, echoing syllables. It was the battalion's private rallying-cry in street fights and bar-room brawls.

The men were almost upon him. In despair he bellowed again, with all his force, 'Bundoo-oo-oo-ooll!'

The big man lunged at him, a short upward jab. Fooks struck at the man's knife hand. The great fist was as hard as wood against his blow; the shock jolted up his arm. Fooks jabbed with his left elbow to keep a second attacker at bay and drove his boot at the big man's knee. They had recoiled, and he was able to draw a long shaking breath and raise his fists again. He shouted once more, his voice rising almost to a scream, 'Bundoo-oo-ooll!'

His heart leaped up within him as he heard, from somewhere behind the walls on his left, the pounding of boots on a staircase. Only the steel studs of ammunition boots could make a clatter like that. He roared joyfully,

'Come on, the infanteers!' A door banged open and a khaki figure dived past him at the three men. He caught a confused glimpse of a wooden club swinging up and over, and from among the whirl of bodies he heard a sickening crack and a man's scream. His rescuer was at his side. The three men rallied. The big man's head was streaming with blood.

'Get back, you bastards!' The shock of surprise almost made Fooks spew; he knew the voice. He croaked, ''Arry!'

Jobling advanced from the wall. The club swung in his left hand. In his right he held a pistol. He drove the three men out of the courtyard. Fooks heard them scuttling away down the street. He whispered, as Jobling came back towards him, 'Gor blind ol' bleeding Riley!'

Jobling asked, 'You all right?'

'Fine. What about you? You been playin' a fine old game, boy.'

'I'm all right. Gave me a bit of a turn, it did, when I heard the old war cry.' Jobling's voice hardened. 'What have they done with him?'

'Who?'

'You know who.'

'Broom? 'E's in the clink. Twenty-eight days' field punishment. Look 'ere, 'Arry, why don't you...'

Jobling uttered the parody of a laugh. 'Twenty-eight days!'

'Why don't you chuck it? You could still get off easy. You 'aven't got a chance if you stay on the run.'

'Twenty-eight days! You knew my kid!'

'What good will it do? You'd swing for it. Your ol' lady wouldn' even get a pension for you. The bloody misery'd prob'ly kill 'er, anyway. First Geoff, then you!'

'Save your breath, mate. And if you see that lump of dung, tell him I've got this all cleaned up ready for him.'

He displayed the pistol. 'And if anyone else comes after me, they'll get a taste of it, too.'

'You're barmy! You're bloody bomb-'appy!'

'I know what I'm doing. If you're a mate of mine you won't tell anyone you saw me. Not that they'll find me, even if you do. I'll be out the back door of this house before you can say "knife".'

''Arry!'

Jobling was gone. The slam of the door died away. The houses looked blankly upon the silent courtyard, and from the distance Fooks heard again the sound of the piano and of singing.

§§§§

Nella took the money. She felt cold and numbed. The notes that she clutched in her hand had no meaning. Nothing moved in her; everything in her being was leaden and dead. The fat little soldier was still speaking. After the freezing shock of his first words, nothing else had reached her. His voice was a faraway gabble that came without sense to her ears.

Her mind was too immature, she was too inexperienced in calamity, to react to what she had heard. There was only a thick heaviness in her head. At moments one thought peeped out of the confusion: if only she could see him: but she was too overwhelmed to give utterance to it. Her fist was clenched round the notes in a rigor like that of death; no impulse of rejection flowed from the brain; her grip was so tight that it hurt. There was only paralysis, and a core of pain in her breast.

The red face was still grinning at her. The voice assailed her, its inflections successively inquiring, expectant, insistent, resigned. Words failed the little soldier; he hung about her, looking into her face with doubt and growing embarrassment. He turned on his heels and she saw him cross the courtyard and go back into the office.

She could not move. She leaned against the wall of the porch in a stupor, all sense of time fled from her. The shadows crept about her and the glare died out of the daylight. The sweat on her body chilled. An unfamiliar coldness crept through her veins and she shivered as if visited by malaria. There was a prickling at the back of her hot, dry eyes. Her intelligence began to stir; terrified little impulses invaded her, to make a scene, to rush in upon him, to do herself violence. The woman in her spoke, but the child in her did not dare. She waited, stupidly. Soldiers hurried by, glancing at her with curiosity. Men came streaming down the stairs out of the billet and went into the cookhouse. Through the doors she heard the clatter and the subdued hubbub of a meal. The meal was over; the men came out, washed their mess tins and dispersed to their rooms. Still she waited in the porch. She could not take her eyes from the office door. Perhaps he was in there. Every time the door opened there was a great wrench of childish hope in her; each time, it was not he who emerged, and the pain rushed back into her.

How long she had been there she did not know. She had lost all desire to wait for him any more: she would have liked to creep away, but she was too weak and dizzy, and her mind was still too stupefied to set her limbs in motion. The sentry said something to her. She took no notice. He spoke again, in a firm but kindly voice. He took her arm and pushed her gently out into the street. She could not feel the pavement beneath her as she moved. She was enveloped in a sensation of dream, and she was sick with terror.

Someone else was speaking to her. She swayed in front of him. It was Tiger. Her empty face did not return his smile. He looked at her uncomprehendingly, and tried to awaken her to his banter. He was asking her to come with him; he was insisting; she felt hostile and impatient. He laid a hand on her arm. His voice was cheerful but overlaid with urgency. His grip tightened, and he tugged at her.

A spasm of fury racked her. She was on fire with pain and loathing. She tore herself from his grasp, spat in his face and ran away like a terrified animal.

Chapter Sixteen

THE next day, when the men had returned from their training. Craddock went shopping with Graziella. She had suggested this in the hope that it would please him; he had always taken a delight in these expeditions that to her was inexplicable on the part of a man. She clung to his arm among the throngs of shoppers, reckless of appearances, rapt and triumphant at her nearness to him. Even in this crowd she was wholly concentrated upon him. All her being was fixed upon him. It was not only with her eyes and mind that she watched; every nerve in her body was awake to him. He was the oak upon which she grew and fed. All the rest of the human race was far away, a swarm of little creatures rushing about on the plains far below the heights on which he and she dwelt, to be regarded remotely with pity and contempt. With her eyes closed she could feel inside her body every impulse of sympathy or passion that he experienced; her fingertips, her arm clasped in his, her flank against his, communicated to her every hesitation, every moment of withdrawal, every flicker of impatience on his part. When he frowned she died for a second.

Today they were close together. They walked heavily against each other like lovers, and their fingers were entwined; yet she felt that she did not live inside him as he lived inside her. Perhaps he was tired after all that marching. Perhaps the two men, Honeycombe and the other man, with whom he had been talking while she waited for him in the street, had brought him bad news. He had parted from them unwillingly and he had said to her, 'We must hurry. I have promised to come back and see them again.' Whatever it was, she knew that his thoughts were not with her.

Beneath her happiness there beat a pulse of anxiety. She could not uncover it; it existed less in the mind than as a bodily uneasiness. In their own relations little had happened to interfere with her triumph; but from the depths of her there came warning signals that she could neither interpret nor ignore; and all about her, in the street, there stirred something that disturbed her against her will. Somehow the explosion had split the street in two. What had become one community was becoming two again. A restlessness was growing among the soldiers; each day they were becoming more immersed in their own concerns. There was a restlessness among the women, too. They did not understand, but they were like a herd in which the panic can be felt for seconds before the moment of stampede. Now, in Graziella, fear was acting like an acid upon her happiness. She strove to please him, to weave herself about him, to blind his eyes to the surrounding world, to fuse him by her ardour into one flesh with her own. The more she tried, the faster the warning signals came. She felt the alarm storing up in her like an explosive force.

They were walking in the shadow of a wall that protected them from the sun. They turned into a gloomy archway: the white glare, the uproar and the overpowering stench of fish hit them all at once as they emerged into the market place.

The market square rose on a slope before them, a sprawling huddle of stalls that jostled each other in a crazy variety of shape and size, tented booths rising beside open barrows, rickety skeletons of woodwork leaning up against painted peasant carts. The unpaved patch in the middle was crowded with fish vendors, who squatted on the sunbaked dirt beside their baskets. People flowed in dark tides on the pavements, in the cobbled roadway, in the spaces between the stalls and the baskets, a sea of bodies broken only by the ramshackle structures around which they swirled.

It was like a crowd scene with titanic arc lights bathing everything in a revealing radiance which showed up the dirty lava walls of the tumbledown shops, drew a white glare from the stretched tentcloth of the booths, and turned the contrasting displays of pots and pans, old clothes, dress materials and foodstuffs into a fluttering, bewildering pattern of bright colours. Against the background of a thousand conversations the screeching cries of the vendors rose in raucous and repetitive rhythms, each in a different monotone. Now in one quarter of the market, now in another, a sudden outburst of noise would prevail above the general din; the bellow of a cheapjack haranguing the crowd from a soapbox; the crack of a whip and the rattle of wheels as a cart breasted the crowd, its driver shouting angry warnings; falsetto snatches of altercation; and, soaking through every nook and cranny in this jungle of noise, the asthmatic braying of a gramophone on a music stall.

Graziella let Craddock tow her through this pandemonium, tugging his arm to stop every now and then while she poked in a basket among the squirming heaps of fish. There were baskets crammed high with sardines, baskets of slender fish that gleamed in streaks of beautiful blue and silver, baskets of fish whose golden scales dazzled in the sunlight, baskets of tentacled squid, of swordfish, of bristly seafruit. She picked and haggled and purchased, joyously deriding Craddock for his squeamishness when he grimaced at the sharp and violent smell which the heat drew off, thick as steam, from the fish.

They pushed on through the tumult of life. Small boys, touting for their sisters, darted among the throng in search of soldiers. An old man made water against a wall. A woman bawled her griefs to a crony, clawing at her breast with both hands while tears streamed down her cheeks. Two Highlanders bargained with a girl in a doorway. The flies swooped in buzzing swarms on to the butchers' slabs. A carabiniere went from stall to stall collecting his bribes. Beggars whined. Crippled ex-soldiers crawled in the gutters, ignored by the sleek, succoured by the ragged and by the Tommies. And over all, the noise, the heat, the glare.

They paused at a haberdashery stall. Craddock rummaged, and selected half a dozen handkerchiefs. He asked the proprietor how much they cost. The man, dewlapped and sweating, told him that they were a hundred lire each; he could have the six for five hundred.

Graziella quivered with joy. This was a chance to help. She whispered to Craddock, 'Do not pay, it is too much.'

Craddock grinned and continued to count out the money. She was dismayed; he could not have understood her. 'He is taking advantage of you because you are a soldier,' she said.

Craddock said, 'Don't you worry.'

She seized his hand before he could pass over the money. She was determined to save him from this foolishness. 'Listen to me,' she cried, 'they are only worth twenty lire each. He is robbing you!'

Craddock flushed and pulled his hand away. He said sharply, 'Mind your own business!'

A great heat of anger overwhelmed her, and she burst out, 'How can you let him treat you like this? He is laughing at you! He despises you! He will boast, when you have gone, of how he swindled the Englishman!'

The obscene, bubbling voice of the vendor interrupted them, 'Shut your mouth, woman! Who do you think you are, screaming at a man like that?'

She lost all control of herself. 'You keep quiet, you dirty thief!'

'Don't you call me a thief!' the man shouted, shaking his fist at her. 'They have plenty of money, these English! You take care to get your share of it, I don't doubt. You be content with what you earn in bed, and don't try to steal the bread out of my mouth!'

A moment ago she would have been terrified at the fury in Craddock's face, but now she was beside herself, and when he shouted, 'For God's sake, shut up!' she answered frantically, 'I will not let you waste your money!'

'To hell with the money! What do you mean by showing me up like this?'

She screamed, 'You great child! Where would you be without me to look after you?' The stallholder intervened again with a torrent of abuse. She flung herself at him, and people crowded round, yelling in a babel of encouragement and imprecation. The man was panting, dribbling from the mouth, as he heaped foulnesses on her. Shrill and relentless, in her element, she leaned across the stall and screeched insult for insult. She was dumbfounded at the way Craddock had turned on her; she was obsessed with the determination to prove herself by saving his money for him; there was a strange sense of relief in her agony, as if she were vomiting emotionally, emptying upon this man all the anxieties that had gathered in her.

She felt a cruel grip on her arm, and she struggled, screaming, as Craddock dragged her away. The crowd closed in between her and the stall. Voices came at her from all sides; wherever she looked there were jeering faces. She wailed, 'You are hurting me!'

Craddock took no notice. He continued to push through the crowds, dragging her after him.

'You did not understand! He said filthy things to me!'

He did not even look over his shoulder. His pace did not slacken.

'You coward!' she screamed. 'How could you let a man speak to me like that?' She struggled, but she could not break his grip.

A calm of despair settled upon her. She felt betrayed, by him and by her own actions. She wanted to understand every fibre of him, and now it seemed to her that she would never understand. Everything that she did must turn against her. She followed him dumbly. Before, she had been borne on the human tide, buoyant with her own happiness. Now the crowds buffeted her as if to sweep her under. She had to run to keep up with Craddock. At every pace it seemed that elbows were deliberately being thrust out to jab her, feet protruded to hack her ankles and throw her off her balance. She stumbled after him, sobbing and trembling. At each blow a fresh pain jolted through her. She was tired. She wanted to fling herself down, among the rubbish, to be trampled. What had she done wrong? She tried, she goaded her brain to try to understand. For the first time the heat oppressed her, the light hurt her eyes. The air, heavy with grime and human breath and the smell of fish, stifled her. She would faint if she could not escape from here quickly. What had she done wrong? She clenched her teeth, aching with humiliation and bewilderment. What had she done wrong? What had she done wrong?

They walked home in sullen quiet. Once they were away from the market he slackened his pace. She slipped her arm through his, and he reached across and took the shopping bag from her. Neither of them spoke. He was relaxed, and the anger had gone from his face. When they came to a busy road he checked her, and said in a normal voice, 'Wait, let the lorry go by, we have plenty of time.' She felt her own confusion subside; she had been cowering inwardly at the fresh outburst of recrimination that she had feared might follow; each time he turned his face towards her she recoiled with dread, but the expected reproaches did not come. Perhaps, after all, he would not punish her. He was such an unpredictable man. Oh, she would never understand him! She leaned pleadingly on his arm, a prey to disappointment, perplexity and torturing hope.

At the door of her house he paused.

'Aren't you coming in?'

'No. I have something to do.'

Fear and suspicion quavered in her voice. 'Will you be long? Pippo, you must come in. You must let me explain.'

His manner softened. 'Truly, it is not because of that. I told you before we came, I must go somewhere. A friend is in great trouble. I will come back later.'

She could not restrain a long sigh of relief. 'Of course! I will wait for you. I will prepare a meal. Hurry back!'

She was alone. She sat down limply on the bed. Her love, her doubts, were a burden too great for her to bear. She shut her eyes, seeking a respite of peace. She must rest; and when she had rested she must think, and plan.

§§§§

'We've got to get hold of him,' said Craddock. 'I went to look for him on my own once, after young Tiger thought he'd seen him. It was no use. But we've got to act quickly now or else he'll be right down the pan. If he kills Broom, well, you know what that means. Even if he doesn't, and he's still on the run when we move out, he'll become a deserter on active service. And you know what that means. He'll be for it either way.'

'He's for it already,' said Honeycombe.

'So far he's only absent without leave. He'll have to answer for breaking arrest, as well, and for taking that pot shot at Broom. Still, what with extenuating circumstances, and all the rest of it, he wouldn't come off too bad. We've got to get hold of him.'

'And turn him in? asked Fooks.

'And turn him in. I could square the captain to say he'd given himself up. That would make it a bit better for him.'

Honeycombe said, 'Well, let's go. We haven't got all day.'

'I suppose you two blokes realize,' Fooks said to his companions, 'you won't 'alf catch it if the redcaps nab us. They can't do much to me. I've 'ad more days in detention than I've 'ad 'ot dinners, and a few more wouldn't make no odds. But you two 'ave got your stripes to lose. You'd both be back in the ranks peeling spuds with me an' Sparrer.'

Craddock told him, 'That's our worry, Wally, not yours.'

Like most of the soldiers in town, they all had 'bootleg' pistols, and they went armed. They searched the whole of the quarter in which Jobling had been seen. They pried into the back rooms of wineshops, shone their torches into the dark recesses of street after street of hovels, pushed their way into brothels, clashing the bead curtains aside and shouting 'Polizia!' or displaying their pistols when a house bully tried to bar their way. They interrogated scared bawds and street-corner idlers. Late in the evening they returned, tired and dispirited; their search had been in vain.

§§§§

Graziella sang as she moved about the room, to dispel her loneliness and unease. She wanted to lift the baby out of his cot and hug him to her, to keep her company, but he was asleep. Nella usually came at this time of the evening. Graziella wished she were here, to bring comfort like a warm little kitten.

She went to the door. She called, 'Have you seen Nella?'

Rosario looked up from a newspaper, and his face came alive with welcome. 'Ciao, Graziella! She was here until a little while ago. All the evening she has been hanging about at the gate of the barracks, but just now she went away.'

'Was she with someone?'

'No, she was alone. She seemed to be in a hurry. I do not know what she was doing there. She was speaking to no one. But it seems to me that she is becoming too interested in the soldiers. People do not talk well about girls who wait for the soldiers.'

'There is no harm in her. And if you do not want people to talk, do not talk thus yourself.'

'I am sorry, Graziella. I meant only to help.' He put the newspaper aside and came towards her, casually but with eagerness. 'Have you been to the cinema this week? There is a good film at the Sala Roma. I saw it last night. It is very sad.'

'I have seen it.' She felt weary and annoyed. She wanted to escape, but she did not know how.

'Did you like it?'

She shrugged her shoulders and grimaced.

'There will be many more good films now that they have begun to send them again from America,' he said. 'The American films are magnificent.'

She did not answer. She leaned against the doorpost with her hands behind her back, looking past him.

He said, 'I saw a funny thing this evening. You know the bald little soldier, who goes with Fat Lina? Their door was open, and I saw him bathing the children. He had one of them in the tub in front of him, all covered with soap. The baby was rolling on the floor, still dirty. The other three were all sitting up on the edge of the table like little dolls on a shelf, all washed and combed. Each time one of them fidgeted he took his pipe out of his mouth and waved it at them like a stick, and shouted to them in English. And, do you know, those children understood him! As soon as he spoke they sat still, and they looked at him with big solemn eyes, and they said, "Yes, pappa".'

She said dully, 'It is very funny.' She was unmoved by the disappointment in his face. To her all men but one were contemptible; Rosario most of all. She knew these conversations, with his mouth uttering banalities and his eyes pleading like a dog's.

He was trying desperately to keep the conversation from flagging, to be with her a little longer. He said, 'I have olive oil in the shop.'

She said to herself, 'I wonder where she is.'

'I could let you have as much as you want.'

'I have olive oil.'

She was about to make her excuses. He spoke again, hastily, 'The children in hospital are out of danger. My mother has been to see them. She took eggs.'

'Your mother is a good woman.'

'She is in bed now. The walk was hard for her. She is not well, her chest troubles her a lot. All night long I hear her struggling for breath. She will not be able to get about much longer.'

'You can manage with the shop on your own?' She was talking absent-mindedly, keeping him at bay with empty words while her thoughts wandered.

'Yes, but she cooks and cleans, and I cannot do that. Nor have I time to look after her.'

The commonplace reply came out of her mouth before she could check it. 'Well, take a wife!' She awoke in a panic: she must retreat before he answered her.

It was too late. He said, his eyes intent on her, 'Who?'

She mumbled, 'Oh, anyone. There are plenty of women,' and sought to back away from him into the doorway. He moved quickly to intercept her and checked her with his hand. There was a terrible urgency in his bearing. 'Graziella,

I must say this.' His voice was hardly audible and the words poured from him so rapidly that they were almost unintelligible. 'It humiliates me. Every word I speak will make my humiliation worse, but now I must speak. Graziella, for the love of God, be kind to me!'

She whispered, 'What do you want?'

'Graziella, please, I beg you, you do not know what my life is like. You have no idea of my torment. I cannot bear it any longer. Be good to me, just once, for an hour, for a little while.' He paused, gasping, and at the sight of the horror in her face the words came tumbling from him again. 'What difference will it make to you? It will not hurt you. It is nothing for a woman!'

She stood as if petrified. He said, in a frenzy of shame, 'Does the idea disgust you, then?' She did not answer. He leaned back from her. The strength and the wild hope died from his voice. 'Do you hate me?'

'No.'

'Do you despise me?'

She shook her head indifferently.

'What then?'

She raised her eyes and looked at him out of their remote depths. 'I do not see you.'

The words were like a blow. He said, choking, 'When he goes away you will be a woman to spit upon.'

She tried to pass him. 'Get out of my way!'

'Graziella, the man who takes you when he has gone will be laughed at by everyone. But I will take you. What is the humiliation compared with my love for you?' She squirmed past him and tried to close the door on him. He jammed his body into the doorway like a beggar. His voice became harsh with anguish. 'I would crawl at your feet! I would let you trample on me!' She forced the door shut. She heard him cry, from outside, 'He will go away!'

His footsteps faded. Through the thin plaster wall that separated the two houses Graziella heard the voice of his mother, querulous and insistent, and his brief reply; the mother's voice again, trailing off into a rumble of coughing, and a snarl of anger from Rosario.

Graziella busied herself spreading a tablecloth and laying out plates. She felt more alone than ever. She could not steady the racing beat of her heart; each time she remembered Rosario's last words the icy fluttering in her breast began again. Mentally she was utterly befogged. She longed for Nella to come and console her.

She finished laying the table and went to stir the pasta in the pot. Her impatience became a physical discomfort. She went about her housework with greater energy, hoping to banish the overtired feeling that oppressed her and to leave herself without time to brood; but time dragged, and the pop and bubble of boiling water, the cries echoing distantly from the streets, the stertorous breathing of the old woman next door emphasized the silence about her and made her solitude more burdensome.

The meal was cooked, the floor swept and the bed unnecessarily remade by the time Nella arrived. Graziella experienced a hot surge of relief as her cousin entered, but she said irritably, 'Where have you been?'

Nella answered, in a flat voice, 'I did not think that you would be alone. Where is he?' She moved about the room, toying with the ornaments on the shelves, as if she were not interested in receiving a reply.

'He is out. He is coming later for supper. Where have you been?'

'Walking.'

'Where?'

'I don't know. Why do you keep asking?'

'Rosario is talking about you. He says that you are hanging about the gate of the barracks.'

Nella's eyes flashed, in the shadows, in sudden pain and fury. 'You have a spy, now, to watch me?'

'No. Why do you shout so? I have never seen you so bad-tempered. Aren't you well, dear?'

Nella turned away with a child's petulant movement of the shoulders. 'I'm all right. Leave me alone. You drive me mad with your questions.' She turned, and a momentary light of interest appeared in her eyes as she studied Graziella. 'You don't look so well yourself. What is the matter with you?'

Graziella glanced at the mirror. A haunted face looked back at her, the eyes red with rubbing, the hair neglected, clefts of anxiety in the full cheeks. She said, 'I have been working, and before that I slept for a while. I must make myself tidy. I am sorry I could not come to see your mother today. I was at the market. Did you give her the flour?'

'Yes. She is making a polenta.' Nella was staring at her with the cunning curiosity of a child. 'I think you are in trouble.'

Graziella pushed her hair up wearily and rubbed the flat of her hand beneath her breasts. 'Oh, I'm all right.'

Nella continued to walk about the room, like a wary little animal keeping out of reach. There was something strange about her today; there was no comfort to be had from her, no relief in her presence after the day's buffetings. Her mouth trembled as she spoke again, but it made almost the shape of a cruel little smile. 'Perhaps your man has left you?'

Graziella forced herself to reply, in a pitying tone, 'Oh, you foolish child! What a thing to say!'

Nella said, with unexpected violence, 'Why foolish? He will leave you. They all do.'

Graziella stooped and painstakingly straightened the edge of the counterpane. 'When you are older you will know what you are talking about.'

'They all do! All the English!' Again it was the child speaking, in a half-weeping anger at being contradicted. 'In any case, they will all go away soon, and you will lose him then!'

Graziella thought that she was going to faint. She was beset; one blow followed another. Why was the child trying to hurt her so? She told herself that she must not lose control, but she could not prevent herself from answering desperately, 'He will not go away!'

'Who is the child now?' muttered Nella stubbornly. 'You know he must go, but you are afraid to admit it, and so you talk like a child.'

Reason fled from Graziella. It was her own thoughts that she was trying to deny, rather than Nella's words. She said, in a harsh, loud voice, 'He will not go away!'

'Stupid, when they are called, they go. Vincenzo was called, and he went. All these, they will be called soon. They will go, and your man will go with the others.'

'He will not go. I have lost one. This one I will not lose!'

'You are mad. He is a soldier.'

'Rosario is a soldier.' Graziella was speaking without conviction, but there was no trace of this in the vehemence of her voice; she found a mysterious relief in hearing the futile words coming from her lips.

'This one is an Englishman.'

'And Francesca's man?' Graziella's voice rose. 'What is he?'

Nella crept closer and looked up at her in terror. 'What is he?'

She heard her own voice, loud and quivering, as if someone else were speaking. 'You know what he is? He is one of those others. Francesca has told me. She knew she could trust me. She knew that I would understand. He is one of those others. They are soldiers. They are more warlike than the English. And Francesca has kept him.'

Nella whispered, 'You are mad!'

'I am a woman, and I know how to keep a man. This one I will keep!' She saw Nella crouching at her feet, looking up at her with big, scared eyes. The tension drained out of her and she said, 'Oh, what am I doing? I am so tired. Put some water in the bowl for me, dear. I must wash. He will be back soon, and I do not want him to see me like this.'

Nella went humbly to the sink. Graziella said, 'You will not tell anyone what I have told you?'

Nella opened her mouth, but her voice had deserted her. She shook her head violently.

'Francesca is a woman,' Graziella said. 'It would be a wicked thing to betray her.' She smiled weakly. 'I will wear the comb, he likes to see me wear it. Find it for me. And you can play the gramophone if you like. I know that pleases you.' She went to the sink and began to wash. 'You will stay for supper with us, and we shall have a good evening.'

Chapter Seventeen

B Y the last week-end in August, the company's training was in full swing. Captain Rumbold was bringing his men up to fighting pitch with the unhurrying certitude and confidence of an orchestral conductor. He measured their progress by the morning run with which he now began each day's training. He had begun by taking them out, dressed only in gym kit, over short distances. Day by day he had added to the weight of their attire and increased the distance until now they were going out for five-mile runs in the sun's full heat in complete battle order, burdened with packs, weapons, grenades and ammunition. At the beginning each run had been an ordeal, a struggle against unwilling muscles and lungs; now he would watch them swinging easily past, without effort, and know that every one of them shared with him the joy of endurance and self-command. They would return to the billet grinning with confidence, all thought of the purpose of these preparations drowned by the blood's hot pride. Even their arms drill was vigorous and precise, although they only had ten minutes of it each day. The captain remarked to Mr Perkington, 'You see, a pennorth of pride does more than a pound's-worth of practice.'

All around them military activity was becoming more intense. Flotillas of landing-craft came sliding into the harbour and anchored hull to hull. Lorry convoys loaded up with petrol and ammunition, and vanished mysteriously to the north. Swarms of bombers flecked the sky throughout the day, and the radio bulletins told of ceaseless raids on the southern tip of Italy. The brigadier was going off to conferences and the colonel was driving to and fro between the companies, with a preoccupied look on his face, checking up on training and equipment. Rumours multiplied.

A Commando unit had appeared in town, and one day it engaged the company in a street-fighting exercise. The exercise was so realistic that it degenerated into a gigantic hand-to-hand brawl among the rubble. The men returned to the billet with sore heads and bloodied shirts, but they were savagely content.

Day after day they practised beach landings. A man was drowned during one of these exercises; his disappearance was hardly noticed; he might as well have gone on leave. The landings, clumsy and muddled at first, became models of timing. The men, old hands and newcomers alike, learned to reach and cross a beach with the dash and the instinctive unity of an attacking football team.

A handful of burned-out men had straggled into the town, a collection of individuals who had wearily carried out certain duties in common but who, each evening, had dispersed and disappeared into the swarming civilian life around them. Now they were drawn together again into a functioning, human unit. They felt a living comradeship again. Each recognized among his companions the same schoolboy exuberance that stirred within him, the sense almost of sport with which each day's fresh trials were surmounted, the banishment of thought. They were storing up energy like fuel.

§§§§

On the Saturday evening, after football, Craddock went to see Graziella. He was tired after the game, and glad to relax in domestic surroundings. He greeted her with constraint; the memory of their first quarrel still survived as an irritant in his consciousness; but, grateful for peace after the heat and the glare and the male excitement of these recent days, he surrendered to her presence, feeling a little guilty when he recalled how he had acted towards her.

She gave him his supper, sat down with him, and ate sparingly and in silence. While he finished his meal she sat back, watching him. She reminded him, as she sat in the shadows with her hands in her lap, of her attitude during the first evenings they had spent together; yet there was a difference. She had been remote, then, and the only expression he had been able to discern in her eyes had been one of inquiry. Tonight there was a repose in her face that told of gratification. Her eyes, profound and inscrutable as those of a cat, were lit only with knowledge, with possession. The talkativeness and the clinging anxiety, which she had come to display as their association progressed, were gone. She was all solicitude, but she no longer tried to intrude. She was content to wait upon him in silence and humility.

She said, 'I have kept some water in a pitcher, in a cool place. I know that you prefer it to wine when you are hot.'

'Yes, I am still hot. Can you see it, then? I took a bath after the game, but I am still sweating.'

'The heat is too great. Here the men do not play football in summer. They work when they have to, and when they do not work, they sleep. But then,' she sighed, smiling, 'the English!'

'We did not play until the sun began to go down. Besides, we are soldiers, we are used to it. Rosario came with us. He enjoyed the game.'

She grimaced, 'That one!'

'Oh, I like Rosario. He is an intelligent fellow.'

There was dissent in her eyes, but she did not answer. He lit a cigarette. She said, 'Go to bed early. It will do you good. There is still some cocoa left in the tin you brought. I will make you a cup in a little while, and you will sleep well.'

'Aren't you going to have any?'

'There is only a little left, and I do not like it much.'

She moved away across the room, and as he spoke to her she turned her head to look back at him with a shy grace that he had never before noticed so acutely. Despite their moments of disharmony, she seemed beautiful in a new way each time he saw her, like a precious stone intricately cut and filled with changing lights and colours. He saw things in her that he had seen neither in his wife nor in any other woman before.

It was hard to remember his wife now, and when he did so it was to compare her unkindly with Graziella. When he saw Graziella standing before him, miraculously still yet relaxed throughout her body, he remembered his wife standing tensed or fidgeting, a picture of impatience or uncertainty. When Graziella walked he flinched at the memory of his wife's firm stride. When Graziella received him with eyes that were like dark pools of submission he remembered his wife's eyes, always anxious or angry or inquiring, always expressing some kind of conflict with his own. When Graziella embraced him hotly he remembered his wife's alternate moods of greed or unwillingness, and her pathetic gracelessness.

He told himself that he was not being fair; that, under the spell of this dream-life between battles, his memory was being warped. He tried to remember the good times, the times that ought to make a man homesick, that were so remote from this alien, sun-sodden island; shopping with his wife on Saturday afternoon, for instance; spending an evening with her among their friends in the saloon bar of the Vicar of Wakefield; Christmas with the family – pudding, paper hats, roaring fire, the room full of warmth and laughter, his wife's face flushed with merriment; sprawling side by side in two deck chairs at Margate. It was no use. He could not make these memories real in his mind. It was the old life, which had become alien; further away, beyond the battlefields, than the stars that sprinkled the night sky. Lethe was not more final, more potent than the narrow Simeto.

Graziella was standing at the stove, fanning the charcoal glow with a tireless, hypnotic movement of her hand. She was looking at him, utterly without thought, and he submitted, living only in the pinpoints of light that gleamed from the darkness of her eyes.

His eyelids drooped. He felt himself succumbing to the warmth and comfort which she wove about him. After a little while he went gratefully to bed. She brought his cocoa to him in bed as if he were her child, and when he had drunk she climbed in beside him. They were lying under a single thin coverlet. He felt her, vibrant, near him, but she did not interfere with his peace. She turned her face to him, scrutinizing him with an air of secret triumph, and put her arm loosely around his shoulders. 'There!' she murmured, when he was comfortable against her. 'Isn't that nice?' There was something in her manner of a mother's placid command.

They talked drowsily. It was good to talk, of the baby's upsets, of English dishes he wanted her to prepare, of his friends and her neighbours, of her childhood and his.

'It feels so good,' he said, 'to be here with you. All my worries disappear.'

'You have many worries. I have seen.'

'Not many.'

'What is it, then, that disturbs you?'

He hesitated. He could not bring himself to talk to her of his wife. Once they had been able to discuss the lives which they had left behind; but not now. He knew that it would ease him to talk to her, in the darkness, of his wife, but he knew, too, that it would hurt her. 'Oh, things happen in the company. Men do foolish things, and I have to punish them. I have to, or they would do worse things and get into more serious trouble. But sometimes they resent it.'

'But they like you. I know. Honeycombe has told me, and women have told me, too.'

'Perhaps. I don't know. Men have curious minds. They are always looking for someone to blame.'

'That disturbs you?'

'It ought not to, but it does. It is weak of me.'

'Ah, no!' she murmured. 'You have the heart of a man, not of a soldier.'

He closed his eyes. 'And there is one of my friends who is in very serious trouble. You do not know him, but I have told you about him. He is the brother of the soldier who was killed the night we came.'

'They have not found him yet?'

'No. He is one of the nicest men I have ever known, very quiet, very thoughtful. I do not know what happened to him.'

'It is not strange, to want to avenge a brother.'

'Perhaps, but we cannot leave him at large to make things worse for himself. I have been to look for him twice. If we are to help him we must find him.'

'I knew that the police were looking for him, but I did not know that you, too, wanted to find him.' She paused. He felt her fingers tighten on his shoulder, and as she spoke he was again aware of the secret triumph in her. 'You should have told me before. If only I had known!'

'Why? What can you do?'

'You should have told me before! Ciccio will know.'

'Ciccio?'

'Ciccio will know. He and his band of ragamuffins, they wander all day in the streets, they steal, they make deals, they talk with everyone, they know every thief, every smuggler, every bad house in this town.'

'It is not possible. One man in all this town!'

'You do not know! There is nothing that these boys do not know about the bad things of this town. Among the bad people here, there is a whole trade of hiding deserters. Ciccio himself has made money from it. He has told me.'

'The little rat! And you people let him behave like that?'

'Who is to stop him, and how? There are many like him.'

'Where is he?'

'You cannot do anything now. In the morning I will find him for you. Perhaps he will tell you something.'

'When I get my hands on him, he will tell me something!'

'In the morning,' she soothed. 'There is time in the morning. Sleep now, darling, sleep.'

§§§§

The oil lamp, turned down, made only a feeble stain of light in the darkness. Rosario lay on his narrow bed by the wall, listening to his mother's wheezing from behind the curtain across the room. It was hot, and the confined space was fetid with the smells of the night and of garlic. On the other side of the wall the murmur of conversation had died down.

He stared up into the gloom until his head ached and curtains of colour swirled before his eyes. These were the terrible hours, endless, when he could not sleep; his imagination raged, torturing his body, seizing on every sound that came from beyond the wall – the thump of boots falling to the floor, the creak of the bed, laughter – to goad his passions into life. He gloated, in agony, on the story that each sound told him, and dreamed obscenities. He sank into that state, on the borderlands of sleep, when the senses remain awake to outward stimulus but the mind is dizzy and released; fresh visions came, to relieve his torment, of triumph and revenge. Disjointed scenes succeeded each other; he was murdering her; he was standing, bloody and victorious after combat, while her lover cowered at his feet and she looked on in wonder; he was saving both their lives and acknowledging their shamed gratitude; he was rich and successful, passing her arrogantly with an adoring woman on his arm and feasting on her discomfiture; he was dead, and she was weeping over him in remorse; he was haranguing the people, denouncing the foreigner and his whore, and the crowd was roaring for blood. There was solace in these dreams, but the pain on awakening was all the greater.

He went over everything that had happened during the day, letting his mind twist good into bad, finding an evil motive for every innocent action. He remembered how he had slouched, alone and unheeded, along the touchline of the football field while the British soldiers had cheered and shouted around him, excluding him from their boisterousness and jostling him without apology. Time after time Craddock had come running past, with never a look his way or a friendly wave. After the game, when the team had come off the field, Craddock had been a hero, the men had surrounded him, thumping him on the back and congratulating him. Rosario, eager to be at his friend's side, to share his triumph and show his status to this crowd, had pushed towards him and tried to walk off the field arm-in-arm with him, as was the way of friends in this country. Craddock had pulled his arm free and said, laughingly, 'Here, I'm not your sweetheart!' What was that, Rosario asked himself now, but a repudiation? What else but an English insult? And why had he said 'sweetheart'? What had he meant? Had Graziella told him? Was he mocking? Rosario remembered the murmuring he had heard through the wall, and the laughter. Oh, if she had told him! If the two of them were laughing at his misery! He reached under the mattress and took out his knife. He pressed the flat of the blade against his chest, shocking himself awake with its icy touch. For that he could kill! He could kill!

He sat up cautiously. He peered across the room, and made sure that his mother was asleep. He reached up to the picture that hung on the wall above him, and slowly moved it aside. Beneath it there was a tiny hole in the wall.

He raised himself, careful to make no sound, and put his eye to the hole. The humiliation was like a whip across his face. Something had driven him to bore this hole in the thin plaster wall, an inexplicable longing to trample on the last shreds of his dignity, to feed on the visible evidence of his own shame. He could see nothing; even when they were awake he could only see a spot of light through the hole, and an occasional blur of black as one of them moved across it. Now there was only darkness.

He hated himself for this. It was the symbol of everything in his life that had become filthy; his love, this room, the ageing heap of decay that snored in the other bed, the sixpenny brothels to which he had to go to vent himself. And they, those two glutting themselves on each other behind the wall, were the authors of his shame.

He lay back, but there was no rest. The visions continued to pass before him.

§§§§

In the morning Craddock and Graziella found Ciccio. He grinned impudently when Craddock asked for information, and held out his hand. 'How much?'

'Come on, what do you know?'

'Cigarettes, money, alla same. How much?' There was a sparkle of cunning in Ciccio's eyes.

Craddock knocked the boy down with the back of his hand. Graziella was dumbfounded. He stood over Ciccio and spoke, briefly but with great anger. Ciccio whined threats and excuses, saw the look on Craddock's face and began to sniffle. Graziella stood by, clutching her hands together in distress. She wanted to plead with Craddock; instead she appealed to Ciccio to speak. Craddock motioned her to be quiet and poked the boy in the ribs with the toe of his boot. He said roughly, 'Well?'

'I will find him,' Ciccio muttered. 'But if I do not go to work this morning I will lose money.'

'When you come back, ask the sentry for me. If you do not come by twelve o'clock I will send the police for you.'

'I will find him.'

Ciccio went; and in the afternoon Craddock, Honeycombe and Fooks set off in the company truck to bring in Jobling.

Harry had put as much distance as he could between himself and his former hiding-place. The address which Ciccio had brought back was on the outskirts of the town, among the warren of rock-and-plaster hovels which sprawled beyond the Garibaldi Gate.

Craddock drove out through the gate. At the crossroads a Military Police jeep was drawn up in the kerb, its crew of four still as a group of statues beneath the sun. 'It can't be far from here,' said Honeycombe nervously. 'If he starts shooting we'll have that lot on top of us in ten seconds. They'd blow the daylights out of him.'

Craddock said, 'We won't give him the chance.'

They turned off the main road and the truck crept into what seemed like a city of stables. There were no streets here, only unpaved tracks, baked into ruts and potholes over which the truck lurched and jounced. A frightening quietness hung over the whole quarter. The windowless shacks leaned on each other as if in sleep. The people squatted in their doorways, looking at the truck in apathetic silence, cloaked like Arabs against the sun, too indifferent even to brush away the flies that crawled on their malaria-drawn faces.

The three men parked the truck and made their way on foot along an alley whose aperture was little more than a dark crack between two houses, so narrow that they had not seen it until they had come abreast of it. Craddock was walking now as if he were on patrol. He raised his hand and the men behind him halted. He sidled along the wall until he came to a doorway. The seconds spun out in the sunlight as he edged himself round the jamb of the door. His movements were almost imperceptible. He looked back and nodded. The other two came on quietly. He laid the back of his hand against his cheek. Their quarry was asleep. He pointed at Honeycombe and at himself; at Fooks, then at the doorway. His companions signalled that they understood. They waited, aware of the loudness of their own breathing. He gave them the 'come on' sign and plunged in through the doorway. Honeycombe leaped after him and Fooks moved forward to block the doorway.

Craddock was half way across the earth floor before Jobling awoke to the thump of boots. Craddock saw the look of panic and hatred in Jobling's face and the hand sliding under the pillow. No time now for comradely pleading. He shouted, 'The gun!' and hurled himself across Jobling's body, groping for the other man's gun hand. Honeycombe dived low, as if in a rugby tackle, scooped the pistol from under the pillow and flung it across the floor to Fooks. Craddock toppled backwards on to the floor with Jobling on top of him, and a flurry of blankets fell away from them. Jobling butted downwards with his head. Craddock felt the terrible impact against his temple and half-swooned into darkness and pain, but he clung on tenaciously. Honeycombe came crashing down on top of them, chopping with his clenched fist at the back of Jobling's neck. Fooks, from the door, could hear from among them only an animal grunting and, from Jobling, inarticulate noises of protest and fury. Jobling broke free. Blood poured from his nostrils and stained the front of his shirt. Fooks came forward and grappled with him, Honeycombe dived for his knees, and they brought him down like a pair of hunting dogs. Pinioned by their arms, Jobling threw his head back, his mouth wide open in a soundless agony. Craddock had picked up the pistol. He measured his distance and brought the barrel of the pistol down against the side of Jobling's head. Jobling cried out, and Craddock struck again. Honeycombe relaxed and said, panting, 'That's it!' Jobling lay in a heap on the floor.

'By God!' said Craddock, feeling his own forehead. 'He's give me a headache, all right!'

They picked Jobling up and carried him to the truck. Craddock kept watch while the other two hid their captive under a tarpaulin and fastened up the tailboard again.

'Where are we going to put him?' Fooks asked, as the truck slowed up outside the billet and turned in through the porch. 'In the guardroom?'

'In the stores,' Craddock answered. 'I want to see what I can do with the captain before we give him up.'

Craddock backed the truck tight up to the door of the stores so that no one could see what was being unloaded, and they hustled Jobling into the room.

'This is the best place,' Craddock said. 'The window's barred. Reckon we'll have to tie him up for a bit, though.'

They bandaged the gash in Jobling's head, bound his hands and feet, and made him as comfortable as they could against a bale of old clothing. 'I'm sorry, Harry,' Craddock said, 'it's for your own good. It won't be for long.'

Jobling glared back. 'You yellow dog! I never thought you could sink so low!'

'We'll bring you some grub in a jiffy.'

They locked the door and went to their rooms to wash.

A half-hour later Craddock came downstairs. He asked the sentry, 'Has the captain come in yet?'

'Just gone into the office, sergeant.'

Craddock went into the office.

'Hallo, sergeant,' the captain said. 'Where'd you get that bruise on your forehead? Girlfriend been biffing you with the old rolling pin?'

'Bit of an accident, sir. May I have a word with you?'

'Yes, I wanted to see you, too. I was just going to send for you. Do you feel like a bit of fun and frolic?'

'Why, what's up, sir?'

'Orders just come through from HQ. The whole brigade's off on a three-day scheme tomorrow. Like the idea?'

'I don't mind.'

'You don't sound very enthusiastic. I think it's a great idea. It's just come at the tight time. Now listen, here's the form. We'll be shoving off at nine o'clock in the morning. The rendezvous is at Paterno, tomorrow evening, and we'll have all the details outlined to us when we get there. It sounds as if we'll be going up Etna way. I've got Porky typing out Orders now. Breakfast at seven, parade for inspection at eight. I want you to go round the rooms tonight and see that the men get their kit ready before they go to bed.'

'Right, sir. Is that all?'

'That's all for the time being. Now, what's eating you?'

'About Jobling, sir.'

The captain looked up in surprise. 'What about him?'

'I've got an idea I might know where he is.'

'Where is he?'

'Well, what I wanted to ask was, if we get him, couldn't we do anything for him?'

The captain took a typewritten sheet that Piggott offered him, signed it and answered, 'You know where he is, don't you?'

There was a pause. Craddock said, 'Yes, sir. I was thinking that we could say he'd given himself up. That'd make it better for him.'

The captain buckled on his revolver belt. 'Let's go. Where is he?'

'Well, what about it, sir?'

'What about what?'

'Fixing it up like I said.'

'Sergeant Craddock, are you trying to bargain with me? The captain strode towards the door. 'Stand to attention and stop this bloody nonsense. Now, out with it, where is he?'

Craddock said, 'We've got him in the stores.'

'Piggott, tell the guard commander to detail an escort, and get me a driver for the truck. He's not our prisoner. We'll hand him over right away. Sergeant, you come with me.'

Craddock pleaded, 'Look, just give us a minute.'

'Don't daydream, sergeant. You're in the Army. Remember? If you want me to overlook the way you're acting, shut up.'

'But...'

'I won't give you another chance. Shut up!'

Craddock followed the captain to the stores.

Chapter Eighteen

T HE battalion toiled up into the mountains. Each time the men looked over their shoulders the panorama beneath them grew wider and more remote; at each halt the air was cooler; but the broad crater that crowned the tiered ranges never came nearer.

The road drew a white line, zigzagging backwards and forwards on itself, up the unending slopes ahead of them. It led them through vineyards, orchards, cool woods of beech, chestnut and pine, fields of tall maize and plantations heavy with the scent of oranges; through farms, through huddled villages and little towns heaped upon the hillsides in level upon level of rippling, russet-tiled roofs.

The noises of the march seemed tiny in this vast, crystal silence; the undulating distances offered to each man, as he looked out from the straggling file, loneliness and freedom. Flocks of goats came rushing down upon them with a music of bells. Oxen moved past with massive dignity, tolerant of the little boys who goaded their flanks with sharp-pointed sticks and urged them on with long-drawn cries of 'Ah-guah! Ah-guah!' The world of crowds was far below, beneath veils of mist. Here each human being was a separate mystery; a black figure looking down on them from the steep terraces; a glimpse of movement against a great cactus clump; a leathery face in a doorway; a woman gliding past in black dress and white headcloth, erect beneath a tall water jar, secret and untouched by their cries of greeting. This was a world without shouting. The women's voices came to them low and lamenting, the men's in harsh animal grunts.

They climbed on, leaving behind them the realm of human habitation. They were passing through a waste of black cinder. This was the zone where the earth made manifest its hidden agonies. Every particle of soil had been burned to death. The mountain's flanks spread beneath them in bulging slopes, pocked by old craters that thrust up their lips like a hundred clamant wounds, scarred by broad tracks where fire had flowed, disfigured by long growths of black lava; a scorched moon-landscape. The sky assumed its proper dimensions, no longer a flat sheet rising behind a solid scene but an infinity of pale space in whose midst they crept. They sang and jested, seeking each other's comfort in face of the revelation that they were less than insects in this universe. But the vision did not frighten; the plains of death that surrounded them were possessed with the peace of death; all problems died here and the mind was liberated.

Sicily lay at their feet, a mass of hill-contours crowded like the corrugations of a walnut, a fringe of flat plain scalloped by the sea. Towns were tiny white clusters, clinging to the hills or spread upon the plain. From these heights men looked down like gods; the rest of the human race was lost to sight; all those multitudes below were too insignificant to catch the divine eye. Sea and sky fed the sensation of mastery. One mirrored the other, the same pale blue; and the clouds floated at eye level, flat-topped and flounced beneath, like ribboned reflections of the Calabrian shore. The meeting-place of sea and sky was imperceptible. There was no horizon, no place where the eye could rest and assure itself of reality. Was this the dream, or was yesterday the dream? The men were not conscious of transition. Only the unreal present was real. They were exhilarated, purified, released.

Captain Rumbold, sitting on a boulder, said to Perkington, 'This is the life, eh?'

Perkington raised his chin from his cupped hands. His eyes were heavy with thought, and he answered unwillingly, 'I could stay here for ever.'

'I don't know about that. I see what you mean, though.' The captain pondered. 'Yes, it's a thought. Ever done any climbing?'

'No. I'm afraid I was never very active.'

'I used to do a bit. Rock-climbing. In the Lake District. There's something about it. I always wanted to have a go at the real thing, you know, Switzerland, but I could never afford it. I started saving up about fifty times, but I was never the thrifty kind. Good Time Charlie, that's me. I read all the books, though, you know, old Smythe's stuff, that kind of thing. About all I ever did read.' He reflected. 'Damn funny, when you come to think of it.'

Perkington's interest quickened. The self-conscious grin on Rumbold's face was something he had never seen before. He had not expected confessions from the captain; for the first time he felt intimate with the other man, and his equal. He said, 'I used to read the old voyages and histories. *Anson, Prescott, Robinson Crusoe, Two Years Before The Mast*. I suppose that was why I was keen on the *Odyssey*. Do you know it?'

'Ancient Greeks, or something, wasn't it? Not exactly in my line.'

'You'd like it. It all took place in this part of the world. As a matter of fact, I was thinking about it just now.'

Rumbold let a respectful moment elapse, uttered a noisy sigh of satisfaction and said, 'Yes, this suits me all right. Funny, you join the Army and you find yourself perched up here. Talk about on top of the world! I'll tell you frankly, I've never had so much fun in all my life. Oh, I had a good time before the war! I made a living, I sodded about, I did all sorts of things, women galore, you know. But it never really meant a thing. Have you ever been having a hell of a fine time, getting on all right with everyone, and yet you somehow want to punch someone on the nose or kick a chair to bits, just through sheer boredom? Well, that was me.'

Perkington, in his turn, became confidential, trying to strengthen this new intimacy between them. 'I know what you mean. I can't say I led your kind of life, but I was fed up, too. I suppose I ought not to talk till I've seen a bit of action, but I must say the war has been an escape for me.' He paused, and asked suddenly, 'Have you ever tried to make sense of life?'

'Can't say I have. The world can go its own sweet way without my help.'

'Well, I did. And the more I tried to understand it, the more of a muddle it seemed. Everything came to pieces in my hands as soon as I touched it. I was taught that all sorts of things were true, and when I looked at the opposites, they were just as true. The university seemed all wrong, my parents and the things they believed in seemed all wrong, my friends seemed all wrong, when I looked at myself I seemed all wrong. The whole darned world seemed all wrong. You see these things, and you feel responsible, but you don't know what to do about it. I spent four years getting an Arts degree, and ended up writing publicity for beauty preparations. The money was all right, but I ask you!'

'Sounds a damn good job to me.'

'I suppose you'd call it that. But every time I picked up the papers and saw what was happening in the world, I felt like a criminal. My job seemed parasitic and useless. I mean, what's the use of living like that?'

'Bit of a philosopher on the quiet, aren't you?'

'Oh, I don't know. Do you want to go back to the old grind after the war?'

'After the war?' The captain screwed up his eyes and stared out across the landscape. 'Anyone can see you're new to the game.' He pointed. 'Look, there's the Simeto.'

Perkington peered down through the haze. He could just discern the dark line winding across the plain. The sight of the river and the captain's words had reminded him of what was to come. The cold feeling crept back into his entrails. He was still a schoolboy, uninitiated.

§§§§

There had been a panic in the Via dei Martiri when the soldiers assembled to march away, but the news soon spread that they were coming back. Nevertheless, without them, the street seemed bereft. Rosario could not remember when it had ever been so quiet before.

He left his mother gossiping with a customer, and walked down towards the waterfront. There was no work for him at the billet today; the place was deserted, with only a handful of men left on guard. The sea was smooth and sparkling. Masts crowded the harbour. Rosario looked at the hundreds of little craft, all long and low, all painted blue and white. Men were moving on their decks.

'They are loading stores.'

He turned at the sound of the low, strong voice. Francesca's man was standing at his elbow. He said, 'Ciao.'

'Ciao.'

Rosario said, 'You are bold, today.'

'Why bold?'

'This is the first time I have seen you walking about in the street.'

'I often walk.'

'What do you fear? To be interned? They have not interfered with me.'

'There is the risk. Besides, I have suffered much with malaria.'

'You are well now?'

'For the moment. But it comes back.'

'I know. If Francesca had gone to the soldiers they would have given her quinine for you.'

'Francesca!' The man laughed. 'She guards me like a she-wolf. No soldiers for her!' He put his hand inside his shirt. 'Here, this pleased you when you saw me making it.' He drew out a wooden crucifix and offered it to Rosario.

Rosario examined it, passing his fingers over the body of the Christ. 'It is a work of art,' he said reverently. 'It is as smooth and supple as the living flesh. One can even see the agony in the face, although it is so small.'

'And the wound in the side,' said the stranger. 'You see the wound?'

'Truly I see the wound. And the fingers clawing in agony at the nails that pierce the hands. It is worthy to be placed in the cathedral. You have seen the carvings in the cathedral? They are the work of Scipione di Guido, a great man. You know them?'

'Yes, I have seen.'

Rosario held the crucifix up before him. 'A man touches a piece of wood, and the spirit breathes from it! To be an artist is to be like God.'

The man said, 'You work for the English?'

'Yes. Why, do you want work?'

'Do you ever work in the port?'

'No.'

'Those are landing-craft, for an attack. Have you seen any soldiers going aboard them yet?'

'No. You are an inquisitive man. It is better not to be thus, particularly when one is in your position and mine.' Rosario held out the crucifix. 'I am grateful to you for showing me this. It grieves me to relinquish such an object of beauty.'

The man said, 'Keep it. I shall make more.'

'Truly? How much do you want for it?'

'It is a gift.'

'A gift? Tell me, what do you want from me? I know too much of the world to believe in gifts.'

The man smiled. 'You are a sour one! We are comrades, of a kind, are we not?'

Rosario dropped the crucifix into his jacket pocket. 'I thank you from my heart. This will make my mother very happy. She will weep over it.'

'I am glad.' The stranger indicated the deserted street with a jerk of his head. 'It is better without them, eh?'

'I am indifferent.'

'Perhaps. But it is better, is it not?'

Rosario shrugged his shoulders. 'Yes.'

'Francesca tells me you have spoken against them.'

'Francesca lies. They are no worse than others. I am not a fool, to speak ill of conquerors.'

'But a man can think, non è vero?' The stranger paused. 'I see the fishing boats are going out again.'

'Yes, there is plenty of fish.'

'Do you know any of the fishermen?'

'Yes, I have friends among them.'

'Good friends?'

'What is a good friend?'

'Friends you can trust?'

'Whom can one trust? Why?'

'Do they go out far?'

'I think that there are limits. Why all these questions?'

The man said, 'Sometimes one must trust. Can a fishing boat cross to the mainland? In one night? It is not far.'

'What do you want?'

'I want to go to the mainland.'

'The Germans are there.'

'Well, the English are here.'

'Why do you want to go?'

'I want to go home.'

'Does Francesca know?'

'What do you care?'

Rosario pondered. 'Can you pay?'

'I have some money.'

'You will have to wait.'

The stranger looked out across the harbour. 'I do not want to wait too long.'

Rosario sucked at his lower lip, and studied the other man. 'I will make inquiries.'

'Good.'

Rosario said, 'I must go back to the shop. I cannot leave my mother for long. It is difficult for a man. Will you come back with me, to take some wine? My mother will want to thank you.'

'Another time. Now I am going for a little walk.'

The man went off along the street that led past the dock gates. Rosario watched, frowning. When the man was out of sight, Rosario sighed, and made his own way home. He walked slowly, deep in thought. He passed the soldiers' billet, paused, and turned back. He asked the sentry, 'When will the company be back?'

'No capeesh.'

'Craddock – il sergente Craddock. Dov'è?'

The sentry shook his head. 'Craddock lontano. Not here.'

Rosario racked his brains for English words. 'Ufficiali? Officers?'

'No officers.'

Rosario asked desperately, in Italian, 'When will they come back? Tomorrow? The day after tomorrow?'

The soldier caught the word domani. 'Not tomorrow.'

'But I have something of great importance to ask him.'

'No capeesh.' The sentry turned away.

Rosario lingered on the pavement for a moment, shrugged his shoulders and went home.

Chapter Nineteen

LATE on Wednesday evening the battalion was spread across a bare hillside, formed up for a mock attack. With the black wall of lava rising behind them in a menacing silhouette, the men looked up from the floor of an infinite cavern of sky into whose shadowed and mysterious depths the bleak slopes fell away beneath them. They lay for hours, talking quietly, while the cold crept into them and the darkness thickened about them. No orders came; only the brief roar of a distant motor cycle charging uphill, a voice raised far away in command, the rumble and crash of a falling boulder; each sound burst out of the night to compel attention, and died in the silence. Men exchanged rumours. The fear of the unknown, so easily aroused, awakened in them. Orders came, but not to allay their uncertainty. The attack was called off. Cold and cramped, they assembled in platoons in the darkness and began to stumble downhill.

Nobody told them where they were going. It was unnerving, trudging and slithering downwards, downwards, like blind men stumbling on the edge of space. The hours crept by, and they marched on, their legs aching with the strain of this descent through the darkness. They halted again, and squatted on their heels. Still nobody told them what was happening. Shouts echoed in the night, and officers congregated mysteriously. They heard lorries crashing and lurching up towards them, and the banging of falling tailboards. Officers came hurrying back to shout at them, hustling them up on to their feet, stirring them again to a confusion of movement. The men milled and thronged in the dark, colliding, cursing and shouting questions. They were herded into the lorries, the officers packing them in, despite a hubbub of protests, until they were jammed to suffocation in the darkness. The tailboards slammed into place, pressing them even tighter. Engines roared again, and the lorries moved off in convoy, creeping downwards like a row of black beetles against the pale edge of the sky.

To the men, crammed upright in the lorries, breathing in each others' faces, dashed against each others' weapons and equipment by every bounce and jolt, it seemed as if they were boxed up in great coffins and being lowered violently into a bottomless grave. The din of engines deafened them. Newcomers to the battalion shouted bewildered questions to each other; they had been flung without warning from one compartment of life into another; they were aggrieved and humiliated. The older hands said nothing, as they swayed and sweated in the darkness; for them the familiar journey into the inhuman had begun again.

At last they saw the sunlight. They glimpsed houses and heard the voices of children. The lorries halted, and the men climbed down, stiff and sick. They were in town, parading outside the battalion's headquarters. Once more the officers hurried away. Fragments of conversation came to them to heighten their suspense. Still unenlightened, they marched off.

Rumbold's company tramped through the streets, glad to be breathing fresh air and moving their limbs again. They turned into the Via dei Martiri. Doors opened. The women appeared, dishevelled from sleep, clutching their babies and welcoming the men with agonized smiles of relief. A soldier muttered, 'Thank God we're home!' The ranks came to life with recognition, with reassurance; but the chill of uncertainty persisted.

They halted, and waited for the command to dismiss. It did not come. Impatience grew in each man like an itch. The officers and sergeants had gone away, and the men leaned on their rifles, hitching their packs higher on their shoulders to relieve the strain. They talked, unchecked by their NCOs. The reinforcements grew more and more garrulous, the veterans more taciturn.

The officers appeared. Captain Rumbold came forward. He shouted, 'Company–'

The conversation died away.

'Atten – shun!'

Rifle-butts crashed. The ranks were still.

'Stannat – ease! Stand easy now, keep quiet, and pay attention.'

Even the women felt the strain in the men's hush, and they quieted their children.

'Before you're dismissed, I've got something to tell you. As from now, the battalion is under notice to move. We've no further orders yet, but all guard duties are cancelled, you'll remain in the vicinity of the billet, and you'll keep your battle order packed. Mail will continue to be collected, but if you've got any letters to write, you'd better get them off now. There may not be time later. There'll be plenty for you to do. I'm putting two platoons on scrubbing the billet down from top to bottom, and one platoon on packing up spare stores and sending them back to Battalion HQ. You'll be allowed out this evening, unless I get orders to the contrary, but I want you all in by nine o'clock, and God help any man who isn't. That's all for now. Don't get excited. It may never happen. Fall the men out, sergeant-major.'

§§§§

Craddock wanted to get away from the uproar, but everyone crowded round him.

Fooks grabbed his arm. ''Ere, sarge, comin' out tonight? Platoon beer-up. Everything's on me.'

Craddock said, 'No thanks, Wal.' It had come. What incredible tricks time and a man's mind played with him! Right up to that last moment when the platoon leaders had crowded round the captain in the courtyard, it had been too remote to imagine. He had even wanted it to come. Why was he always discontented with what he had? Now that it was here he dreaded it.

Ling moaned, 'Bleed'n' cheek! What they wanna pick on us for?'

The sergeant said, 'Cheer up, Sparrow, every mile's a mile on the way to Bethnal Green.' That was a lie if there ever was one! Every mile was a mile further away from the land of the living, into a wilderness whose milestones were graves. Bethnal Green – Slough – a wife, a daughter – did they really exist beyond the mists?

One of the reinforcements asked him, 'Do you reckon we're for it, sarge?'

He answered, 'Maybe, maybe not. There's plenty of false alarms in this business. Take those buckets upstairs.' It was like having a limb torn off to think of telling Graziella. In these last three days away from her, he had realized how much she meant to him. He had been happy enough by day, in the heat of action, but at night, lying alone in his blanket beneath the stars, he had ached with misery at being apart from her. He had dreamed of the embrace of her limbs, all softness and strength; of her satin smoothness, and of the fire in which she enveloped him; of her subtlety and her simplicity; of her fury and her submission; of her healing silences and her profound understanding. She could behave like his slave and make him feel like her child.

Tiger came up to him. 'Sarge, old Rosario's outside. He's asking for you. Says it's important.'

Craddock looked up at the windows, wondering where he could hide for a while in solitude and peace. 'Tell him to go and take a running jump. I'm busy.' He could not face her. In their first encounters it had been little more than friend-ship, than sympathy, that had made him want to bring her to life. It was only in their last few times together that he had come to recognize that something more than enjoyment burned in her. The life which had flowered in her was his own. When they were together her eyes were on him all the time; she could see nothing else but him. In her room she moved about him like the moon about the sun. When he laid his hand on her breast he was filled with awe at the frantic beating of her heart. To leave her would be to wrench the life out of her.

Tiger came back. 'He says he must see you.'

He could not tell her tonight. It was not so much her passion he needed, for one last night, as her calm. Perhaps he would think of a way to hint, to prepare her. He said, 'Let him wait. You go on upstairs.' The boy looked wan. 'What's up, kid? Not worried, are you? Why don't you go out with Fooksy and the boys tonight? And get your hair cut. You look like a bloody violinist.'

Honeycombe appeared. Why couldn't they leave him alone?

Honeycombe said, 'Well, this is what you wanted. Glad we're shoving off?'

Craddock said, 'I'm not sorry.'

Honeycombe studied him. 'Going to see her, Joe? You can stay the night if you want to. I'll look after things here. I can always give you a call if the balloon goes up.'

Craddock said, 'I reckon I will. Thanks.'

§§§§

An hour passed; then another. Rosario walked back to the shop, hovered in the doorway, unable to take his eyes from the gateway of the billet; returned, as if drawn by something beyond his power, to the billet; walked back to the shop; and returned again.

Soldiers hurried to and fro past him, ignoring him. They were loading a lorry, with much noise, in the courtyard. They were plodding up and down the stairs with ammunition boxes on their shoulders. They were emptying buckets of dirty water down the drains and heaping piles of rubbish in a corner. Men pushed him out of the way, or shouted to him brusquely to stand aside. He felt the purpose in all this activity. They were men, preparing for a man's job. They did not look upon him as one of their kind. All recognition, all kinship had faded from their eyes. He was less than an outcast, standing slackly in their midst; he was only an obstruction. He had seen the blind fear in the women's faces today. It was not for him. They, too, looked through him as if he were not human. These incomprehensible women, who had once nodded approvingly when they thought of his courage in finding his own way back, alone among all their men, from this war they hated, even they at this moment despised him because he was exempt from the hated ordeal.

He asked himself again and again, 'What business is it of mine?' He tried to put out of his mind the thing that was worrying him. He told himself that they were going away, at last they were going away, and the street would be quiet and free once more. Graziella – his throat constricted at the thought – Graziella! Graziella! – she would be alone, stricken, humbled, creeping to him for comfort and for protection. She would be another man's leavings. He would taste that other man's kisses on her mouth. What did it matter? They would soon be gone; they would soon be gone.

He walked back to the gate and, for the third time, timidly asked the sentry if he had seen Sergeant Craddock. 'Andate via,' said the sentry, 'he's busy.' Why could he not forget it? Why could he not keep away? 'What business is it of mine?' he asked himself again. He looked for Craddock among the thronging soldiers, stifled by the impatience and the resentment that warred within him. What he knew, he told himself, it might be something of importance; it might be the bombshell that he could explode in the midst of all their indifference. They would all pause in their activity, and look his way, and whisper. Craddock would listen attentively, would put eager questions, would clasp his hand in warm gratitude. Graziella would gaze at him with big eyes. And that Francesca, how she would suffer! He waited, and waited, and waited.

Craddock came out through the gate. His face was heavy with care. His eyes rested on Rosario for a moment in recognition, but without greeting, and he walked past. Rosario was overwhelmed at the same time with relief at seeing him, and with resentment. He laid his hand on Craddock's arm and said, 'I sent messages, but you did not receive them.'

Craddock paused unwillingly. 'I received them.' His face was unyielding.

Rosario suppressed the quiver of anger that intruded into his voice. 'I have been waiting for hours.'

'I am busy. What do you want?'

'There is something I must ask you.'

'It will have to wait. I am busy.'

'It is about Francesca's man. Have you never been suspicious of him?'

Craddock looked impatient. 'What riddles are you wasting my time with now?'

'No riddles. Have you never noticed that he is afraid to appear in the street?'

It was clear that Craddock was not listening. He was looking away, towards *her* door, and his whole body was poised to move on. 'Have you never asked yourself why?' Rosario asked desperately.

Craddock looked at him with unconcealed scorn. 'Perhaps it is because he is a deserter,' he said in a rough voice, with a cruel emphasis on the last word.

A great heat of fury was mounting inside Rosario. He could not control the shuddering of his breath as he said, 'He has spoken to me.'

'Well, why tell me? Was it such an honour?'

Rosario was choking, but he could not tear himself away now. 'He was asking me questions about the soldiers. He wants to go to the mainland. I tell you he plans some harm.'

'What harm? Everybody is asking questions about the soldiers.'

'But let me tell you...'

'Tell me tomorrow!' Craddock said violently.

'Tomorrow!' Rosario shouted. 'Where will you be tomorrow? Is that the way to talk to a friend?'

Craddock was already walking away. He said thickly, over his shoulder, 'Friend! You make me sick!'

He disappeared into Graziella's house. Rosario watched, speechless and shaking. His whole body was shaking horribly, as if the malaria were upon him. Hot tears of anger rolled down his cheeks; he could only breathe in gulps. If he had had his knife with him he would have plunged it into that broad back, to avenge his bruised manhood. He made his way back to the shop, dreamy with hatred. He went to his bed and fumbled beneath the mattress. He heard his mother's wheezy voice from behind her curtain, coming to him from an infinite distance, a noise in his ears without meaning. He could hear the two of them, already, beyond the wall. He paused in his search and listened, his whole body rigid, his head thrown back, his mouth open; listening, like a dog.

Chapter Twenty

A FAN of daylight opened across the floor as Craddock entered the room. Graziella, her back to him, lay on the bed in an ugly heap, with her face pressed into the pillow and her legs tucked up beneath her out-thrust buttocks. She stirred as the light touched the pillow, raised herself on her hands and looked at him over her shoulder. Craddock heard the door creak behind him as he closed it with his heel. Graziella was looking at him as if the daylight had blinded her; her smile of welcome, as the shadows flitted over her face and advanced across the room behind the closing door, seemed to be an afterthought.

The room was almost dark now. Craddock said, 'Well, I have returned.'

She swung her body round, lowered her feet to the floor and stood up, with tired movements.

'Aren't you glad to see me?' he asked.

She nodded absently. Her smile deepened, but there was something forced in it. She came into his arms and let him kiss her. She moved away into the room, and he followed her, noticing with perplexity her bowed head and her embarrassed, secretive smile. She seemed to be oppressed by private thoughts. She took down a decanter and a tumbler with automatic movements, and poured wine for him. The clink of glass and the gurgle of the wine were loud in the silence. She said, 'Do you want to eat?'

'No.'

'Are you tired?' Her voice was uninterested. 'Did you have a hard time?'

'No.' He drank his wine, feeling less sure of himself every moment.

She went to the mirror, shook her hair out and began to comb it energetically. 'Little happened while you were away. Filomena's baby has been born, a little girl.'

Now it was Craddock who was silent.

She went on chattering, 'It was not a difficult birth, the child is so small, it is like a little doll.' Her voice was hard and bright. She tore at her hair with the comb. 'It displeased you to find me like this? You surprised me, coming thus. Earlier I was prepared for you, but you did not come.'

Craddock stared into his wine-glass.

'Ecco!' She turned to face him again; passing her hands back tenderly over her hair. 'See how it shines!'

Craddock smiled painfully. Her eyes were intent upon him; all the animation went out of her and she turned away again, her hands against her waist, cleaning one thumbnail with the other. When she looked at him again, her eyes were dulled as though by an anaesthetic. 'You are going away.'

'How do you know?'

'Everybody knows.'

He said, 'It is too soon to know.'

'It is not certain?'

'Not yet.'

'And you? What do you think?'

He heard her laboured breathing in the silence. Her eyes were compelling. He braced himself with a long breath and said, 'We shall go.'

She was still working at her fingernails, frowning down at them as if nothing else concerned her. She asked, 'When?'

'I do not know.'

'Soon?'

He hesitated again. 'Very soon, I think.'

Again the silence, and her quick, harsh breathing. He said, 'You must not sadden yourself. We both knew that it had to happen.'

Her bearing was listless. There was no sign of interest in her eyes. He felt that although he was standing before her she could not see him. He repeated, 'We both knew that it had to happen, non è vero?'

Her eyes opened wide, replying in mute pain and resentment, as if he had struck her violently on the forehead. When she spoke, he could discern only a muffled irritation in her voice. 'I heard you the first time.' She rubbed her hands, the fingers pointing straight downwards, up and down her skirt; it was a habit of hers. She cried suddenly, 'Why do you talk to me like that? Do you think that I am a child?'

He said helplessly, 'Then what is there to say?'

She looked past him in silence; then she said, in a strangled, unconfident voice, 'Stay with me.'

He held out his hand to her, and pleaded, 'Graziella!'

She ignored his hand. She said again, this time in a clear and decisive voice, 'Stay with me!'

'You do not know what you are saying.'

'I know what I am saying. It is simple. Stay with me!'

He said gently, 'Try to be calm.'

'Try!' She spoke with fury. 'Oh!' She pressed her fists against her breast. 'Here, how do you feel here? How can you breathe? How can you smile? What a beast is a man! To part is nothing to you! For you love is only a game of deceit! You feel nothing, nothing, nothing!'

He was ashamed of the feebleness of the only words he could summon. 'That is not true.'

'It is true! It is clear that you do not know me. You would not have spoken thus if you knew me. But I know you. I know every movement of your body and every beat of your heart. I know every look on your face and every thought in your head. Do you think you can lie to a woman? You have enjoyed yourself with me, and if you feel a little sorry to leave me, you tell yourself that there will be more women. Look at you! Your mind is not occupied with what I am saying. Already you are thinking of journeys, of battles, of adventures. It is of no use that I cry out, that I empty my heart to you! There is no love or pity in your eyes. I see nothing there but disdain, but hatred for this woman who throws herself in your path...'

Craddock interrupted her with a force that rendered him almost inarticulate. 'That is not true! What – what do you want me to do? How can I show what I feel? Do you want me to cry like a baby? Will that make you more happy?'

'Contenta?' she echoed derisively. 'Listen to the man! What a word he flings at me! When he is gone I shall be a woman ruined and empty. But no! There is not a thought in his head about what will become of *me*!'

'And me?' Craddock burst forth. 'Have you thought of what is going to become of *me*?'

'No!' she taunted, the tears streaming down her face. 'Of course not! I have not lain awake at nights, while you slept, and let the hot tears fall on your body, thinking of the wounds that might torture it! I have not felt dread in my heart every time I saw a crippled soldier crawling on his stumps up the church steps! I have not looked at your face and remembered the face of the madman who once stared at us in the street!'

Craddock muttered, 'Oh, my poor Graziella!' He went towards her and reached out for her, but she backed away from him, and sat huddled on the bed, sobbing furiously. She gasped, between sobs, 'Why do you think I want to keep you? Only to bring me food? Only to buy me gifts? Only to make love with me?'

'Graziella,' he said, 'I did not think that. I do not want to hurt you.'

She sat up, wild and trembling. 'Then stay with me!'

He shrugged his shoulders hopelessly. 'What use is it for me to talk? Again and again you say the same thing. You tell me that you are not a child, but you refuse to think, you say the same thing, again and again, like a child.'

'Why like a child? Other men have done it.'

'Deserters!' he said with loathing.

'Deserters, yes! Whom are you going to desert, your comrades or me? If you knew what love meant, there would not be any doubt!'

Craddock could bear no longer to be hounded both by her and by his own unhappiness. 'For the love of God!' he said violently. 'You talk like a crazy woman! Doubt? There is no doubt! I am a soldier. You have known that all the time.'

'I know one thing now,' she jeered, 'that I did not know before. You are afraid! You are afraid to be hunted! You are afraid to be shot! You are afraid of your comrades! You are afraid of love! You are a coward!'

He strode across to the bed and seized her roughly by the shoulders. She threw her head back and glared up at him in defiance. He shouted, 'Mad one! Listen! I am not afraid. It is not out of fear that I fight. You! – You pretend to understand! You do not even begin to understand a man!' He threw her back on the bed. 'I am a man. You cannot expect me to be otherwise.'

'Rosario is a man. He did it!'

'Rosario! That – thing – a man!'

'And the German?' she shrilled, utterly beside herself now. 'He is not a man? He is not a soldier? They are soldiers, they are better soldiers than all the others, they are better soldiers than the English!'

'What German?'

'Francesca's German!' She was showing her teeth like a cat, crouching on the bed, spitting the words up at him. 'Ha! The big man knows everything! The woman knows nothing! Well, there is something you did not know. Even a German soldier will desert for the woman he loves, he deserts because he is a man, a real man!'

'Francesca's German,' echoed Craddock, hesitating, remembering. He turned on her again, 'You fool! He is no deserter! There are hundreds of Germans on this island, who were left behind in the retreat. They wait, in civilian clothes, for the chance to escape. Every day, in our battalion, we are warned about them, told to watch for them. Deserter! Even now he is preparing to leave his darling Francesca and to escape to the mainland. You see,' he said, leaning over her and speaking with great bitterness, 'they are soldiers, too. They fight to the end. They are men.'

She was coiled on the bed, not moving, but panting quickly and following him with her eyes like a trapped animal. 'By God,' he thought, in the midst of his anger. 'she's lovely!' He said, 'But he will not escape. In five minutes he will be behind bars.' He turned towards the door. 'Graziella, I shall come back soon. Try, for the two of us, to calm yourself. Force yourself to think, and you will see reason.'

She let him take a couple of paces, watching him in disbelief; then, with a hoarse cry of protest, she flew after him and flung herself upon him. 'No!' she cried, 'You must not betray him. You will break Francesca's heart. Leave them in peace.'

He tried to pull her arms from about his neck, but her fingers were locked behind his head and the whole weight of her body lay upon him. If he had broken free she would have crashed in a heap at his feet. He said, 'Let me go!'

She moaned, 'I will kill myself if I have betrayed her!' She thrust her body up against his and tightened her arms about him in a feverish embrace. 'Afterwards, do what you like afterwards, but stay with me now.' She was crying again. Big tears fell quickly and silently and splashed, scalding, on the backs of his hands. Her face was close to his, imploring, and she smothered him with kisses. He muttered, 'Let me go!' – his voice scarcely audible. His legs were weak as if the bones were going soft, and the blood raced through his veins like molten metal. 'Afterwards, afterwards!' she panted. She was fastened upon him like a beast upon its prey. He was overwhelmed by the yielding pressure of her body. He could see nothing but her great eyes close against him. He could hear nothing but her heartbeats and his own. Resolution, anger, all thought, melted away in the blaze that enveloped him. She bore him backwards, her will irresistible. She wept and babbled over him as they sank upon the bed, and in the gasping laughter that came from her throat, there was compassion and triumph.

§§§§

Rosario heard it all.

He moved away from the wall, trembling. He felt sick and soiled.

He waited for a moment, irresolute, and in that moment he felt that his opportunity had passed. How could he break in on them now? Even if he killed the Englishman; even if he killed them both, thrusting his knife down and down and down again into his own defeat, into his own shame, into his own uselessness, he would not look less the fool; the cuckold who had never even been a husband!

There were still sounds coming through the thin wall; the creak of the bed and – for Rosario it was the breaking-point – a low, throaty laugh from Graziella. His legs nearly buckled under him, and the pain leaped and bit inside him like a fox sewn up in his vitals. He strode out into the street, stood for a moment blinking in the sunlight and swaying in front of her door like a drunkard. The hilt of the knife burned in his hand. His mind became clear; a great, obsessed emptiness. He turned away from her door and went lurching across the street.

He was half-blind with the sweat in his eyes when he halted outside the door of Francesca's house. He kicked the door open. Francesca and her man were sitting at the table, eating. Francesca looked up, her face blank with surprise. The man looked at Rosario, saw his swaying stance, his lowered face. Without panic the German reached for the short, black-handled knife which was plunged into a loaf on the table. He did not take his eyes from Rosario's face as he rose, and, with a shove of his foot, sent the chair scraping back from beneath him.

Francesca screamed.

With the back of his free hand Rosario wiped the sweat and the shame out of his eyes. He jeered, 'Ciao, tedesco!' and advanced into the room.

§§§§

Across the road, Craddock heard Francesca's scream. A few moments later there was another scream, even more high-pitched. It echoed somewhere in the back of his consciousness, and he recognized it, as apathetically as if it were a note of music, as a man's death-scream. But Graziella was holding him, and he was lost in a fiery haze.

Graziella lay beside him, supine and slack like a gorged animal, staring up at the ceiling with unseeing, triumphant eyes. Her hand was moist and soft in his. Her breast rose and fell, slow and powerful as the sea. A distant clamour came to him from the street, shouts, screams, running footsteps, sounds without meaning that were lost in the shadowed room. He felt drugged.

He rose. His legs were unsteady for a moment; then the strength returned to them. He wandered aimlessly up and down as he tidied his clothes, frowning and silent.

Graziella did not move; the heaving of her breast quickened and her eyes followed him as he walked to and fro. He went slowly to the door. The set of her face did not change, but the points of light shifted and flickered in her eyes, and a dozen different women looked out in succession from their depths.

He said, 'Goodbye, Graziella.'

She turned her head slightly. Her dark eyes were flecked with a yellow fire of contempt. She stared at him as if she were pronouncing a silent curse upon all men. He went out.

In the street, he felt stunned. He was not aware of the pavement beneath his feet. The clamour around him still did not reach him, and the growing crowd on the opposite pavement had no significance. Only dimly aware of his mission he walked across the road. He pushed through the crowd, reached the two soldiers who barred Francesca's doorway with their rifles, looked over their shoulders, and discovered that he was too late.

Chapter Twenty-One

WHEN the soldiers awoke the next morning and opened the outward windows of their billet to enjoy the cool, fresh air, there was something about the view across the sea that mystified them. More men came to the windows; then they realized; the harbour was empty of landing-craft.

They went downstairs for breakfast, where two pieces of news awaited them; the first, that at four-thirty a.m. British troops had landed on the coast of Southern Italy; the second, that their own battalion was under twenty-four hours' notice to move and was confined to billets.

The great machine was rolling again. Aircraft roared overhead, ships crawled northward against the skyline, columns of lorries rumbled through the town. The machine was rolling. When would they be fed into it?

Nobody knew where they were going. Even Captain Rumbold was puzzled, for they were not travelling northward, in the stream of the invasion, but south, by rail, to Syracuse, where they were to go aboard ship. Where to? He shrugged his shoulders and told his questioners to get on with their duties. Some said that they would go to Italy, to reinforce the invasion. Some pointed out that they had been practising beach landings for weeks, and that they might very well be headed for some fresh assault at a new point on the Italian coast. Some spoke, with dread, of the possibility that they might be bound for the jungles of the Far East, and recalled recent rumours of mysterious bales of equipment locked up at battalion headquarters. Some optimists ventured the old, evergreen guess – they were going home. Men can cope mentally with the grimmest of prospects if they know, at least, what awaits them. Soldiers, in their journeyings, are denied this consolation. To the men in the billet that day, all ahead was dark. They busied themselves with their preparations and the building echoed with their merriment.

§§§§

Craddock received permission from the captain to visit Rosario, who was in hospital with a shallow knife wound across the stomach.

He walked past the closed door of Graziella's house, feeling numbed and indifferent. He did not want to see her. He would have been embarrassed if she had appeared suddenly to confront him. They had nothing more to say to each other.

He reached the hospital and found Rosario. After they had exchanged greetings, Rosario said, 'Have you come to have a look at the fool?'

'Are you not glad that you killed him?'

'Yes, I am pleased. It is a paradox. I am pleased because I showed myself a man. But it is the thought of a child, to content oneself thus. When we do the greatest and the most terrible things in life, we are children.'

'But it was a good thing to do. He was a German.'

'German, Italian, Englishman, what is the difference? If you seize a man by the shoulder and say, "Look, there is the enemy," he will go, no matter at whom you point. "The enemy", that is what he always needs. Perhaps he is seeking someone on whom to inflict his own misery.'

'That does not make sense to me.'

'It does not make sense when a drum beats. But what do you feel inside when you hear it?'

'That is not why we hate the Germans. We know why we fight them. Do you not feel angry when you think of what they did to poor little Aldo?'

'They alone did not do it!'

'It was their bomb. It was their minds that planned it, and we do not want such minds to rule the world. What they did to Aldo they would do to the world. What future has the child, without hands, because of them?'

'As good a future as any of his countrymen. He will make a good beggar.'

'Many of your countrymen do not think like you. In the North, there are already Italians fighting the Germans. I have heard it on the radio. There are entire brigades of Italian partisans, and heavy battles are being fought between them and the Germans. Are they not right to fight?'

'Ask them. They know. I do not know.'

Craddock insisted, 'Will you not fight again?'

Rosario opened his mouth to answer, pondered, and

grinned a little. 'I do not know... Perhaps... It was futile for me to run away from the war. Each of us is at war all the time. In the big war, all the little wars are fought. Is that why you came to see me, to ask me all this?'

'No, idiot. I came with these things.' Craddock gave him cigarettes and chocolates. 'Is there anything else you want?'

'Yes.' Rosario turned his face away. 'Graziella.'

Craddock rose to his feet.

'You see,' said Rosario hoarsely, 'I am not proud, eh?'

'I'm going now. Get better quickly.'

'Why?'

Craddock said, 'You ask too many questions. And because you cannot find the answers, you decide that nothing is of any use. I know a lot of people like you. They hide from life behind words. It will do you good to fight.' He held out his hand. 'Well, so long!'

Rosario took his hand and said, 'Goodbye!'

§§§§

Harry Jobling rose to his feet and stood respectfully to attention when Captain Rumbold entered his cell.

'All right,' said the captain, 'sit down. How's your head?'

'It doesn't bother me, sir. They took the stitches out yesterday.'

The captain passed him a cigarette. 'It's all right, you can smoke while I'm here. They treating you all right here?'

Jobling grinned ruefully. 'I'm not grumbling.'

The captain lit his own cigarette. 'Well, you did a silly thing there, lad.'

'I know.'

'Feeling better?'

Jobling grimaced. 'No use cryin' over spilt milk.' He reflected. 'I don't know what come over me.'

The captain said, 'Well, it's over and done with. Did you know the battalion was shoving off?'

'Yes, the sentry told me.' He said, timidly, 'I suppose there's no chance of my coming with, I mean, under escort or something?'

'Not a chance. You're booked for a court-martial.'

'I mean, couldn't the colonel fix it up? You know.'

The captain shook his head.

'I'm not whinin',' Jobling said. 'I'm not worried about what's coming to me. It's the thought of staying here when the battalion's moving. The battalion, well, I mean, it's like your home, isn't it?'

'We've been doing what we can,' said the captain, 'that's what I came to tell you. I thought you'd like to know. I've left behind a long statement of evidence that I collected from the chaps at the billet. Between you and me and the old doorknob, it's quite a work of art. Anyway, it ought to do you a bit of good. And the colonel's put in a deposition about your character that makes you sound like Saint John the Baptist. You won't recognize yourself when you hear it.'

Jobling said, 'Thanks. What d'you reckon I'll get?'

'No idea,' said the captain. 'It depends on who they appoint to conduct the court-martial. That's something no one'll know till after we're gone. Anyway, we've asked for you to get a quick trial. If you box clever and keep your mouth shut, and put yourself across as a good boy, you ought to be able to count on a suspended sentence.'

'That means I'll come back to the battalion.'

'Yes, straight from the courtroom. Then, as long as you kept your nose clean, you wouldn't hear any more about it.

But the moment you stepped out of line, even for the most trivial offence, back you'd go to clink, to serve out your term.'

'You wouldn't have to worry about that, sir.'

'Well,' said the captain, 'that's the way it is. Don't count your chickens. You never know what might happen. But with a bit of luck, that's how it'll work out.' He grinned. 'So I hope to be seeing you soon. In the meantime, keep your chin up.'

'Thank you, sir. And...'

'Well?'

'Good luck to you and the lads, sir.'

'Uh! Uh!' said the captain. 'Don't you know it's bad luck to say that? Cheerio!'

§§§§

Nella had spent her two thousand lire. For a week she had carried the money about with her, until the notes were soggy and crushed. Whenever she saw her mother, haggard and bent, creeping about in rags in the dirt and gloom of their home, she wanted to give it to her, but she was afraid. For days she gazed into shop windows, where already the profiteers were displaying handbags, dresses, shoes and underclothes for sale at inflated prices. She was tantalized but scared. At last she plucked up the courage to spend all her money on something of which she had dreamed for years – a pair of high-heeled shoes. She came wobbling out of the shop tremulous with joy and fear; joy because she would share with Paloma the admiration and envy of all the other women; fear because she still had to face her mother. However, she consoled herself, her mother, who never ventured more than a few hundred yards from their own street door, would never know how much the shoes had cost, and any silly story would satisfy her.

It gave Nella an unsteady, exalted feeling to walk in these shoes. She had to be careful of her balance, and the backs of her calves were strained. It seemed to her that the shoes had made her twice as tall. She was filled with an unreal, up-in-the-air sensation. She was still lonely, but after a week the dumb shock had worn off. No deadlier, comprehending grief had taken its place, but a perverse pride in her adventure. Imagination had falsified her memory, suppressing the things that she did not want to recall and weaving over them a concealing garment of fantasy. She walked in pride at the secret knowledge of her womanhood, looking down at the swarming children who seemed as remote from her as her own childhood, and dreaming in the sunshine.

A little fearful because she would have to account for the shoes, but bursting with gossip and self-importance, she called on her cousin. Graziella lay like a dead woman on her bed; Nella tried to arouse her, at first with chatter, then with apprehensive questioning, but Graziella, her face as still as a mask, only looked at her indifferently. Nella came away, frightened.

Wandering disconsolately on the waterfront, she met Ciccio. She tried to assume a scornful, grown-up air, but he looked at her like a knowing old man and said, 'Where did you get those shoes?'

They had confided in each other for years. It was from Ciccio that she had learned, even in childhood, about all the dark jungle of life that crowded in on their sunny playgrounds. It was to him that she went with her questions about the ways of men; he kept her informed of all the scandals of the town. They perched on the parapet above the rocks, and she poured out her story. She spoke rapidly, wondering at the feeling of relief that grew within her and warmed to real pleasure, as she unburdened herself. She became excited; her eyes sparkled as if she were describing a film that had charmed her. She heard her own voice telling of a passionate wooing, of her lover's tenderness and adoration, of his eagerness to obey her caprices, of a sorrowful parting. She had told him to be brave, she said, but he was inconsolable; and as she spoke, tears gleamed in her eyes, for she believed herself; this had become the real memory.

She was flushed and happy when she finished, her eyes glowing reminiscently. Ciccio was watching her with a sceptical grin. He said, 'And how much did he give you?'

She would have exaggerated, boasted of her lover's fantastic generosity, but she had already admitted that all the money had gone on the shoes, and Ciccio would know to a lira what they cost. She answered, 'Two thousand.'

Ciccio made a derisive noise. 'Only two thousand. How many times did he have for that?'

'It was not a payment,' she said sullenly, 'it was a gift. He wanted to give me more, to buy me clothes, but I would not let him.'

Ciccio scowled at the cigarette which he held between his fingers. 'Very romantic! Do you think I was born yesterday? You are a fool, you have thrown money away.'

'I did not do it for money,' she insisted. 'And the girls who do it for money only get fifty lire.'

'You know a lot about business!' he jeered. 'A woman is glad to get fifty lire, but for a fresh girl of your age there are men who will pay much more.'

She did not answer.

'You could make a lot of money,' he said.

She looked at him in fascination and alarm.

'What is the use of fine shoes when you run about in that dirty dress. It is a child's dress. It hardly covers your knees. And what do you wear beneath it but a dirty pair of drawers? You could have silk underclothes.'

Terror and indecision seized her. She bit her lip, staring at him.

'I know an officer who would give three hundred, for each time, for you.'

She whispered, 'For each time?' For so brief and pleasant a duty. For sinning – oh, for doing what all women had to do, look at them all! Her brain whirled.

'Three hundred. Naturally, you would have to give me something.'

'Oh,' she murmured, hardly aware that she was speaking, 'I would buy you whatever you liked.'

'Fool, I am not a child. I do not want presents. I want my share of the money. Would you give me a hundred each time?'

She nodded dazedly.

'Well, what do you say?'

She was afraid to answer. Cold little fingers of panic moved about inside her. Then a dazzling revelation came to her and drove the scared feeling away. She need never be what she had dreaded to become, one man's beast of burden, taken in her youth from the sunshine and stabled for life in a dark hovel. She could be free, independent, like those Englishwomen in the newspaper, like those Americans in the films. She could have dresses and shoes and money of her own. Her mamma, her poor mamma with the lines of misery deep in her face, could always have bread and wine on her table, could go to church with a purse so well filled that her offerings would make the other women murmur with envy and the priest clasp his hands in admiration. Nella said, in a childlike ecstasy, 'Take me to this officer.'

Chapter Twenty-Two

SIX a.m... Craddock opened his eyes and stirred in his blanket. He saw the open window, the sunlight on the wall; he arched his body in joyful recognition of the familiar and pleasant surroundings, of a new day. The air tasted as sharp and sweet as an iced drink in his mouth. He relaxed, unwilling to emerge from sleep, and let the sounds of awakening life come to him from across the rooftops – a dog barking, cocks crowing, the shouting of workmen, and the wordless, wavering wail of a woman's song. Each morning he enjoyed these first seconds of languor, when the radiant world welcomed him back from the caverns of darkness, showing off to him all its beauty and tranquillity.

His mind awoke, and he remembered: *this is the last time*. The buoyant pleasure went out of him. He felt sick and cold. He closed his eyes and fought to expel for a few moments the leaden misery, to sink back into the blanket's warm oblivion. It was no use; his brain was already working as remorselessly as a quick-ticking watch. He cast off the blanket and pulled on his boots.

He woke Honeycombe, went down the corridor banging at doors, packed his gear with feverish vigour; memory was amok inside him and he was trying to stun it with activity. He rolled his blanket, pulled it round his pack and fastened the straps over it, tightening them with savage energy. His equipment was piled in a corner now, ready for the march, Honeycombe's in another. Otherwise the room was empty; all trace of human habitation and repose had vanished. His soul was empty, too. Other men were on their feet. The rooms rang with the stamping of feet, the thump of falling packs, the clatter of weapons, and impatient voices. The building which, while they had lived in it, had muffled their everyday noises with its walls, protested against their departure with a frenzy of echoes. The hunt music of the peaceful world around them, drowned by their clamour, no longer beguiled them.

Craddock stood on the landing and shouted, 'Rise and shine! Downstairs, my lucky lads!' His men streamed past him, grinning at him. The rush was like the noise and movement of a war dance, quickening the blood to new impulses of vigour and enthusiasm. He followed them out into the street. For a moment the cold numbness returned: *this is the last time.* Pride returned at the sight of the company forming up, the shuffling ranks closing into a neat, solid block of khaki that filled the whole length of the street; the straight lines of helmets swathed in dun sacking, the straight lines of rifles, the straight lines of packs, the straight lines of red faces.

It was a single organism into which all individualities and all worries vanished, self-sufficient and aloof from the untidy throng of civilians who surged around it as a tall ship is from the sea through which it cleaves. He took his post in front of his platoon.

§§§§

Seven a.m. ... The sun had risen. The air, saturated with heat, became still, and shimmered with the brilliance of full morning. The men squatted in rows upon their packs, eating from their mess tins a last meal of stew which the cooks had prepared in a boiler pitched on the pavement. The captain had ordered the billet to be emptied so that the last fatigue party, which was busy now, could leave it spotless, a final reminder to its returning tenants of the ways of the British.

The civilians were all awake. Everyone was out in the street to see the soldiers go. Families crowded in their doorways, chattering with the subdued and expectant gaiety that is seen before the start of a horse-race. People hovered on the fringes of the parade and took heart, one by one, to penetrate the ranks, until the street was a disorder of khaki and black. Couples drew apart, each pair – burdened soldier and full-skirted woman – standing close together with bowed heads. Here and there could be seen a whole household crowding round a soldier, embracing him and talking volubly to him as if it were their own son who was being taken from them. Other soldiers squatted with children perched on their knees or huddled in the crook of their arms, feeding them from their mess tins.

Captain Rumbold watched the children gathering like a horde of ravenous sparrows. 'Damn fools,' he said to Perkington, 'giving their food away. God knows when they'll get their next meal. We'll have to stop this.'

Perkington said, 'Just you try!'

Rumbold deliberated. 'We can't upset 'em now,' he said. 'There's only one thing to do.' He turned to the sergeant-major. 'How are we fixed for grub?'

'There's a whole crateful of tins still unopened, sir.'

'Tell the cook to tip it all in. Sergeant Craddock!'

'Sir?'

'You speak the bloody language. Tell the Eyeties to get plates and line up on the pavement. God damn it,' he said desperately. 'let's have a party! Come one, come all, and bugger the income-tax! Aren't we the bloody onions?'

Craddock spoke to the people near him. They screamed the tidings to their neighbours. There was a wild rush to the houses, and in a moment an unruly queue was jostling on the pavement. People came running with plates, jugs, saucepans, washbowls, jam tins, ornamental vases, kettles, cauldrons – anything that would enable them to carry away as big a share as possible. One small boy peered happily over the rim of a chamberpot. The cooks stirred and ladled and sweated over the steaming boiler, while the people came and went with their overbrimming portions, squatting on the pavements to join in the feast, shouting to each other in extravagant gratitude and bringing the soldiers sweetmeats, bowls of pasta and bottles of wine to make a real holiday of the occasion.

Paloma, who was standing with her arms round the shoulders of two sturdy soldiers, whispered excitedly with her companions. Without warning she rushed upon Captain Rumbold, threw her arms round him and kissed him heartily. She drew back, laughing, to view his embarrassment, but the captain seized her in a murderous hug, planted his mouth on hers and crushed her to him, lifting her strapping body from the ground as easily as if she were a child. She thrashed at the air with her legs, making choking sounds of laughter and protest in her throat, and when at last he let her down she clung to him, limp and breathless. The captain turned her round and dismissed her, amid the cheers of the company, with a slap across the buttocks. She scurried back to her admirers in the ranks, screaming, 'What a man! If only I had known him earlier!' The wine flowed. People were laughing and talking everywhere. For an hour there was festa in the street.

§§§§

Eight a.m. ... The animation had died away. The women were quiet and nervous, the children fretted, the soldiers were oppressed by the growing heat and by the lethargy of waiting. Tiger, looking punier than ever, was panting already under the weight of his full kit. Fooks sat, tipsy and almost asleep, with his head in Paloma's lap. Ling peered from beneath his helmet like a tortoise from beneath its shell, with the expression of a little boy who is waiting to be caned. His gear hung about him in disarray, and he held his rifle from him like something alien and unwanted. He was a comical sight among all these soldiers. His woman towered over him moaning with grief and plucking at her bosom, while the five children stared at his unaccustomed appearance with their little faces upturned in solemn silence. Craddock stood looking at the closed door of Graziella's house. He tried to ignore the sense of loneliness that touched his heart among all these leave-takings. He felt stifled and depressed, becalmed between two states of feeling. Close behind him were all the human emotions which he feared

255

to contemplate; ahead, near enough to beckon but still out of reach, were the pleasure and relief of action. Fearing the one and unable to attain the other, he felt merely wretched, stirred only from time to time by a wave of irrational resentment at the obstinate stare of the closed door, or by a prickle of impatience as the ordeal of waiting dragged on. He said to Honeycombe, 'I wish to God we could get out of here.'

Old Buonocorso was shuffling among the ranks, collecting cigarettes in his hat and bestowing in return a torrent of servile thanks and farewells. Craddock watched him dully. He had hoped that Aldo's mutilation would shock the old man back into life; he had wanted to appeal to him to take up once more his responsibilities and give these stunned, bewildered people the leadership they needed; but he felt no desire to speak to him now. He only said, dropping a packet of cigarettes into the old man's hat, 'Goodbye, old man. And look after Aldo, for he cannot look after you any more.'

Buonocorso said, 'Someone will look after us. I thank you for bringing him the dog. It has given him hope.'

'I am glad that one of you has hope,' said Craddock harshly. 'There is enough need of it here.'

The old man bobbed a gesture of resignation. 'It was a beautiful thought, to give him the dog. Goodbye, and a good journey.'

Craddock looked away, across the street, at the closed door.

Nella was standing before him, pathetic in her war-paint and her high-heeled shoes. Craddock took both her hands and drew her gently towards him. He said, 'You have come to say goodbye?'

She looked up at him with big, piteous eyes, and nodded. She whispered, 'Graziella is weeping in the house.' She withdrew her hands from Craddock's and reached into the bosom of her dress. 'I wanted her to come,' she said. 'Are you angry with her?'

Craddock smiled and shook his head.

She opened her hand. A silver chain lay heaped on a crucifix in the palm. 'Will you wear this?'

Craddock nodded, and sank down on to his heels, putting his hands about her waist. 'For you?'

'For her.' Nella hung the chain round his neck. 'She says, you are not with God, but God will be with you.'

Craddock sighed, and kissed her on the cheek. She began to tremble under his hands. He straightened up and said, 'Go back to her now.'

She hurried away, crying. As she went, Tiger stepped forward and laid his hand on her arm, but she scampered on as if she had not felt his touch. The door closed behind her.

§§§§

Nine a.m.... The ranks had been cleared. The soldiers stood stolidly over their rifles, wiping the sweat from their faces and looking with silent indifference at the crowd which fidgeted in a subdued panic on the opposite pavement. The roadway was wide and empty between them.

Into the dull timelessness of waiting there intruded a new sound; the disorderly surge of distant marching. The noise grew, and the men grinned uneasily at each other. The battalion was on the move. This was 'A' Company, coming along the waterfront on its way to the station. Their own turn would follow. 'A' Company came tramping past the head of the street, and the noise of its passing, caught up in a roaring echo between the walls of the street, stirred them.

The sound died away. 'A' Company must be filing into the station now. Time dragged once more. The men's eagerness began to subside; they were oppressed by their own impatience and by the scorching heat. A hush lay on the street, broken only by snatches of whimpering and an occasional flight of hysterical laughter from among the women.

'Company...!'

The torpor lifted from the soldiers as the words of command came to them. They slung their rifles and turned to the right. There was no time to think. Craddock felt a last, quick wrench of pain, then the ranks ahead began to move, and he moved with them, uplifted by a great flood of relief. As the men moved off, there was a moment's hesitation on the pavement, before the people started off alongside the column, in full cry. Craddock was suddenly glad that his last memory of Graziella would not be as one of this crowd of frantic women running clumsily along the street.

There was a comfort in marching. The thunderous tramp, the rhythm of his own legs, the weight of his equipment, the sight of the pack bobbing in front of him, were all part of an old, instinctive routine which carried him along without the necessity of thought. Some of the men around him were gloomy, some were grinning and calling to their followers on the pavement, some had already relapsed into the slack-mouthed apathy of the marching soldier.

The buildings and the dusty trees moved past as in a dream. The babbling crowd on the pavement was in another world. Familiar sights had become strange again; and the soldiers, inhabitants yesterday, had become passing strangers.

Orders were shouted. The men in front could be seen coming to a stop and unslinging their rifles, and the rest of the column piled up in a disorderly halt. The khaki ranks dissolved into a mass of men squatting in the station yard. The officers hurried away; time passed – ten, fifteen, twenty minutes. The men showed no signs of restlessness, but made themselves comfortable, enduring this new delay with the patience of animals. Some of the women drew near once more, but few of the men responded. They were losing the ability to recognize anything outside themselves.

They climbed to their feet again and began to file, by platoons, into the station. The dilapidated waiting rooms mocked them with echoes as they hurried through. Here and there a man hesitated, cluttering up the narrow entrance with his equipment as he looked back for a moment, panic stricken. Then he would hasten on, leaning forward beneath the weight of his gear, to emerge again into the pitiless sunlight of the platform. A tall, white wall cut them off for ever from the world which they could still hear beyond. The platform was military, with the colonel and a group of Movement Control Officers standing against the wall swishing their sticks. The shouts that echoed from one end of the platform to the other were military, as inhuman as rifle shots.

'What platoon, sergeant?'

'Eight Platoon, sir!'

More shouting, 'Up the front, Eight Platoon, come on, come on,' Craddock ran, and heard the platoon clattering behind him. There was relief in running and in feeling his pack jerking up and down against his shoulders. He opened a carriage door and bundled the men in. 'Come on, come on, get in and don't talk so much. Move up, there. Move up on that right-hand seat, there's room for more. Two more. Come on!' He slammed the door. There was relief in hearing the door slam. He opened the next door. 'Come on, look sharp!' He slammed the door. A third carriage. 'Come on, come on, wake your ideas up, Ling!' He climbed into the compartment, slammed the door from the inside and said heavily to Honeycombe, 'Well that's that!' He could still feel the slam of the door inside him. The crucifix burned like an icicle in the groove of his chest. He shouted out of the window, 'Eight Platoon all in, sir!' Mr Perkington scurried away, with a terrified schoolboy eagerness, to report.

He sat down, and did not look out of the window any more. He wanted to unburden himself by shouting Graziella's name. There was a dusty, cindery smell in the carriage but his nostrils were cloyed with a strange, remembered scent. Honeycombe was sitting opposite, looking at him. Honeycombe asked, 'All right?'

He answered, 'All right.'

The fragrance was tormenting his imagination, stirring unwelcome emotions that did not explain themselves to him but which inflicted pain.

Men were crowding at the windows, looking out as if they had just arrived. The station buildings were a barrier that they could never cross. In a moment the mysterious gap of the years would begin to open out.

The train jerked. Men were flung together, and steadied themselves. A flash of remembrance came to Craddock. He knew now what the scent was. He saw again, more clearly than the carriage in which he sat, more sharply indeed than the scene had appeared in reality, his first glimpse of Sicily. It was two months – two lifetimes – ago. Their landing-craft was idling through the shoreward swell. The sun rose, and the heat and the motion of the craft made the men seasick. The sergeant stood up in impatience. He saw the sea heaving silently about them, a shimmering silk of indigo and silver. He saw ahead, swinging slowly towards them, the continent to which their army was returning: a strip of shore, clusters of white houses, low wooded slopes, and behind, line after line of hills dark against the dawn pallor. Out of the stillness there came a single breath of breeze, and on the breeze was borne this haunting fragrance, the pungency of oranges, the bitterness of almonds, and the minty odour of wild herbs. The breeze died and the smells of oil, vomit and hot metal arose again.

The train began to move. He asked Honeycombe for a cigarette. The clatter of wheels quickened and the platform buildings slid past. A swarm of children had climbed up on to the embankment to shrill a last farewell, and the men shouted back from the windows. Some were already settled in their seats, unwrapping their haversack rations. The sergeant leaned across to Honeycombe for a light to his cigarette. His face was between Honeycombe's cupped hands, and he did not raise his head to look out of the window.

There was a last shower of chocolates and caramels from the windows and a last clamorous response from the children. The train gathered speed and passed round the bend. Now there was only the blank end of the rear truck. Now it was gone.

The last tremor died from the rails. The sun's glare, pitiless, blanched the blue sky, glittered on the deep blue sea, reflected, dazzling, from the walls of the tumbled white houses and drew an oven heat from the bleached pavements. The last tremor died from the rails. Now there was no sound in the blinding white sunlight; no sound but the weeping of women.

Afterword

John L. Williams

ALEXANDER BARON was, arguably, the great British novelist of the Second World War, and for a while he was also the most popular. The three books in which he covered the conflict – *There's No Home*; *From The City, From The Plough*; and *The Human Kind* – received glowing reviews and sold in vast numbers on their first appearance on the bookstands and in book club editions.

That these titles have receded from view, rather than becoming established classics – on a par with, say, the wartime books of Evelyn Waugh, Graham Greene or Olivia Manning – seems as mysterious as it is unjust. Perhaps it is due to Baron's concern with the infantryman's point of view, rather than the officer class. Or perhaps it is that Baron's style is so effortlessly simple and unsensational that it is easy to overlook the virtuosity of the writing. Or maybe it was the author – a very private man, who shied away from any attempt to propel him towards literary celebrity. But whatever the reason for the novels' decades of neglect, it has one great benefit: we are now able to rediscover them without any preconceptions at all.

Baron was certainly well placed to write about the war. He
fought in two of its bloodiest campaigns, the invasion of Sicily
in 1943, as a member of Montgomery's Eighth Army, and the
D-Day landings of 1944. He was there when the bullets were
flying and the landmines exploding. He suffered both physically
and, afterwards, mentally. He started writing about the war as
a form of therapy, to make sense of the horror in which he
and so many others had been immersed. He wanted, above all,
to make sure that no one forgot that this was a war that had
been fought and won by the common man.

The first of Baron's war novels, *From The City, From The
Plough,* appeared in 1948 and was an immediate hit: the
leading literary critic of the time, VS Pritchett, called it 'the
only war book that has conveyed any sense of reality to me'.
It reminded the reader that the most dramatic events of
the war were fought not by a warrior elite but by ordinary
working-class men, most of whom would have been happier
at the dog track or on the farm than on the battlefield.
Instead, these reluctant soldiers were plunged into a conflict
that was all too likely to kill them, but one that they faced
with the traditional weapons of the British working class: black
humour and strong tea.

There's No Home, the follow-up, was published in 1950 and
it's a wonderful example of a writer sidestepping the reader's
expectations. This is a war novel all right, but it's one that
contains no scenes of armed combat. This despite the fact that
it's set in Sicily, where Baron had been in the thick of bloody
battle, clearing mines off the beaches while under constant fire
from the Germans. But, rather than reprise the action scenes
of *From The City, From The Plough*, Baron decided to write about
one of the war's lulls, the events that immediately followed the
capture of Sicily, when his regiment spent a couple of months

garrisoned in the town of Catania, waiting to be sent into battle on the Italian mainland.

Remarkably, for what was ostensibly a war novel, Baron chose to make his focus the fortunes of women during the conflict. More remarkably still, for a book written by a British infantryman who never moved past the rank of corporal, this decision had its roots in his reading of Friedrich Engels, whom he had read while doing his military training in 1940.

But then, Alexander Baron was no ordinary infantryman. By the time he joined up in 1940, he was 22 years old and had spent all his adult life to date in the service of the Communist Party. Born Joseph Alexander Bernstein, he grew up in a secular Jewish family in East London, becoming a teenager just as Mosley's Blackshirts were starting to mobilise in the area. Like many others of his generation, he was politically radicalised by this experience and joined forces with the most vocal opponents of fascism in the East End, the Communist Party. Although he was never a card-carrying Party member, he publicly positioned himself on the left wing of the Labour Party.

Obviously bright and able, Baron was soon singled out for advancement by the Party. He was dissuaded from going to Spain to fight in the Civil War on the grounds that he was too valuable to risk. By 1939, he was the editor of the Party's youth magazine, Challenge. That was the year that war broke out; it was also the year of the Hitler-Stalin pact, which meant that Baron was obliged to go from passionately advocating war against the fascist menace to passionately advocating that Britain stay out of the war.

The situation was a shameful nonsense that gradually began to undermine the young firebrand's political commitment. In 1940, he received his call-up to the army and found himself thrilled at the prospect (he had, in fact, already attempted to join

the RAF but had been instantly rejected when the recruiter saw
his glasses). At first, he attempted to rationalise his excitement
by persuading himself that he was training for the Communist
revolution that was to come; and as it turned out, in 1941, with
the German invasion of Russia, he was indeed able to fight in
good conscience as both an Englishman and a Communist.

Baron's reading matter, as he went through his army training
as a member of the Pioneer Corps, included Engels' *The Origin
Of The Family*. In his (as yet unpublished) memoir, *Chapters Of
Accidents*, he comments:

> I was struck by what this book had to say about the position
> of women in society. I had formed a generally high opinion of
> the men around me; perhaps the soldiers and the civilians I met
> in different countries during the war were more congenial to
> me than the 'people of a new type' among whom I had felt so
> isolated during my last year with the party. But my juvenile and
> puritan soul was grieved at the to-me insulting way in which they
> spoke about women. I bought a school exercise book and wrote
> by hand a pamphlet on the Woman Question. I started by asking
> if it was right to refer to a woman as a piece of cunt. Men who
> had read it accosted me to talk about it. Some came into my
> room to have an argument; all these discussions were serious.

For the first year of Baron's military training he and his fellow
members of the Pioneer Corps were preparing for a German
invasion. For Baron this period was an opportunity to learn
about life as it was lived outside the magic circle of committed
Communists that had been his world since childhood:

> I had come into the army as ignorant of human nature and full
> of illusions as a schoolboy, having been preserved as one by my

years in the party machine. Since then both my ignorance and my attachment to the party had diminished, but only slowly, for I clung to them, being reluctant to acknowledge that people lived largely for the satisfaction of simple brute instincts. I was still repeatedly taken aback by what I saw of sexual behaviour which was like that of dogs trotting about in the street. I remember one occasion when we picked up an Air Force girl while we were travelling in the back of a covered truck. She was fair and pretty. I took her to be the kind of girl toward whom one ought to be protective. Soon she was lying on the floor with her legs up, giggling and gasping pleasurably. Among the men who went to her were some I had thought to be faithful husbands. She dropped from the tailboard outside an Air Force camp and walked off, as bright as ever, while the men waved and called cheerful goodbyes after her.

I thought, how do they know? Why are they so sure of each other? How can all these transactions take place so instantly and confidently without a word being spoken? I decided that I lacked some kind of psychic antennae that other people possessed.

We can see right there the seeds of what made Baron the writer he became – a determination to understand how people act: not how they say they act, or would like to act, but how they actually act when under pressure. And, of course, there could be no time of greater pressure than those war years. Also, as we will see, the matter of 'the Woman Question' stayed with Baron. It was clear to him from the start that the war was impacting not only on the men charged with fighting it, but also on the women around whose lives it swirled.

During this training period Baron applied to become an officer but was turned down on political grounds. He became increasingly frustrated, feeling he was marking time while the action went on all around him but, with the Allied victories at Stalingrad and El Alamein, things began to look up. In the summer of 1943 Baron's battalion finally got the call to travel overseas and in July landed in Sicily as part of Montgomery's Eighth Army. Operating as sappers, they cleared the beaches and battlefields of mines while under constant enemy fire, and fought on until the Germans were ousted from the island.

With the Axis withdrawal on August 17, Baron and his comrades moved into the town of Catania, where they remained for two long, hot, summer months. At first they were simply resting after the rigours of battle, but soon they started to explore the town in which they were billeted, and before long to strike up relationships with the locals. During this period Baron wrote regular letters home to his mother and father which offer a remarkable insight into the actual experiences that would eventually provide the basis for *There's No Home*.

It's a measure of the man that his first letters, written in July while still in the midst of warfare, ask his mother to send a copy of Hugo's *Italian in Three Months* and an Italian English dictionary. When the fighting finished in late August the first request in his letter home is for copies of the New Statesman. And then, after a brief discussion of the weather – talk of military matters was expressly forbidden in letters home, lest they fall into enemy hands – he describes about his recent reading:

> I'm just reading Jane Austen's *Northanger Abbey*. The book is a real refuge from the sweat and slog of this life, with its calm unruffled style, its early nineteenth-century heroines and its storm in a teacup adventures. As a matter of fact I am always staggered when I think of Jane Austen. Here was a parson's

daughter, born in the country a century ago, educated at home, never seeing the outside world — yet she saw right through the social stupidities that she lived amongst, and the snobbery and shallowness of the minor rural gentry.

It's an arresting notion, that of the young soldier, swept up amid the blood and dust of war, not just escaping into the lost world of Austen's England but also seeing beyond that into Austen's ability to find the universal in the most particular of milieus.

Six weeks later, Baron's October 15 letter to his father shows how quickly life has moved on in Catania:

I have been 'adopted'. I have been going of late to the house of a docker and his wife — very fine and simple people, with whom I've become very friendly indeed. He is a broad-shouldered handsome fellow, who talks very intelligently (+ often very poetically). His wife, who must have been beautiful when she was younger, is still pleasant and cheerful of countenance though worn (as all these women are) by a lifetime of work and grief.

They are desperately poor and I try to eat in there as rarely as possible, Sometimes, however I have to, to avoid offending them. I stayed for supper the other night, for instance. They put out a spotless white tablecloth and beautifully pressed and embroidered napkins. We had fried fish, olives and bread, cheese, wine and grapes. It doesn't sound much, I know, but to a family where the husband's pay is 2/6 a week, it's a feast.

I was invited out last night too. Laurie (my friend) and I spent the evening with the family of two very pleasant and attractive Italian girls we know (It's all right, there's no danger of me coming home with a wife and family!). We learned to play cards in the Italian fashion…

Here, as you will find out, are the seeds of *There's No Home*, and the central relationship between Sergeant Craddock – a heartier, more confident version of Baron – and Graziella, a 'very pleasant and attractive' Italian girl (among Baron's wartime papers there's a teasing photograph of an Italian girl, perhaps the model for Graziella). Apply the clear eye that Baron so admires in Jane Austen and the result is a book about the horror of war which takes place almost entirely on one small street in a Sicilian town, a long way from the front line. In this novel, unlike the Russian epic, war and peace are not two separate narrative strands but have become indivisible. *There's No Home* also offered Baron the perfect opportunity to introduce his concern with 'the Woman Question'.

It has long been a cliché to suggest that war is a man's game, that if women ruled the world there'd be no more conflict. On one level this is patently absurd: warrior women from Boudicca to Condoleezza Rice have not shied away from armed conflict. What is true, and what Baron dramatises brilliantly here, is that for the most part women and men experience war in very different ways.

At one point Sergeant Craddock receives a letter from his wife, full of desperately cheery news from home But home now seems almost unimaginable to Craddock after what he and his comrades have been through. The only reality is that of the moment, this strange eye-of-the-storm period of quasi-domesticity among the Sicilians. And so the letter serves only as a reproach:

> At the sight of the envelopes he had felt a stab of resentment;
> it was a fresh blow from the outside world, at the sealed,
> timeless life he was leading. But the letters touched at his heart
> and aroused a sense of guilt. He tried to remember home.

After all, he told himself, it ought not to be so hard. It was only – how long was it? – Good Lord, it was only four months since they had sailed. It had been easy to remember home on the warm decks on the troopship. Home in those days had been something of which to talk and sing sentimentally. It had been easy to remember home in the first days ashore, on the white, wandering roads, passing through the deserted ruins of towns, lying among the olive trees in the green hills. Every letter had brought a beautiful pang. Where had it all died? On the plains, yes, on the parched white plains where so many men had died. The heat had killed it; the stink had killed it; the noise had killed it; the endlessness of the whole thing, the twitching, fear-burdened, obsessed endlessness, the days when men were afraid to move from their oven holes and the nights when the sky had been lit with great jagged flashes and flares had winked like traffic lights in the darkness. Home – he tried, clenching his fists, to remember.

The men in *There's No Home*, the British soldiers, aren't macho blowhards in love with fighting; they want nothing more than for it all to be over. But they are nonetheless propelled forwards; they know there's a war waiting for them and that they will, sooner or later, be in the midst of it, participating rather than hanging around on the sidelines. They feel the imperative of narrative, the need to move forwards.

The women, on the other hand, want life to stand still. They have all lost men to the war: husbands and lovers, fathers, brothers and sons. Their domestic lives have been upended and yet they have carried on. When the British soldiers arrive in Catania, they are incorporated into this powerful domesticity; and if the women there had their way, there they would stay, simply replacing the men they'd lost. The women essentially want the narrative to stop – they reject the headlong linear drive of the war story, preferring the circular mode of the soap opera. And in the end, of course, they lose: it's the narrative of war, with its relentless forward march, that triumphs, disrupting their precarious domestic life and tearing the men away from them once again.

In spite of this, what lends *There's No Home* its power, its sympathy and its tragedy, is that Baron – and his proxy, Sergeant Craddock – understand and respond to the demands of the women. Looking back many years later, Baron wrote:

> The women of Sicily were to be the subject of my second novel. They lived a life of their own. They were more natural and knowing than English women. Those over forty all wore black. Those a few years older than that had faces as aged and seamed as my grandmother's. The girls wore short print dresses faded by much washing. They walked clack-clack down the street on wooden sandals. They had a quick energy of movement and voice, emotions and tempers that flared easily, and a way with men that was at once wary and frank.
>
> Once, in some back-street hall, I sat squeezed on a bench among an audience of women who were all weeping loudly. The cause of their grief was the film we were watching, *Wuthering Heights*. They rocked in sympathy with Cathy Earnshaw. From all parts of the dark hall they cried, 'Ah, la poverina, la poverina!'

The contrast between the (mostly) emotionally volatile Sicilian women and the (mostly) phlegmatic British squaddies could easily be the stuff of stereotype, but in Baron's hand it seems, instead, to be elemental. There's a scene towards the end of the book when Graziella, in an attempt to bind her lover closer, prepares a huge feast for him and one of his friends (a meal, incidentally, that resembles very closely one described in Baron's letters home). Instead of being pleased, however, Craddock is repulsed by the huge plates of oily and, in some instances, barely cooked food, and by the unabashed appetite of Graziella who gorges herself on her share, mopping up all that remains. With dismay he learns that she has walked fifteen kilometres into the countryside to her uncle's farm to beg for food, leaving at sunrise and returning on blistered feet only an hour earlier; hence her hunger and the hastily prepared dishes. Craddock's terse rejection of this sacrifice triggers in Graziella an overwhelming grief that both obscures her character — normally careful and dignified — and echoes the earlier theme of voraciousness.

> There was an empty second, then a sudden vomit of sobbing burst up from deep inside her. She wailed, in a cracked voice that forced itself through the thickness in her throat, 'I wanted to please you.'

On this occasion there is a rapprochement between the two of them, but we, the readers, know that it cannot last, that their narratives are doomed to diverge. And it is a measure of Baron's talent that, in the end, we don't know who to pity more — the men heading into the horror of war or the women left behind. Out of an instinctive empathy with women as well as men, Baron has fashioned a novel that is at once masculine and feminine, a war story and a love story, an affirmation of the human spirit, and a tragedy: in short, a book about the whole of human life.

The wide-ranging scope of *There's No Home* made it clear that Alexander Baron was not simply a war novelist. His next novel, *Rosie Hogarth*, was set in peacetime, in Islington, and told the story of a man returning from war to find his world much changed. It was the first of what have become known as his London novels. His 1952 novel, *With Hope Farewell*, was about a Jewish Londoner; set between 1928 and 1948, the war inevitably played a part in it. And a year later, he went back to the war in earnest for a third and last time with *The Human Kind*, a wonderfully well-wrought set of linked, evidently autobiographical vignettes. A decade later it would be filmed by Carl Foreman as *The Victors*. However, in the film the soldiers are American, rather than British, and Baron himself was most unhappy with the result.

All of his early novels sold well. The three war books, in particular, were ideally suited to the democratic new wave of British paperback publishing, and became key Pan Books titles of the time. But Baron was never comfortable with literary celebrity. He used to tell the tale, with some relish, of how his hardcover publisher, Jonathan Cape, decided to throw a party for him in his grand Bedford Square offices. Taking the bus in from Hackney, he was overcome by nerves and stopped off at King's Cross for a quick shot of Dutch courage. Three more shots later he arrived outside the Cape offices, saw the party in full swing through the windows of the first floor, promptly turned round, and went home.

Throughout the 1950s Baron continued to put out first-class work. Following *The Human Kind* he drew a line under the war and thoroughly enjoyed himself with a couple of historical novels: *The Golden Princess* and *Queen Of The East*. After these technicolor entertainments Baron returned closer to home for the most cultish of his novels, *The Lowlife*, a beautifully observed and understated study of an East End Jewish gambler that deals subtly with the consuming guilt of those Jews who took no part in the war. It's also one of the first British novels to include as characters members of the new wave of Caribbean immigrants. On a grander scale was *King Dido*, an historical epic about the Jewish gangs who held sway in the East End in the years before Baron's birth, and one of his own favourites.

Baron then began a parallel career as a scriptwriter, one that was ultimately to take over from his novel writing. His first successes were the East End anarchist drama *The Siege Of Sidney Street* and the western *Robbery Under Arms*. In the 1960s, he became increasingly involved with TV. He was a regular writer on Play For Today, wrote mainstream dramas like *Poldark* and, in latter years, a number of classic adaptations for the BBC – *Jane Eyre*, *Oliver Twist* and *Vanity Fair* among them. Appropriately enough, perhaps the best loved of them was his 1981 adaptation of Jane Austen's *Sense And Sensibility*.

Baron's novels continued to appear until the early 1970s, most of them set in the past. His last published novel, *Franco Is Dying*, returned to the present with the story of an ageing ex-Communist who revisits the battleground of the Spanish Civil War at the time of Franco's long-drawn-out death.

It is Baron's darkest work, a requiem for the years of grand ideals and untold deaths. He also wrote an unpublished sequel and an autobiography, and when I first met him in the 1990s, to interview him for a national paper, he was working on a history of communism. However, it is the war trilogy for which he will ultimately be remembered: three books offering proof positive that there need be no contradiction between the serious and the popular.

Meeting Baron at his home in Temple Fortune, north London, I encountered a shy, courteous man, though one with a dry wit and a piercing intelligence. He was a devoted husband and father, who maintained a keen interest in literature, politics and the arts. At the time there was a revival of interest in his work: he was pleased, if not a little bemused, to be included in Iain Sinclair and Chris Petit's eccentric East End TV film *The Cardinal And The Corpse*, alongside such other fine London writers as Derek Raymond and Emmanuel Litvinoff. He was not, however, keen to be pigeonholed as any kind of cult writer. He had spent long enough in a very large cult and had little enthusiasm for new ones. Crucially, though – and unlike many former Communists – he had never drifted to the right. Although his experience of the war robbed him of his initial zeal, it also instilled in him a profound belief in the essential decency of ordinary people. He developed a tolerance for the weaknesses of both men and women trapped in difficult circumstances, and a monumental suspicion of those in power touting big ideas.

Gradually, over the next few years, I became friends with Baron and came to know the warmth and kindness of this very private man. He took a gratifying interest in my writing and left me with the abiding lesson that a writing life is about the work and not the surrounding flim flam. Baron died of cancer in 1999. I had seen him just a few weeks earlier and he'd seemed in fine form. The disease took him unnervingly quickly, though at least he avoided prolonged suffering.

The following week I wrote an obituary for *The Guardian*. I concluded with a sentence I see no reason to change: 'His work is characterised by a humanity that deserves to endure.' And that humanity is never more apparent than in this, his second novel, *There's No Home*.